Pride Publishing books by S. J. Coles

Single Books
Blood Winter

I0658885

BLOOD WINTER

S. J. COLES

Blood Winter
ISBN # 978-1-83943-932-2
©Copyright S. J. Coles 2020
Cover Art by Erin Dameron-Hill ©Copyright December 2020
Interior text design by Claire Siemaszkiewicz
Pride Publishing

BLOOD WINTER

Dedication

For Anna And Hannah, my partners in
lusciousness

Chapter One

Sparks waterfalled to the concrete floor, spattered, guttered and died into nothing around my boots. The air was filled with the firework smell of welding and my face was sweaty and itching under my mask. The radio twittered away on the shelf but I hardly registered the newsreader's dull, professional catastrophizing. I rarely did. The real world didn't intrude here and that was just the way I liked it.

"You'll need to grind that back."

I straightened and accepted the mug Clem held out without replying. I knew it needed grinding. He knew I knew. I'd stopped being Clement Dalgleish's apprentice and become his partner more than a year before, but the old man hadn't changed much more than a pair of socks in all the time I'd known him.

I sipped the coffee, grimacing at the slightly oily taste, and checked over the rust repairs on the 1969 Morris Oxford, my sweat rapidly cooling in the chill air. When further commentary wasn't forthcoming, I looked up to see Clem staring at the radio, his heavy white brows drawn together

"What's wrong?"

"Nothing," he grumbled, glaring into his own mug. "Just this shit."

"The coffee?"

He grunted and jerked his head at the radio. I made myself focus on the flat, English voice.

"Whereas there has been no direct link established between the disappearance of what are now being called 'Blood dealers' and any registered haemophiles, anti-haemo protest groups are labeling them 'revenge kidnappings', executed in retaliation for the capture and abuse of haemophiles at human hands. Haemophile Blood-dealing is still a highly controversial topic, sparking heated debate on both sides with no satisfactory resolution in sight. The public is now demanding a review of the investigation into Shelly Morris' murder, which is still popularly believed to be an act of haemophile violence.

"Haemophile spokesperson Ivor Novák has assured the government that all haemophiles registered in the UK abide by their registration laws and would never take matters into their own hands, but the human public remains far from reassured."

I switched the channel. A jaunty pop tune rattled out of the tinny speaker. It set my teeth on edge, but the round lines of Clem's large frame eased. He ambled back to the open bonnet of the 1964 Austin Healey and bent into the cavity. I stared at the radio a moment longer, something unwelcome ghosting under my belly, then shook my head and strode across the workshop to turn the bar-heater on.

"Any idea what that'll do to the electric bill?" Clem grumbled from the depths of the Austin's engine.

"It'll be snowing before the end of the month," I replied, taking the air filer from the tool rack. "Personally, I'd struggle to work if my fingers dropped off."

"Wear gloves," he retorted, but he was staring into the Austin's engine and I knew he wasn't even aware he was arguing with me.

I started to file back the weld on the Morris, relieved that whatever had been unsettled in the air had gone.

"Alec. *Alec*." Clem had to bark my name twice before I heard him over the grind of the filer.

"What now?"

Clem nodded toward the front door. A dark, heart-shaped face framed by black curls was pressed against the glass, frowning into the dim interior. She waved as I approached the door, a smile warming her face.

"We're closed."

"Very funny," came her muffled reply. "Let me in, will you? It's bloody perishing out here."

I unbolted and opened the door, shuddering in the gust of winter air that rushed in with her. "What are you doing here, Meg?"

"I'm on my way back to Glasgow," she said, smiling that wide, brilliant smile of hers. "Been up to Inverness for a meeting."

"You're a long way off the A9."

"So even social calls aren't allowed anymore?"

My gaze slid over her shoulder to where Clem stood chewing on something and watching our exchange with interest. I nodded to an interior door and led her through to the cluttered kitchen.

"Uh, drink?"

"I'd kill for a coffee."

I fired up the coffee machine. It rattled and shuddered as Meg shed her powder-blue coat and cashmere scarf.

"You're looking thin, Alec," she said. "Is everything okay?"

"Of course it is."

"You've not been ill? The damp in that old place —"

"Meg" — I cut her off — "I'm fine. Was there something you needed?"

She pressed her lips together, her sloe-black eyes full of concern. "It's just been a while. That's all."

"I've been busy," I said, pouring coffee into our least filthy mug.

She wrapped her hands around it but didn't drink. "So business is picking up?"

"It's steady."

"Well, that's good news." She raised the mug, sipped and her face twisted.

"Yeah, I know. It's all the Aviemore Co-op stocks. But it's strong."

She took another careful sip. "I'll need it if I'm gonna stay awake long enough to get home."

"How's everything with you?" I said, because all I could hear in the silence that followed was her waiting for me to ask.

Her smile broadened. "Good, thanks. Really good. I got the division leader position and we're expanding. I get to hire an assistant."

"That's great."

She narrowed her eyes. "You don't even remember me telling you about the division leader job, do you?"

I raised my eyebrows. "'Course I do. You mentioned it the last time you rang."

"Which was?"

"I don't know. A few weeks ago?"

She raised her eyebrows. "Try three months, Alec."

I fought a sigh. "I'm sorry. This place… It keeps me busy."

"It keeps you isolated. Well, that and your nonexistent broadband."

I clamped my mouth shut on the immediate reply. "Okay, Meg, you've checked in on me and I'm clearly alive. Is there anything else?"

She set the mug aside. "I just can't get my head around why you barely come down anymore. It's been forever since you and David—"

I scowled. "Meg—"

"Let me finish," she said, firmly. "It was painful, sure. He hurt you. I know that. But cutting yourself off from all human interaction isn't healthy."

"What about Clem?"

"He barely qualifies as human."

"And what if I've decided I don't like humans?"

She sighed. "Believe me… I know how much my brother can screw people up. But when I think of you out here…" She cast her eyes around the messy kitchen then out of the window to the rolling hillside and the gray sky hanging low over the black mountains.

I took another long moment to marshal my response. "I like it here."

"You never used to."

"It's different now."

She nodded, but I could tell it was more in acknowledgement than agreement. "So long as you're happy."

I schooled my face. "I'm happy."

"All right. I believe you. Just do me one favor?"

I eyed her warily. "What sort of favor?"

She flashed her smile again. "Get your best suit dry-cleaned. You're coming to a club opening with me at the end of the month."

I blinked at her. "I'm *what*?"

"A new nightclub. Lure. It's opening right in the middle of Glasgow, a super-exclusive, members-only deal. It's the Ogdell-Paiges' newest project. The likes of Angus Mackie and Mayor Frederick are going."

"Who?"

She tilted her chin. "Don't be obtuse. This is a big deal, Alec."

I pinched the bridge of my nose. "Don't you think we're a bit old for nightclubs?"

"Speak for yourself."

"We're the same age."

"Uh, excuse me. I'm a full six months and four days younger."

I sighed. "I don't know —"

"Seriously" — she cut me off — "some of the top legal firms in the country are sending people, not to mention the politicians and business executives going for the social kudos. And *I* was the one who got the invite. Me. Not Bryce, not Sofia, but *me*, Megan Carlisle from Nowhere, Newtonmore." Her face grew serious. "This is my chance to bring in some big-name clients of my own. It's important, Alec."

"Why do you need me?"

"For moral support. Because you know how to talk to these sorts of people. And, well" — she gave an awkward shrug — "because they want to meet you."

Heat rose to my face. "They *what*?"

She held up her hands. "Don't bite my head off, okay? Word got around that we were at primary school together. I met Olivia Ogdell-Paige at a conference and you came up in conversation…"

"The only reason anyone like that would want to meet me—"

She made an impatient gesture. "No one's going to make a move on Glenroe, Alec. We've already established that legally no one can, though you still haven't convinced me that it wouldn't be a bad thing."

I made an indignant noise.

"It's not about the estate," she said in a gentler voice. "They're just interested in you."

"I'm not interesting."

"You're coming with me, Alec," she said firmly. "I want you to spend time with people. Real people. And, well"—her eyes softened—"I miss you."

I chewed on that for a moment whilst glaring at the wall.

"Please?"

I let out a breath and nodded.

She beamed. "That's the spirit. Here." She produced a fountain pen and marked the *Autospares* calendar with a large X on the last Saturday of the month. "It's official. And no hotels. Stay with me. Come for the whole weekend. We'll make a proper thing of it. Okay?"

"Okay."

She screwed the lid back on her pen in a deliberate manner. "Try not to jump too high in excitement, Lord Aviemore. You'll pull a muscle."

I fetched her coat but paused before opening the workshop door.

"What is it?"

I took a breath. "Have you heard from David?"

A pause. "Why?"

"Have you?"

"Please don't put me in this position, Alec."

"I just want to know he's safe."

"Safe?"

I ran my hand through my hair. "I heard on the radio that dealers are going missing in London."

"*Blood* dealers. David was never into Blood. Was he?" she added, eyes widening slightly.

"No. But he was headed down a bad road."

"He's many things, but he's never been a dealer, Alec...of any sort."

"I know that," I said, hearing the lie.

She chewed on the inside of her cheek for a long moment, her dark eyes haunted. "He's fine," she eventually said, "as far as I know. But we don't talk much these days."

I nodded and opened the door. Meg strode across the workshop floor, her neat heels clicking on the concrete. She turned at the front door, eyed Clem warily then leaned in and said in a low voice, "Look after yourself, you hear?"

"I will," I said, trying for a smile of my own. She examined me for another long moment then kissed me on the cheek, briefly surrounding me with the delicate scents of cinnamon and coconut before returning to her sporty electric-blue Mazda. She waved again, then the car was zooming down the twisting lane, its roar gradually fading to nothing in the cold air.

"Sweet on you, that one is."

"What?"

"She likes you," Clem said. "Always has, by my reckoning."

I tried to figure out if there was anything more than the usual truculence behind Clem's words, but his face was as readable as bearded granite. I went back to smoothing down the body work on the Morris, refusing to think about what I'd gotten myself into.

Clem left when it started to get dark, repeating unnecessary reminders to lock up properly. I heard the cranky growl of his ancient Land Rover coughing to life, then the rumble as it drove away. I took a second to enjoy the utter silence that enveloped me — the silence that only ever came from being truly alone — then locked the workshop and made for the path leading up the hillside.

I bent my head against the wind. It smelled like snow. The winter-brittle grass hissed against my overalls. I startled a deer in a patch of scrubby heather. It bounded up the path and was gone.

Glenroe was little more than a darker patch of gray against the slate-colored slope of mountain. The boarded windows watched me like dead eyes. I reached the overgrown track that passed for the driveway and spotted a wooden plank splintered on the weedy gravel. Craning my neck, I spotted where it had fallen from — one of the windows in the turret on the west wing — and cursed.

Mentally logging the job for another day, I followed the track through the sprawling bushes around the side of the house. I was shivering by the time I got the key into the side door. I shut it on the swirling wind and stood for a second in the enclosed quiet. The passage was dark and the silence complete. I couldn't even hear the scuff of rats in the walls. It was too cold even for vermin.

My footsteps echoed on the stone flags. I didn't look into the faces of the dead people who smiled at me from photo frames on the walls whilst I strode through the dust-shrouded rooms to the kitchen. I hurriedly shut the door on the rest of the house and flicked on the light, the strip bulb humming as it came to life. The rickety table was covered with engine parts. The counters were piled with mismatched crockery, books and old copies of *Classic Motor*. There was a three-year-old calendar on the wall that I'd kept because I'd liked the photo of Buachaille Etive Mor that they'd used for July. Hiking up that mountain with David during our good summer was still one of my fondest memories, though I rarely admitted it, even to myself. I lit the wood-burning stove, switched on the kettle then the radio, clicking the channel over from another report of the London disappearances. I went through to my bedroom next door — what had been some of the old staff quarters — to change whilst the stove warmed water for a shower.

The wind was hammering at the windows when I emerged. By the time I was dumping my dirty dinner plates into the sink, I'd almost managed to forget about Meg. Then I caught my reflection in the darkened window. No wonder the sight of me had concerned her. My cheeks were hollow, my blue eyes lackluster and dull, the skin under them smudged gray. I scratched at a week's worth of stubble and pushed back my over-long hair, scowled and turned away.

* * * *

Two more restorations came into the workshop the following week. I worked into the night almost every day, much to Clem's bemoaning of our electric bill. But progress was steady, which pleased the clients, and I was able to sink myself into the work and forget everything else, which pleased me.

The weather got colder and darker. We had four solid days of heavy rain. Puddles appeared in the Glenroe hallway and I lost an entire half-day to patching up a new gap in the roof. It was only when I was working out a new labor schedule on the workshop calendar that I realized Meg's club opening was the next day. I guiltily checked my mobile where I'd left it on the workshop windowsill, the only place it got signal. I had two voicemails and a string of increasingly impatient texts.

I've not forgotten. See you tomorrow.

I sent the message then returned to where Clem was grouching over the corroded exhaust of a vintage Sunbeam. I helped him remove it and spent the rest of the day fitting the new one, refusing to think about what the next day might bring.

* * * *

The drive from Glenroe to Glasgow was the best part of three hours on a good day. Saturday dawned in sheeting rain and howling wind. It took me well over two hours just to reach the main road, splashing through rushing run-off and crunching over rain-loosed gravel and branches. There was virtually no other traffic, even when I reached the A9, but I still drove my faithful X-Trail slower than was necessary, scowling out into the gray curtain of rain with a hard knot in my stomach.

The traffic increased as I approached the city. The knot tightened. The buildings jostled together and glowered down at me, soot-stained and dark with rain. Pedestrians filled the pavements, battling with umbrellas or hurrying along in waterproofs and overcoats, heads bent against the wind. Everywhere there were people…thousands of people. The noise and the sights crowded in on my brain. I wondered how I'd ever managed to live there.

When I finally reached Meg's building, she welcomed me into the open plan, terracotta-painted apartment with a warm hug and a relieved expression.

"You didn't think I was coming, did you?"

She shrugged but had the decency to blush a little. She cooked us dinner in her chrome kitchen, a light but incredibly good dish of Thai chicken with lemongrass served with a really *very* good dry riesling. I virtually inhaled it, grudgingly admitting that it made a welcome change from microwave curries and corner-shop red.

"Good?"

I nodded, swallowing the last mouthful of wine.

"I've ordered a car for nine p.m.," she said. "Now don't bunch up." I hurriedly schooled my face. "You never know, Alec. You might even have fun. Stranger things have happened."

I muttered something noncommittal and took myself off to the guest bathroom to shower, concentrating on not thinking about the fact that the photograph of Meg and David that had been over the bookcase was gone. I'd never let myself think about how his leaving might have hurt Meg too, never let myself think too much about how it might have all been my fault.

"*There's* the Alec MacCarthy I remember," Meg said when she joined me in the sitting room an hour later. "You look great."

She was being nice. I looked…better. I'd stopped at a barber on my way in and had brought one of my black suits that still just about fit. The shirt was new and I'd worn the charcoal Armani tie she'd sent me for my thirtieth birthday. It was the first time it had been out of its packet. It was a nice tie, and I still remembered how to do a perfect Windsor knot, but the mirror over Meg's ornate bathroom sink had showed it around the neck of a hollow-eyed stranger with pallid skin and a grim expression.

"Thank you," I said, managing a smile. "You look wonderful."

That, at least, was true. Meg had long ago cornered the market on looking effortlessly exquisite, even in the backward little town we'd grown up in. A high-paying job and healthy lifestyle certainly hadn't harmed her graceful entrance to her thirties. She'd chosen a silver-gray gown that complimented her walnut-colored skin, oiled her ebony curls into decorative braids and wore a very simple but startling pair of platinum earrings that accentuated her long neck. She'd probably spent a large amount of money and time on her subtle makeup, but her wide, white smile was all she really needed.

"Thank you," she said sincerely, holding my gaze for such a long time that I wondered what else she might be trying to say. She held out her elbow. "Shall we?"

Night had fallen in all its streetlight-tinged glory. There were shouts, laughing, sirens and the squawking of car horns. It had stopped raining, but the air stank of wet tarmac and exhaust fumes, and the chill was damp and pervasive.

"Remember that some of the people there tonight know my boss," she warned as we climbed into the waiting BMW. "Or could be my future bosses. Or clients."

"I'll behave."

She pointed a dusky-pink fingernail at me. "Promise me?"

"Why am I invited again?"

She patted my knee but didn't answer.

Lure had been built into a renovated building near Glasgow Central station. Seeing the vast Victorian façade, which I'd known only as an exhaust-blackened ruin, newly sand-blasted and lit up with projections of slowly rotating stars whilst people in dinner suits and gowns sauntered to the entrance, was unsettling, like I'd stepped into a different time. Meg's eyes shone. Several large gentlemen in suits checked our names and IDs on various lists on the way in. They all eyed me and my driving license with varying degrees of uncertainty before waving me along.

We were beeped through the security scanners then funneled to a bejeweled and gowned woman wearing a pair of incongruous blue medical gloves.

"Good evening, Madam. Sir. A very small and painless blood test is required to enter this evening."

"A blood test?" I said.

Megan elbowed me in the side. "Of course," she said, holding out her hand. The woman took Meg's finger and pressed it briefly to a palm-sized device that clicked. Meg winced then put her finger to her mouth. The woman examined the screen of the device for a moment. When it flashed green, she smiled and handed Meg a tissue.

"Welcome to Lure."

Meg inclined her head and moved on whilst the woman repeated the process with me. I felt the tiniest prick against the pad of my finger. I was handed a tissue to clean the tiny bead of blood after her screen had again flashed green.

"They're not taking any chances," Meg murmured as she guided me through to a cavernous, glittering hall.

"What are they afraid of, exactly?"

"What do you think?" she whispered before falling into awed silence as we were swept by the crowd through to the atrium bar. The vast space was decorated with muted LED lighting, an understated color scheme and simple yet clearly eye-wateringly expensive furniture. The arched ceiling had been restored to its nineteenth-century glory, navy and gold tiles glimmering like a night sky. The rhythmic beat of a chart dance tune thumped through the air. At least a dozen handsome bar staff served the milling clientele with drinks in long-stemmed flutes and heavy-bottomed crystal tumblers. It smelled like new paint, overpriced aftershave and champagne. Everyone was beautiful, richly dressed, smiling broadly, dripping with jewels and designer accessories and exchanging witty, sexually charged banter with abandon.

I hated it instantly.

Meg squeezed my arm and I smoothed my face. "It's very loud," I called over the noise.

"Everyone's here," she said, gazing around. "*Everyone.*"

"Everyone in the world, it seems like."

She gave me a mock-glare. "Let's get a drink."

I let her take me the bar where we were served by a beautiful blonde with a lilting Slavic accent. Meg searched the room over the rim of a glass of gin and tonic the size of a goldfish bowl. The bartender handed me my tumbler and I sipped the single malt appreciatively, grateful that there was at least something here I could enjoy.

"There's Mayor Frederick's son," Meg said in my ear, nodding over to a man who was standing at one of the tables. "And he's brought his mistress. How interesting." I made a noise of acknowledgement and took another mouthful. Meg sipped too, continuing to scan the crowd. "There," she said, pointing. "Olivia Ogdell-Paige. And I think that's her brother. Come on."

She slipped away without even checking to see if I was following. I finished my drink, willing the alcohol to give me strength, ordered another then wove through the crowd to join her. She was shaking hands with a very tall, very thin woman in lavender and white with platinum hair pulled into what looked like a painfully-tight chignon.

"Ah, Miss Carlisle, of course. So glad you could make it. This is my brother, Jon," she said, indicating the hard-faced man next to her, who was so much shorter and stockier that nothing except the identical way they watched everything like hungry hawks would have convinced me they were related.

"Mr. Ogdell." Meg held out her hand. "It's a pleasure."

"Pleasure's all mine," the squat, mousey-haired man replied, his mouth turning up as his narrow eyes flickered over Meg.

"I think I told you at the conference that Jon's firm is looking for representation," Olivia said. "I've recommended your firm, Joseph & Arthur."

"That's wonderful," Meg said. "We are expanding right now, so soon will have even more capacity to—"

"Yes, we're starting another subsidiary," the short man interrupted. "Redeveloping old property in the north, mainly. I heard J&A might be a good fit."

"I'm certain we will be," Meg said with her warmest smile, subtly pinching my thigh. "Mr. Arthur was hoping to attend to discuss this in more detail with you but unfortunately couldn't make it tonight. But this is my friend, Alec MacCarthy."

Both the Ogdells turned their suddenly slack faces toward me.

"Well, I owe you a drink, Olivia," Ogdell said, holding out his hand to me. "The legendary Viscount of Aviemore himself."

"'Alec' is fine," I said flatly, shaking his wide, hot hand.

"You'll have to forgive us, my lord," Olivia said, her pale eyes round and shining. "But this is like meeting a ghost...or someone from a storybook."

"The title really isn't necessary," I replied, keeping my voice level with an effort. "And I promise the reality is less than fantastical."

"Alec doesn't stand on ceremony," Meg put in. "But he was so pleased to be invited along tonight."

"Did you know our father knew yours quite well?" Olivia went on, not even looking at Meg. "He was a barrister on a number of your father's cases."

"Christ, yes, I remember old Judge MacCarthy," Ogdell said, eyeing me with wary curiosity. "Dad had him over for dinner once or twice. Hard-assed bugger. Scared me shitless."

"He was a formidable man."

Ogdell barked a laugh. "I'll say. Dad said he was the toughest old boot to ever take the bench. There was no getting anything past him. He meant it as a compliment, of course. We were all terribly saddened to hear about what happened."

"Yes," I responded flatly.

"You've not followed in his footsteps then, Alec?" Olivia inquired sweetly.

"I'm not interested in the law."

"Alec runs his own business, restoring classic cars," Meg put in.

"Ah, now we're talking," Ogdell beamed. "Dad's got that old Jaguar up on blocks in the back garage, gathering dust. Such a waste. Where are you based, Alec? Maybe I could have it sent through for you to take a look."

"My workshop's on my estate," I said after a pause. "Glenroe Motors. You can google it."

I wasn't sure if I imagined the gleam that came into his eye. "I shall."

"Quite a turn-out tonight," Meg said, gesturing at the around the bar.

"Yes, better than I expected," the short man observed. "With all that rigmarole on the door, I half-expected everyone to turn back."

"Don't be flippant, Jon," Olivia said with a delicate frown. "People want to feel safe. That's all."

"Lure can't afford bad press in its first damn week," Ogdell muttered, with the air of one repeating a much-trodden line of argument. "If anyone gets a sniff that we're screening members—"

"It wouldn't stand up in court for a second," his sister interrupted. "Health and safety legislation is perfectly clear."

"I don't want haemos in my club any more than you do," Ogdell grated, whilst Meg and I awkwardly pretended not to listen. "But they've got representation now. They're passing laws as we speak."

"Until they make it illegal, Lure is a human-only club. I'll not have my members at risk. Alec"—Olivia pointedly turned to me—"why don't I show you the rest of it? Let these two talk business."

She took my arm and led me away before I could answer. I cast a longing look back but Meg had already drawn Jon Ogdell into conversation.

"Now, tell me all about Glenroe," Olivia crooned as we passed into a smaller room with lissome girls on pedestals wearing nothing but tacked-on gemstones and undulating in time to slow, swaying music. "I've only ever seen it in pictures."

"It leaks," I muttered.

She waved for the attention of a waiter. "There are parts of it that date back to the sixteenth century, I believe? And are there really caves under the house?"

I watched her narrowly, but all I could see in her face was polite curiosity. "Yes."

"Used for everything from hiding priests to smuggling, if I remember my history." Her eyes glinted. "Dad often talked about the Cairngorms. A beautiful spot. He loved the hiking—and the hunting, of course. You must have had a wonderful childhood."

Luckily, our drinks arrived so I was able to sidestep replying. I sipped the whisky and pretended to watch the nearest dancer as she did something inventive with a pair of LED streamers. Olivia continued to chatter sweetly to me, practiced nothings that kept the conversation going without me having to make any input at all. I recognized the tactic from a hundred formal gatherings I had been forced to attend growing up and was more than pleased to let her think she was charming me whilst I concentrated on my drink.

"Do you want to get away from the crowds?" she said when I'd emptied my glass. She was obviously watching me closely.

"I think I'd better go find Megan."

"Oh, no need." Olivia's cool smile showed all her straight, white teeth. "I know where she'll be."

"You do?"

"We have a VIP room on the top floor. If I know my brother, Miss Carlisle is already there."

Uncertainty coiled in my belly. I nodded for her to lead the way. She eased through the crowds to a lift that blended into the wall. The thump of bass from the lower levels faded as it sighed upward. The doors opened onto a small, inmate space, softly lit and decorated in warm reds and creams. It was stuffed with comfortable couches and loungers, some in small, screened alcoves in the walls. There was a bar in one corner and about a dozen people sat on the sofas or stood talking together with their heads bent. A card table was set up in the middle with several people smoking and playing poker.

"Lord Aviemore!" I winced and turned to see Jon Ogdell at the bar with two other men and a fairly rigid-looking Meg. "Come and meet some friends of mine."

"You okay?" I murmured to Meg.

She smiled warmly at me, though the edge in her expression didn't quite fade. "I'm this close to signing him. You having a good time?"

"Alec," Ogdell barked before I could answer, slapping my shoulder and pulling me closer. The edges of his words were starting to slur. "Mystery Viscount and Lost Laird of the Cairngorms…" I set my teeth as he indicated the older of the two men. His steel-gray hair was cut severely short and there was a sharp-eyed expression in his pale eyes. "This is a business associate of mine, Hans Karlsson."

The man held out a thin, dry hand, which I shook with a polite nod. "Pleasure," he stated in a rich, deep voice.

"Karlsson is a very old friend. A very good friend to have," Ogdell said, giving me a wink. "And this," he continued, indicating the tall, slim figure just behind him, "is another good friend and perhaps one…more to your taste? Brody Harris."

"Hey there," Harris said with a swaying Californian twang, shaking my hand more warmly than Karlsson. He had ocean-blue eyes and a devastatingly beautiful smile, his teeth extra white in his sun-browned face. "I'm sorry. I don't know what to call you?"

"Alec is fine," I said.

"Think I can handle that."

I told myself I was imagining the intentness of his gaze, but I wasn't imagining the effect it was having on me.

"Jon says you're some kind of aristocrat or something?"

"No. Not even slightly."

"Really?" he said, tilting his head, sculpted auburn waves brushing his forehead whilst his eyes searched my face. "I mean, all the English seem like lords to me, but there's something especially…lordly about you."

"I'm not English."

"No," he laughed. "Of course not. Scottish, right? My apologies."

"You'll have to forgive Mr. Harris," Ogdell said. "He's not been over here long. Brody, you'll just have to think of a way to make it up to his lordship."

I flushed furiously. I opened my mouth but Harris laughed — a light, unfettered sound — and drew me aside.

"Ignore him. He's drunk."

"Drinks are on me," Ogdell called and the bartender began gathering bottles from behind the bar. "What say we all get comfy? Joining us, Alec?"

"I wouldn't want to impose —"

"Nonsense," Ogdell said, gesturing. "I don't want it said I don't know how to throw a party. This way."

He made for one of the booths, his sister at his side talking animatedly into his ear whilst sliding glances at me.

"What's going on, Meg?" I whispered.

"Nothing," she said, squeezing my arm. "They're just starstruck."

"They're setting me up."

"For what? A date?"

I glared at her.

"What's your problem? Tall, toned and handsome not your type?"

"Meg —"

"Come on," she said, pulling at my arm. "I'm sure he doesn't bite. Not without asking first, at least."

I let her drag me to the table, where I was wedged in next to Harris. His hip was warm against mine. The waitress came over with the drinks and I swallowed more whisky, the pleasant burn now starting to fuzz the edges of my awareness.

"I bet you've got better stuff in your cellars, huh?"

I tried to read the American, but the only thing evident on his face was curiosity. "My father preferred wine. But he drank most of that himself."

The waitress returned with a glass board on which sat a silver dish of white powder and a miniature serving spoon.

"This is direct from my man in Columbia," the old European, Karlsson, said with a paternal smile. "Please, everyone" — he gestured — "help yourselves."

"*Now* it's a party," Ogdell said, spooning the white powder onto the board.

"Only the best for you, hey, Jon?" Harris said with a wickedly charming half-smile.

"It pays to have high standards," Ogdell said, scraping the cocaine into lines with a credit card. "I'm sure Lord Alec would agree."

Meg watched everything with a carefully schooled expression. I knew then that she must be a brilliant lawyer. Ogdell bent and snorted the first line.

"Good?" Karlsson asked.

"Hell yeah," Ogdell laughed, blinking and pinching his nose. "Here," he said, pushing the board toward Harris. "Tell me how that shit compares to the stuff you got for the wrap-up party."

"Don't mind if I do." Harris leaned in, his leg brushing mine, and snorted the second line. Blood rushed into his cheeks. He grinned. "Okay, that's some good shit."

Olivia took her own line with the delicate precision of someone sampling an expensive perfume. "Alec?" she said, holding her nose and pushing the board toward me.

"Not done that in years."

"Go on," Harris said, winking. "Live a little."

I felt Meg's eyes on me but could also feel Harris' leg pressing against my knee. He wore an encouraging smile. The alcohol was swirling through my mind. I pulled the board over. The coke burned and stung my nose and throat. Blood rushed to my head. Electricity crackled through my brain and down my neck. It stirred memories that would have been painful, had I been sober.

"Good, huh?" Harris murmured.

I nodded, swallowing the sharp taste in the back of my throat. When my focus returned, Ogdell was handing around glasses of champagne. I drank mine and held it out for a refill. The meaningless chatter bubbled on around me. Harris drew me into a conversation about the classic Ford Mustangs he kept at his home in Santa Monica. He'd shuffled closer to me and was watching my mouth as often as he watched my eyes.

My throat was suddenly dry. I swallowed what was left in my glass, trying to remember how many I'd had.

"Alec, do you want go?" Meg's steadying hand was on my arm.

"Did something happen?"

She shook her head. "No, I just think Mr. Ogdell is, well…beyond business now."

Ogdell was snorting more coke. His face was ruddy and his eyes watery. He beamed at Karlsson, nodding and waving his flute for more champagne.

"You going?" Harris asked.

"Yeah," I replied, glancing at my watch. "Yeah, it's late."

"I'll walk you out."

"That's really not necessary."

"I insist."

Meg raised her eyebrows and we slipped away together. The public levels of the club were heaving, hot and far too loud. My pulse thundered in my throat and the sweat stood out on my forehead. It was a relief to get out into the cool night air.

"I'll call a car," Meg said, taking a pointed step out of earshot.

"It was nice meeting you, Alec," Harris said, holding out his hand. His wavy hair was just the perfect amount of disheveled. He'd undone a button on his shirt, revealing a smooth sweep of brown collarbone.

I shook his hand, fighting to loosen my tongue. "You, too."

"I may be going out on a limb here, but how long are you in town for?"

I took a second to steady my voice. "Until Monday."

"Uh-huh. So…you wanna meet up tomorrow?"

I rubbed my mouth, staring at the pavement beneath my dress shoes. "I'm sorry. I don't know what they told you about me—"

"Just that you were cute." His smile tilted up on one side, dimpling his cheek.

"I don't date."

"No?" He raised an eyebrow. "What do you do?"

"Car'll be here in five," Meg said, rejoining us with a questioning glance "You joining us, Brody?"

"I better get back to the party," he said, his smile still in place. "But maybe I'll see you tomorrow?" He was holding out a card. I stared at it for a long moment then took it.

"Goodnight." Meg shook his hand. He put his hands in his pockets, nodded at me then sauntered back inside.

"It was worth you coming after all."

"I'm not calling him."

"No?"

"No."

"And why not?"

"I have to go on Monday."

"So?"

I rubbed my temples. My head was starting to pound. I kept my mouth shut.

"Go on, Alec. Tell me why you won't see him."

"I don't trust him…them. Any of them."

"Oh my God," she said. "Seriously?"

"That man Ogdell is a *property developer*."

"One interested in hiring *my* firm."

"So, what? Them knowing I was gay and just happening to invite along a good-looking surfer-type who, wow, is *also* gay? That was all, what? Coincidence?"

She shook her head. "Alex, Brody Harris *works* for Jon. He manages his West Coast office in the states."

"That doesn't change my point."

She stared at me a moment longer then looked away. "Living up in Dracula's castle for so long has made you paranoid."

"I wasn't paranoid about Bastle and Hisks — or that Visions Inc. before that? They all try the friendly routes first — the invites, the gifts, the exclusive offers. Then they move in with the less-friendly ones."

"This is nothing to do with you, Alec…or Glenroe. *I* was invited tonight. I took you along as a favor."

"I thought I was the one doing *you* the favor."

Her face was full of equal parts hurt and anger. "David wasn't the only reason you stopped doing drugs. Remember?"

I closed my eyes, guilt sour on my tongue. "I'm sorry."

The car drew up. Meg got in without speaking. She spent the drive back messaging on her phone and not meeting my eye. I turned Harris' card over in my hands and didn't speak either.

Chapter Two

By breakfast, Meg appeared to have forgiven me, more or less. She warmed croissants, made a pot of very good coffee and chattered about her plans for her new department.

"You really should call him."

I blinked, realizing I'd been staring at Brody Harris' card on the counter. I finished my coffee, relieved to feel it start poking holes in my hangover. "That wouldn't be a good idea."

"Come on, Alec," she said, gently. "So what if he works for a property developer? No one's saying you need to marry the guy. Just have lunch. What's the worst that could happen? You told him yourself you're heading home tomorrow."

I chewed on the inside of my cheek. "What about you?"

"I'm sure I can manage without you for a few hours."

I turned the card over in my hands a few times before catching the knowing spark in Meg's eyes, so I retreated to my bedroom to make the call. Two hours later I sat shifting in the seat at a table near the window of a Mediterranean restaurant, still not entirely sure what I was doing. I talked myself into and back out of leaving three times before Harris showed up. He smiled at me across the busy room whilst hanging his coat. I caught myself watching the way he moved, all strength and controlled confidence. He was in tight black jeans and a blue shirt that brought out his eyes. He sat and smiled at me in a way that made my skin ripple.

"You came. I owe myself a drink."

"Meg virtually kicked me out the door."

He smiled wider. "Well, I guess I owe her a drink then. You can drink it for her." He caught the attention of the waitress and ordered tapas and a bottle of rioja. Harris poured whilst he continued to watch me closely. "It's not too early for you?"

I took a mouthful instead of answering. It was rich and fruity and went some way to easing the lingering fog of the night before, though not my strung-up nerves.

"You don't talk much, huh?"

I swallowed. "I've not got much to talk about."

"Sure," he said, "an estate in the Cairngorm mountains, a famous father, a title, land, educated at Cambridge. Nothing of interest there."

The knot had re-formed in my belly. "Have you been googling me?"

His eyes glittered. "Mainly image searches." The blood rushed to my face and farther down my body. I coughed, internally cursing my dry spell, and he grinned. "But your Wikipedia article is informative."

"I have a Wikipedia article?"

"Sure," he said with an easy shrug. "But don't let it go to your head. Jon has one too."

"What about you?"

He laughed. "I'm not important enough."

"I mean…" I fumbled, glancing around the crowded room. "Tell me about you."

The food arrived whilst he was giving me another of his loaded looks. I busied myself with olives and battered squid rings, waiting for him to speak. He didn't until I met his eyes. Then he leaned forward, poured more wine and began to talk about Santa Monica, his work renovating hotels, his cars, his boat. None of it was anything that I would normally find remotely interesting, but his voice was smooth, his manner easy, his face open and so ready to smile that I both stared and listened intently.

It was what David had been like, at the beginning.

The thought caught me by surprise. I paused with a forkful of spiced potato half-way to my mouth. I laid down the fork and finished my wine, my throat suddenly dry. Brody ordered another bottle as the waitress cleared our plates.

"Are you trying to get me drunk?" I said, stupidly.

"Not exactly," he replied, filling his own glass then mine. "But last night you seemed to relax more after your drink. I like you relaxed."

I made myself hold his look. "Is Ogdell making you do this?"

"Do what?"

"*This*," I said, gesturing between us.

"Jon's my boss," he replied easily. "He pays me well, but not well enough to make my private life any of his business."

I watched him for a long moment. He watched me right back, still smiling. "I'm sorry," I said, looking out of the window. "Property developers and me? Well…we usually have different agendas, let's say."

His honey-colored brows drew together in a slight frown. "If I wasn't so sure this was something very important to you, I think I'd be offended."

"Sorry. I don't do this much."

"Do what?" he asked, his smile back.

"*This*," I said, gesturing again.

He laughed. "What? The brooding Heathcliff thing doesn't have all the guys in the neighborhood lining up at the door?"

"There are no guys like me in the neighborhood," I murmured, swirling the wine around my glass, "and there is no neighborhood."

"You're not a virgin, right?"

I gave him a look.

"Okay, okay. I figured not. Look… I'll lay it all out, shall I?" He put his elbows on the table and leaned close, lowering his voice. "I would very much like to kiss you right now." I froze with the wineglass to my lips. "I'd like even more to take you back to my hotel for the evening. And I think you'd quite like that too." I gripped the glass tighter. "But if you wouldn't, say the word. I'll pay the check and you can head back to your castle and carry on roaming the moors or whatever it is you do for fun. I'll let you go with no hard feelings, other than a little disappointment, to which I think I'd be entitled."

My skin was hot. It had been so long since anyone had looked at me that way. The neglected parts of my body and brain were clamoring for attention. His hot blue eyes held mine for a long time, but when I still hadn't spoken, he sighed and gestured to the waitress for the bill.

"Shall I get us an Uber?" I heard myself saying.

He grinned. "You do that."

* * * *

Brody's hotel suite was one of the finest that the Blythswood Hotel — if not all of Glasgow — had to offer. The furnishings were dove-gray and white. The bathroom gleamed with marble and glossed ceramic. There was a large kitchen area and several big-screen TVs, and the delicate smells of Egyptian cotton and branded hand soap were threaded in the air.

I barely noticed any of it. Brody had a full mini-bar and a chrome cigarette case filled with Karlsson's finest cocaine. He talked and laughed with the easy grace of someone who'd never doubted anything in his life. He made it so easy not to think. I battled daily with the effort of not thinking, but Brody took the fight right out of me, leaving me prone, unburdened and raw in all the right places. His smile was warm, his skin was hot and his body that of someone who had grown up in the sunshine and the sea.

We didn't talk much. When we did, he did most of it. Like Olivia, he knew the art of holding the conversation without having to say anything of significance, which was good because, under it all, I knew we had nothing of any significance to say to each other.

We started as soon as he shut the door. First it was hands and mouths, hot and heavy. We rid ourselves of our clothing without breaking stride. I heard buttons ping free but didn't know if they were from his shirt or mine, and I didn't much care. He drew me onto the bed and we groped each other with increasingly demanding need. The small part of me that wasn't completely caught up in the moment was quietly pleased when I didn't come the minute he touched me, so long had it been since I'd done this with another human.

His mouth tasted like wine and cocaine. His skin tasted like salty ocean air. I breathed him deep, bright and hot, like a midsummer's day on a sunbaked, foreign shore, unfamiliar and yet entrancing. I sank myself into it, reveling in the touch of his knowledgeable hands and the sound of his arousal-tightened groans. But when he drew me on top of him and whispered in my ear that he wanted me to fuck him, I had to pull away.

"What's the matter?" he said, voice gravelly with need. "I've got protection."

"It's not that," I managed to get out. He pressed against me and the friction as his body rubbed against my cock made me gasp.

"Then what is it?" His breath was hot in my ear. "I'm guessing you like to top, right?"

"Yes," I rasped into his neck. "I do... Christ, I do. I just..."

He put his finger under my chin and lifted my face to meet his eyes. "It's cool," he said, smile dimpling his flushed cheeks. "Too soon, I get it. I'm a patient guy. Next time, then."

I swallowed his smile with a deep kiss and he reached for me with both hands. I came in hot explosions of white light, like breakers crashing on a beach, the sound of him calling my name as he joined me nearly drowned out by the rushing in my ears.

He grinned up at me from the pillow, his cheeks flushed and eyes hot. He drew me down, kissed me deeply and rolled me under him.

"I hope you're not done yet, Lord Aviemore," he purred in my ear. "We've got all night, you know."

* * * *

When I came to, an unknowable amount of time later, darkness had fallen. I sprawled on the bed, my skin cooling in the air-conditioned air, feeling pleasantly empty for the first time in…a long time. Even the fading swirl of alcohol and coke felt mild, warm and comfortable.

"You need to come down from the mountains more often," Brody drawled whilst searching out clean glasses for more whisky. "Clearly you don't get the chance to *relax* as often as is healthy."

"You sound like Meg."

He chuckled softly. The bed dipped as he sat, holding out the glass to me. "Seriously, though. What's it like?"

I sipped the whisky. It was good. Not my favorite, but good. "What's what like?"

"Living at Glenroe."

"It's quiet."

"And you like it quiet?" he ventured.

I shrugged one shoulder. "I'm used to it."

He shifted a little closer. "And it doesn't freak you out? Living alone, in the middle of nowhere?"

I took in his serious expression. "No. Should it?"

It was his turn to shrug, but it seemed some of the easiness had left him. "It would freak me out these days, with vampires out of the closet and all."

I raised my eyebrows. "Vampires?"

"Haemophiles...whatever."

"There's no such thing as vampires, Brody," I said, smiling.

"They're not so sure there's any difference back home."

"No," I said carefully, looking at my drink instead of him. "I heard that."

"Seriously," he said again, shifting closer still. "You feel safe up there?"

"There are no vampires in the Cairngorms," I said, trying not to sound too desultory. "And no haemophiles either."

"Caves, mountains, crumbling castles? I would have thought it would be perfect Dracula territory."

"You've read too much Stoker. They live in purpose-built communes, down south. There are none registered this far north."

"What about the unregistered ones?"

I shook my head. "Tabloid scaremongering." He raised an eyebrow. I couldn't help but smile. "Seriously, Brody. You come from a country where kids take guns to school and you're scared of things that go bump in the night?"

He looked wounded. "It's just freaky, okay? At least guns we understand."

I drank more whisky. "Well, I've never seen one. Hard to be freaked out by something you've never seen."

"Boogie-monsters aside," he went on, smiling again, "you don't get lonely?"

"Now you sound like Meg again."

"You mention her a lot," he said after a pause.

I tried to see if there was anything going on his face, but I was tired, a little drunk and far too sated to engage in any effort figuring out subtext. "We're friends."

"Good friends?"

"Old friends."

"Uh-huh." I couldn't tell if something had shifted in the air. He was, if anything, even more beautiful lounging against the headboard with his blue eyes heavy, his hair tousled, his surfer's body—straight out of a swimwear catalogue—toned and tan against the white sheets. But his quiet now had a different quality.

"Why do you want to know?"

He laughed, laying a warm hand on my thigh. "Jesus, Alec, relax. It was just a question."

"I should go." I hadn't meant to say it. But then it was out there, hanging between us like black smoke, and I realized it was true.

"Sure," he said, easily enough. "It's late. I should get some sleep before my breakfast meeting. And I'm certain that if you stay I won't get much sleeping done."

I managed a half-smile and started searching amongst the discarded clothing for my jeans. I dressed, trying not to hurry, but Brody seemed unaffected. He rinsed the glasses, said goodnight, went into the bathroom and shut the door. I heard the shower start. I stood holding my shoes, trying to untangle what exactly had happened.

* * * *

"You're overthinking it," Meg said. She hadn't stopped grinning since I'd dragged myself out of the spare bed the next morning for what breakfast my abused stomach could handle. "It was just sex. Good sex, by the look of you."

"Hey," I scowled, stirring the coffee, "let's not."

"Oh come on," she said, setting down a bowl of sliced fruit and yogurt in front of me. "It's just what you needed. Admit it." I grumbled something under my breath and picked up the spoon. "Are you going to see him again?"

"No," I said quickly. Then added, "I don't know."

"Do you *want* to see him again?"

"I don't know."

She dropped her spoon into her bowl with an exasperated gesture. "Honestly, Alec. You are useless."

"I just… Forget it."

"What? You just *what*?"

I pushed the berries and nuts around in the yogurt. "He's not. *We're* not… I don't know."

She sighed. "You're worse than a woman." I glared at her. She grinned then looked at the clock. "I've got to go to work. You gonna be okay getting back?"

"Yeah. I got enough sleep, I think."

"Perhaps you should have got less and stayed a little longer." I leveled another bleary look at her. She beamed and kissed me on the cheek. "It was good to see you, Alec."

"Thanks for having me." I managed a more genuine smile.

"Let's not leave it so long next time, okay?"

I nodded, not trusting myself not to lie. She patted my shoulder and left. I finished the fruit and left too, a tangible weight leaving my shoulders as I drove out of the city.

I passed the drive deep in thought about the events of the previous days and looked forward to the relative peace of my normal routine.

Clem had a lot to say when I finally dragged myself into the workshop so late that afternoon that it was starting to get dark. The fact that we barely had enough work for one person, let alone two, was not something he ever let bother him. I felt better for the long, hot shower I'd taken at Meg's and for being back in my overalls in the chilly, drizzly mountain air.

I could still feel the heat of Brody's hands and hear the sound of his laugh. It had been good, I decided. Invigorating, like a day at the seaside. But I couldn't deny that I felt more like myself with the peaks glowering over me, the smell of heather dripping with the cold rain in my lungs and the crumbling hulk of Glenroe squatting like a broken boulder on the bluff above the workshop.

I tried not to analyze that too closely.

The rain continued, grew colder and turned to hail. More holes became evident in the hall's roof. I was forced to do temporary patch-jobs with tarpaulin when it became too cold and slippery to be out on the slates for long. The days grew shorter. Our last two restorations were sent back to their owners and nothing else had come in. I began to mentally prepare myself for another long, cold winter.

I was unpacking bottom-shelf wine and tins of beans into the larder and trying not to think about another winter subsisting on little else, when I stopped, listening. The noise came again. I moved into the dining room, straining my ears until it came a third time. There was someone knocking on the front door—the one I never used.

A frisson of disquiet ran up my spine. I approached the door after discarding the half-formed notion of retrieving one of my father's shotguns. Through the whorled glass I could just make out a figure on the step. The bolt clanked and the key screeched. I heaved but the door didn't budge. I wrestled with the lock a moment more, heard a louder clunk then dragged the door open. It scraped an arc in the dust and dead leaves on the tiles, the hinges screaming like banshees.

Brody stood on the step, looking utterly surreal, sunny and well-dressed against the backdrop of drizzle and wind-swept mountainside.

"Alec," he said, smiling brightly, "I was beginning to wonder if I'd got the wrong castle."

"What are you doing here?"

My tone caused his smile to slip. "Jon sent me."

I blinked. "Why?"

He frowned. "I've brought his Jaguar. He said he'd arranged it with you."

"Well, yeah," I said, craning my neck to scan the empty, weed-riddled drive. "Did Clement not take it in at the workshop?"

Brody frowned harder. "Sure he did. But he said you were up here, so I thought I'd take the chance to come and, well... Did I do something wrong?"

I shifted on my feet. The shadows of the house felt heavy behind me. "I don't normally use this door."

"I'm sorry. I didn't know."

"I'm not used to visitors."

"No kidding." He was angry now, his brow creased, mouth suddenly a hard, flat line.

"Do you want to come in?" I said, but the silence had been so long that it shouted forced politeness.

"Only if you want me to."

Heat rose in my face. "Of course."

He examined me for a long moment then stepped inside. I heaved the door shut and clanked the heavy locks back into place.

"Wow," he breathed, gaping at the grand staircase then up to the vaulted ceiling and the filth-encrusted chandelier. "This is really something."

"Coffee?" I hurried to the kitchen but Brody followed slowly, staring around at the shrouded furniture, the paintings stacked against the walls, the yawning fireplaces, the leaves that had drifted around mountains of moldering books and tarnished silverware. The brightness of the kitchen made him blink. I sensed him examining the clutter as I turned the kettle on and hunted out the coffee.

"I gotta tell you that this is nothing like I imagined."

"Reality rarely is," I said. When I finally had the coffee ready, he took the mug with an irritatingly sympathetic expression.

"I'm making you uncomfortable."

"No, you're not," I lied.

He sighed and pulled out one of the plastic chairs from around the table. "Did I misread this?"

I shifted on my feet, staring into my mug. "It's not that."

"Then what is it?"

I set my drink aside untasted and made myself sit opposite him. "I don't get visitors."

"You said," he said, casting an eye around my tiny, chaotic living space.

"You don't understand." I heard the words like they were coming from someone else. "No one comes here. This place… It's not…"

He leaned forward in his chair. "Go on. Tell me."

I ran a hand through my hair. "No one but me has set foot in this house for years. Not since…"

He tilted his head to one side. "Since your dad died?"

I glared at the table, angry with myself for reacting.

"That's a long time not to have anyone in your house."

"It's not my house."

A pause. "Your dad didn't like you having people over, huh?"

"No."

"Especially not…*guy* people?"

The bottom fell out of my stomach. A red fog was boiling just under my skin. If he'd have tried to comfort me, reason with me, draw me into talking, I'd would have kicked him out, slammed the door and resolved never to think of him again. But he didn't. He just sat there calmly, his expression mild, his blue eyes warm.

"What about your mom?" he asked eventually.

"She left when I was five."

"And where is she now?"

"I don't know."

"You don't maybe wanna try to find her?"

"She never wanted to find me."

He sipped his coffee. "It was just you and your old man then, huh?"

"Until I went off to boarding school."

"What happened to him? Jon wasn't clear."

"He drank himself to death." I finished my coffee and put the mug aside with an air of finality.

"But you don't want to sell?" He asked it carefully. It was a natural-enough question. It always was.

"Is that something Ogdell wants an answer to?"

He didn't react. "No. I'm just interested."

"Again. Why?"

He paused a moment, face very still. Then he sighed and shifted, leaning in to look into my face. "What happened to you, Alec?"

I fought back images of Dad's drink-reddened face, ordering me out of the house. Of David, lying in a drug-induced coma in a hospital bed, all tubes and sallow skin. The property developer goons who had hammered on my door day and night. I breathed until I could control my voice. "I'm fine. I just don't want to sell."

"Okay," Brody said, with a half-smile, putting his hand on my arm. "Okay. I'm sorry I upset you."

"You didn't," I replied then, after a moment, with more feeling, "You didn't, Brody. I upset myself."

"Yeah, you did," he said, tone light again. "So you wanna come see this car or what?"

I glanced out of the window at the gathering dusk. "It's too late to start any work today. Clem'll have all the paperwork ready for you to pick up on your way back out."

"Oh. Sure." He sounded hurt again. He glanced at my bedroom door then back at me, raising an eyebrow. "But I do believe you and I have some unfinished business?"

I dropped my gaze, rubbing my neck. "You can't sleep here, Brody. There's no room."

Half his mouth turned up in that devil's grin. "Who said anything about sleeping?"

My blood stirred. I remembered his skilled hands and the summery smell of his skin. My chest tightened, but the thought of having him, having anyone, under this roof was a more efficient buzzkill than a bucket of cold water. "I...I'm sorry."

"Okay," he said, easily enough. "I get it. Not here. That's fine. I can live with that." He leaned in so close I could feel his breath on my face. "So how about Jon's hunting lodge? Jacuzzi bath? King-size bed? Would that put you more at ease?"

"What are you talking about?"

His smile broadened. "The other reason I'm here. Jon wants to invite you to a weekend at his new place. He's bought a lodge just on the border of the national park. It's only about an hour and a half from here. They just finished doing it up last week."

I stared at him. "Jon Ogdell has bought a place in the Cairngorms?"

"Only on the edge. I think Jon likes the idea of the countryside, but anything this wild, well..." Brody cast a glance out of the window at the slate-strewn mountainside and white threads of rushing burns. "Let's just say he likes his comforts."

"Why here?"

Brody laughed. "You're worrying too much, Alec. Jon's always doing this. His current thing is aspiring to be the landed laird — like you, I guess, but more like the storybooks. Either way, he's having a party and you're invited."

"Why?"

"Because he likes you. And because I like you."

"You do?" I asked before I'd thought it through.

"Sure," he said with a smile so charming it couldn't possibly be real. "Tendency to imagine the worst aside, you're intriguing. Not hard on the eyes either, as I'm sure you know."

I searched for words but couldn't find any.

"Your friend Meg'll be there."

"She will?"

"Naturally. She's Jon's lawyer now. She'd like to see you, right?"

"She would…"

He was looking at me expectantly. I thought about getting away from the drafty, cold house to somewhere with unlimited hot water and good food. And Brody. Willing, gorgeous, easy-going Brody. Brody who made it so easy to forget, even if, deep down, I had the sneaking suspicion that it was all he was good for. "I'd like that."

He beamed. "That's great. Next weekend, okay? I'll email the details."

"No," I said, rummaging in the kitchen drawers for a notepad, "I don't get good Internet. Can you write it down?"

He laughed and took the notepad. "Yeah, Jon couldn't deal with the reality for sure, caves or no caves." He scribbled an address, date and time on the piece of paper.

"He knows about the caves?"

"Everyone knows about your caves," he said, holding out the paper. "Glenroe has a Wikipedia page too, you know."

"Property developers have said they would be a lucrative tourist attraction." I watched him carefully.

"They're right. But they're *your* caves." He smiled. "Just wait, Alec. You think Jon throws a good party in the city? Wait until you get him out in the middle of nowhere with no neighbors and nowhere to run."

"That sounds ominous."

He took my hand and drew me closer. "Don't worry. I'll look after you."

"You're not scared of the boogie-monsters?" I joked.

"Not at Auchallater Keep," he replied, something glinting in his eyes. "Jon's more than prepared."

I couldn't untangle that one, but he was looking at me like he was going to kiss me. I thought I wanted him to, but I knew that if he did, it wouldn't stop there.

He saved us both by pulling away. I showed him out through the side door, directed him down the path then watched him pick his way through the heather to the drive. I couldn't deny the relief I felt when I shut the door and the silence of the house was restored. But neither could I deny the flicker of something heated that had lit within me, knowing I was going to see him again. I frowned into the shadowed hallway, wondering whether I should be worried at how easily he seemed to be able to change my mind.

I shook my head, waited until I was sure he'd be gone, then made my way to the workshop to examine Jon Ogdell's Jaguar. My mood lifted further when I found the thing a virtual wreck. The panels were rusted, the engine clogged and corroded, the soft top rotting on its broken frame. It had no tires, bent axles and the whole thing was caked in a thick layer of dust that had set into the wax and would need sanding back. It could be a big enough job to keep us going for the winter.

Even if that did mean signing a contact with Jon Ogdell. I shook my head. Meg's voice was in my ear, saying I was paranoid.

'You can't ever just see good luck for what it is,' she'd said to me more than once, most recently in connection to Brody.

When I turned out the light that night, the dark emptiness of the house was heavier than it had been in years. I thought I heard my father's heavy, stumbling tread on the grand staircase. Then the scrape of a vampire's fingernails on the window. It was nonsense. I was alone. Completely alone, just as I liked it.

It was a long time before I fell asleep.

* * * *

I wasn't sure what I was feeling as I lowered myself into the passenger seat of Meg's Mazda a week later — anticipation and trepidation in equal measures for sure. But what I found more alarming was how much I was thinking about Brody.

Meg teased me mercilessly. She had plenty of time to do so since the drive to Ogdell's lodge took almost a full hour longer than it should have been. Snow had finally begun to fall, feathering through the air and coating the twisting lanes in a thin layer of white, slushy powder.

"I could have driven myself, you know," I finally said, cutting her off mid-taunt.

"Cinderella drive herself to the ball? I wouldn't dream of it. What would the prince think?"

"It's not —" I grumbled for the hundredth time. "Jon Ogdell invited me, not Brody."

"You don't like Jon."

"You don't either. Which is worse, since he's your client."

"Yes, but unlike you, Alec MacCarthy, I can hide what I'm thinking."

I sighed. "So what do you think we can expect at this thing?"

"Like the club opening but dialed up to eleven, I expect," she said, a trifle doubtfully. "Fewer people. More drugs."

I eyed her warily. "Do you actually *want* to go?"

"Yes," she said slowly. "He's invited some business partners. It's important that I go. And besides, I wouldn't want to miss the chance to see your romance burgeon and blossom."

"Meg," I snapped.

"Oh, relax and let me have a little fun, will you? It's been long enough."

"Can't you just focus your energies on your own love life?"

"I don't have time for one," she said after only a second's hesitation. "That's why I have to live vicariously through you."

"I hope you weren't doing that whilst I was with your brother."

She laughed. It was only a little strained. "No one envied you that particular shit storm." I fidgeted, suddenly uncomfortable. "You're not nervous, are you?"

"No," I replied, looking out at the worsening weather with an answering chill building in my belly.

"I thought you wanted to go."

"I want…something…" I stared out into the swirling snow. "I'm not sure what."

"Well I'm sure, between Jon's wine cellar, the luxury guest bedrooms and Mr. Harris' willingness, you'll get it figured out."

It was dark by the time the Mazda pulled into the smooth swoop of snow-dusted driveway in front of the opulent hunting lodge. I stared out at the towering stone facade with my mouth open.

"It's huge," Megan breathed.

"It's an old keep," I said quietly, taking in the tall walls, the porticoed entranceway and many lighted windows. "It used to be a ruin."

"There can't be much of the original left?"

"That stonework used to be the tower," I gestured to the rough section to the right of the front door. "Fifteenth century. I'm surprised he got planning permission."

"Jon Ogdell usually gets what he wants."

I tried to unpick if there was a warning in her tone, but she wasn't looking at me as she undid her seatbelt. I hurried after her through the swirling snow. The wind was picking up, icy cold. Black clouds had closed overhead. Meg swore as her carefully arranged hair whipped about her face. She hurried to ring the bell.

"Will you be…indulging tonight?" she asked, too casually.

I blinked. "Is that as personal as it sounds?"

"You know what I mean," she said more firmly, eyes fixed on the wooden door.

"No," I said, quietly. "You were right. There was a reason I stopped getting high."

She gave me a grateful glance, then a tall man with a bald head, a blank face and a smart suit opened the door.

"Megan! Lord Aviemore!" Jon Ogdell bustled forward whilst the butler took our coats. He was in a tailored, if tasteless, tartan smoking jacket. His smile was wide, his small eyes glittering. "You made it. I was wondering if you would. The weather's turned fouler than Egyptian brandy."

"Jon," Meg said, flashing her smile and shaking his hand. "Thanks for having us."

"Please, it's my pleasure. And, Alec, good to see you again. How's the Jag coming?"

He didn't let me answer but chattered on, ushering us through a large, brightly-lit hall, soft and warm with a plush, forest-green carpet, to an equally sumptuous sitting room. I breathed in the smells of synthetic leather and wood smoke. Deep, evergreen sofas and armchairs were arranged around a roaring fire. A gigantic flat-screen TV reeling a slideshow of photographs of the mountains was mounted on the wall. Top-of-the-range speakers fluted Vivaldi into the air. If it weren't for the tartan upholstery on the throws and cushions, we could have been in any luxury hotel in any part of the world.

Olivia rose from her chair, smiling broadly, holding out her thin, white hands. She was clad in a delicate lemon yellow that, along with the oversized pearls at her ears and neck, only succeeded in accentuating her wan complexion.

"Alec... So glad you could come," she said, clutching my cold hands in her warm, dry ones and once again ignoring Meg. "Jon's so eager to know what you think of his new place, aren't you, Jon?"

"Always enjoy entertaining the gentry. You know that, Olivia. Champagne?"

Meg and I accepted our glasses from the butler, who had appeared silently at my elbow.

"Shall we join the others in the dining room?" Olivia twinkled.

We followed her through to a vast dining room containing a mahogany dining table so deeply polished and loaded with silver and candles that it was almost too bright to look at. I shook my head to rid myself of the memory of stepping into the Glenroe dining room during one of the prolonged dinners my father had made me attend. I remembered my stiff collar interfering with the swallowing of the endless courses of pretentious food. The air would be heavy with cigar smoke and conversation that was painfully boring where it wasn't blisteringly impenetrable and, of course, there was always far too much wine, followed by port, followed by brandy. That was back when he could still afford to feed fifteen guests and didn't drink alone.

I blinked and the vision was gone. This room was lighter and the tableware newer. The people were brightly dressed, younger and smiling.

"This is my husband, Matthew," Olivia sparkled, indicating a tall, square-faced man at the end of the table. He inclined his head, then Olivia also introduced about half a dozen other unremarkable people, who I almost immediately forgot the names of.

"And Hans you know already," Olivia finished as the Swede inclined his head from where he sat near Jon, his pale eyes fixed on me.

"Good to see you again, Lord Aviemore," he purred in his swaying accent.

I examined him but couldn't see past his eyes. "And you."

Brody rose from his seat near the fireplace with a wide smile. He looked ready for a photo shoot for Versace or Ralph Lauren in his exquisitely tailored dinner suit. I was suddenly very aware that my own hung a little loose on me and that the wind would have pulled my always-unruly hair into even more disarray. At least I still had a good razor at home.

"You sit next to Brody, Alec," Ogdell said, so pointedly that I was embarrassed for both of us, "and Stanley can start wheeling in the food."

"Is he drunk already?" I murmured as I took my seat next to Brody. Meg sat opposite, already deep in conversation with a good-looking woman sat next to Karlsson. I regarded the woman closely, trying to remember if she was an MP.

"The champagne's been flowing since lunch," Brody murmured, glancing around the room at the chattering gathering. A telltale flush riding on his cheeks told me he'd not resisted following Ogdell's lead. "You look good." He wore a rakish smile.

"Thanks," I returned awkwardly. "So do you."

His smile grew suggestive and my blood started to rush.

I drank sparingly at dinner. The food was excellent and Brody was good at helping me relax, but the conversation with Meg was still repeating in my head. I decided I needed to know what I really wanted by the end of the evening, rather than just what my body wanted. Brody seemed disappointed every time I waved away the wine bottle, but he covered it quickly.

When the cheese course had been cleared away and the port was being poured, Ogdell stood, a little shakily, from his place at the head of the table.

"My friends. I want to say thank you for joining me here tonight and helping me christen Auchallater Keep. I always say a house is only as good as its hospitality, and I'm grateful for you all for coming to let me know how mine measures up."

There were some calls of encouragement, clapping and clinking of forks on glasses. Brody pressed his leg against mine under the table.

"To friends, to neighbors"—he raised his glass to me—"and to a night we'll never forget." People drank the toast and clapped. "And on that note…what do you say we move on to the main event?"

There was an enthusiastic response, then everyone stood and followed Ogdell out of the room. I questioned Brody with my eyes, but he merely smiled a devilish smile and followed suit.

"What's going on?" I asked Meg as everyone crowded into the hall.

"I don't know," she murmured, keeping her face carefully blank. Ogdell had stopped at a secure-looking door, its heavy frame and key-code lock pad incongruous amongst the luxurious furnishings. The rest of the party were murmuring excitedly and a little nervously. Brody squeezed my hand but his eyes, glinting, were fixed ahead.

Ogdell thumbed in a code and a light above the door changed from red to green. He swung it open and proceeded down some stairs. We followed. A hush descended as we stepped into a brightly-lit subterranean room with a bare concrete floor and walls.

I craned my neck, trying to see over everyone's heads. There was some sort of table in the middle, some machinery next to it and a large refrigeration unit next to that. I frowned, trying to figure out what I was looking at. Meg had gone very still.

"Oh my God," she breathed, then covered her mouth with her hand.

"What is it?" I said, then the cluster of people shifted and I was able to see. It wasn't a table. It was a hospital trolley. And there was someone strapped to it. No. *Something*. Something living, though the only indication of life was the juddering rise and fall of a thin chest under some ragged, stained clothing. Not human. The shrunken, boney thing couldn't have been a person and still be alive. But alive it was. It shifted, causing the guests to take a hurried step back.

The skin was a shade closer to gray than flesh. Blue veins like cords roped over the backs of claw-like hands. The thin wrists were shackled to the trolley in an almost comically unnecessary display of security. It was hard to see much of a face behind a black mask, which obscured the mouth and nose. A tube protruded from it and fed into one of the sleek, unfathomable machines at the bedside. The eyes were closed, the eye sockets sunken and shadowed. Fine hair, in a shade of blond so white that it was almost blue, fell back from the skull-like face and tangled on the trolley, plastered with sweat and dirt. Small tubes, dark with liquid, protruded from both exposed forearms and fed into another machine, which purred and reeled unfathomable readings on a small display.

"Here it is, ladies and gentlemen." Ogdell was slurring, a hungry smile on his wide face, his rapt eyes fixed on the machine rather than the captive.

"How did you get a donor?" the woman Meg had been talking to at dinner asked in an awed voice. "The security controls are so strict…"

"Hans can get his hands on anything." Ogdell beamed at the older man, who bowed slightly.

"This must have cost you thousands," another guest murmured, staring at the donor with the same expression of part awe, part fear.

"Tens of thousands," Olivia put in, her expression pinched. "Jon, we need to feed it."

Ogdell opened the refrigeration unit, revealing rows of blood bags. He took one and fastened its tube to the machine, turning a little release tap. The bright red blood flowed down the tube into the creature's mask. The thing twitched and shuddered. Its eyes flickered.

"Relax, everyone," Ogdell said, waving and airy hand. "It's pumped with enough sedative to take down an elephant. And we've taken every precaution." He nodded to a large handgun mounted on the wall. "You're quite safe. I promise."

"That's enough now, Mr. Ogdell," Karlsson said, and Jon took away the half-full bag.

Olivia shook her head. "It's even thinner than yesterday. We're not feeding it enough."

"Liv, we've been through this," Ogdell muttered whilst the rest of the guests stepped closer and talked in hushed whispers. "Karlsson says half a pouch every three days."

"That is the perfect balance of nutrition and sedatives, Mrs. Ogdell-Paige," Karlsson said smoothly. "Any more than that and it could gain enough strength to fight the drugs and the restraints."

"I don't want the biggest investment of the year expiring in my brother's basement because you two men are afraid to feed it."

Ogdell's face went red. He drew his sister aside and hissed at her. She hissed back. Her husband attempted to placate her with a hand on her arm but she threw him off and left the room, head held high and a blotched flush across her pale cheekbones.

Ogdell straightened his bowtie and flashed his smile at everyone. "Shot of Haemo Blood, anyone?"

Chapter Three

I watched in a daze as Ogdell turned a tap and filled crystal shot glasses with a thick, red liquid, so dark that it was almost black. A curiously heady scent filled the air, somewhere between red wine and late autumn bonfires. The creature on the trolley jerked, white eyelashes flickering against the rounded bones of its eye sockets.

"Is it awake?" I heard someone ask in a quavering voice.

"It's impossible to sedate them completely," Hans Karlsson intoned like someone delivering a biology lecture, "but the balance of sedative in its feed combined with the correct level of nutrient-deprivation keeps it well under control."

I turned away as Ogdell handed the shot glasses around to the wide-eyed guests.

"Come now, Alec," Brody said in my ear. "Not squeamish, are you?"

"It's alive," I breathed.

"Of course it's alive. Can't get Blood from a dead donor." He frowned at the look on my face. "What's wrong?"

"It's *alive*," I repeated.

"Now don't you worry, *my lord*," Ogdell drawled, coming forward with a tray of shot glasses filled with dark Blood. "Hans knows everything there is to know about managing donors. It's not any danger, I promise."

"It looks like it's in pain."

Brody laughed. "It's not human, Alec."

"Come, come," Ogdell said, holding out the tray. "This is not in the spirit of the party. Here."

"I'll pass," I said.

"Me too," said Meg, with slightly more grace and a much warmer expression than me. "It's a bit too much for me, Jon, if you don't mind. I have court on Monday."

"If you're sure," he said, grinning at Meg, who smiled, inclined her head and hurried from the room. The other guests were filtering back upstairs with their glasses, breathing in the scent of the Blood and chattering excitedly, any initial reservations quite forgotten.

Brody and Ogdell stood looking at me expectantly — Brody holding his shot, Ogdell holding out the tray with a broad, foolish smile.

"I swear to God that you've never tried anything until you've tried this." Ogdell's glance slid to Brody and back again. "It's at its absolute best when enjoyed together…if you know what I mean."

"Not for me," I said firmly. "Thank you," I added when their looks darkened.

"Suit yourself," Ogdell said, slightly mollified. "But you don't know what you're missing."

Brody was watching me with something in the back of his gaze that I didn't entirely like. He held the glass out to me so I could smell it. The overly-sweet, thick fragrance filled and dizzied me. My heart sped and my blood throbbed in my temples and groin. Brody's slow smile oozed suggestion.

"And that's just the smell," he murmured.

I swallowed, my mouth suddenly dry. "This is wrong."

"Alec," Brody said with exaggerated patience, "it's not a person. It's barely an animal. Besides, it's not our fault drinking its Blood is better than fucking." He held the glass out.

"Thank you. No."

His face hardened a second before he shrugged. "Fine." He leaned in and brushed his mouth over my ear. "But I'll bet you any money you change your mind."

I shivered. He gave me another wicked smile then made for the door. I glanced back once more at the twisted figure on the trolley and hurried from the room.

The butler was drawing the curtains across the windows when I returned to the sitting room. The snow was already piled inches high on the sills and I could hear the wind howling in the chimney. The fire in the grate danced and sizzled in the cold, snowy gusts.

No one else had noticed. They were sprawled in the deep chairs and sofas, drinking from their shot glasses, breathing heavily, grinning and laughing. The volume of conversation had risen by the same amount as the tone had lowered. The champagne was flowing and the entire gathering lounged with hooded eyes and suggestive smiles, flushed cheeks and heaving chests.

They ran their hands slowly over the soft furnishings and each other in dazed fascination. The staining the Blood had left on their lips gave the whole spectacle an otherworldly, ghoulish air. I spotted Meg in a corner with one of the younger men mouthing in her ear.

She caught my eye and smiled at her companion. "One moment," she said and we stepped out of earshot. "I'm so sorry, Alec. I had no idea it was going to be a Blood Party. I swear."

"Not just a Blood Party," I breathed. "They've got a living haemophile tied up in the basement."

She winced. "I thought only the dealers kept donors. I'm sorry, Alec. I didn't know."

"I believe you," I said, staring over the gathering with a mixture of bewilderment and growing revulsion.

"It's not as bad as some of the things we went to back in the day," she said softly, like she was trying to convince herself. "At least no one here's gonna OD."

"And the thing they're torturing downstairs?"

"No one's bothered," she said softly, gazing around the room.

"Aren't you bothered?"

She swallowed. "Olivia said if it wasn't down there, secure, Blood or no Blood, it would be out at large somewhere, killing people."

"That sounds like something she's read in *The Sun*."

"Or something she tells herself to justify all this."

"Oh no," I said, looking over at Ogdell's sister, one arm draped around her husband's shoulder, the other around Brody as she mouthed at his neck. "I don't think she feels the need to justify anything."

Meg followed my gaze to see Brody tilting Olivia's head back and kissing her feverishly. I felt sick.

"He doesn't know what he's doing," Meg said quickly. "He's high, Alec. That's all."

The threesome got up and went to the door, Brody throwing me a long glance over his shoulder before closing it behind them.

"I'm sorry," Meg said again, putting her drink down. "Shall we leave? I've not had too much to drink. I think I could drive."

I lifted a curtain and gazed moodily out onto the snow spiraling through the air and the branches of the trees thrashing in the wind. "We can't go anywhere in this."

"Christ," she said, looking over my shoulder. "If this keeps up, we mayn't even be able to leave tomorrow."

"I'm leaving tomorrow," I stated, "even if I have to walk."

She tactfully did not point out that we'd not brought boots or coats or anything suitable for hiking through the mountains on a good day, let alone in the snow. I accepted a glass of whisky from the butler and chose one of the chairs away from the remaining guests. Meg sat with me to start but was eventually drawn away by a man who Olivia had said was an actor from television, and a fresh glass of champagne. She appeared to relax a little.

I could not. The longer the party went on, the more I found it unnerving and inexplicable that anyone else could smile, laugh or fuck, as those upstairs were undoubtedly doing, knowing what was in the basement.

I accepted another glass of whisky and wondered again if *I* was the weird one. Haemophiles weren't human. Everyone agreed on that much. I ate meat and drank milk. In the online debates, some argued that there was no difference between that and drinking

Blood, except that it was now illegal, of course. On paper, anyway.

Clem got twitchy whenever the reports of conflict and tension, sometimes violence, came on the radio. The unsolved murder of Shelly Morris had been in the papers for months. I only got my impressions of the wider world from Meg, but she'd implied that people were being more careful with what they said since a few charges of human-on-haemo harassment, slander and assault had been successfully tried in court. But the general feeling of abhorrence-tinged-with-fear was just as dense now as it had been when haemophiles had first emerged from their secluded communes and announced their existence to the world.

I'd always told myself it would never touch me at Glenroe. It was yet another ugly reality to separate myself from. But reality, I was coming to realize, always had a way of catching up.

I decided I had to see it again. If I could look at it as they looked at it, as a *thing*, I might at least be able to make it through the night without going crazy. Meg had disappeared off somewhere with the handsome actor. Brody was still upstairs with Olivia and her husband.

I was unsure how I felt about that, beyond the obvious. The alcohol and rich food layered over the prickly sense of unease created a tangle of emotion that was quite complicated enough without adding wounded pride and jealousy.

I put down my glass and slipped from the room. The corridors were unnervingly quiet, the only sound the storm gathering force outside, like a monster roaring in the distance. I found the security door and stared at the keypad dumbly. I was only just getting my head around my stupidity when I heard footsteps and laughter down the corridor.

I ducked through the nearest door, discovered a coat closet bigger than my bedroom and pulled the door to. Through the gap I watched Ogdell approach and key the code in, Olivia, disheveled and swaying slightly, at his heels. Her husband, Matthew, came just behind her, gazing around with dazed fascination.

"No more tonight, Jon. I mean it. You'll kill it," Olivia said.

"Relax," he drawled, pushing the door open. "The bastard's still got plenty of juice."

Olivia's spluttering protests were cut off when the security door shut in her face. She glared at the metal before her husband guided her back down the corridor. I held my breath. Ogdell re-emerged with more shot glasses filled with red-black Blood and sauntered off, humming to himself. I darted out just in time to catch the door before it closed. It was utterly dark on the stairwell. When my feet hit flat ground, the illumination from the machines allowed me to find a light switch.

The haemophile's face was turned to the wall. Its shallow breathing rasped behind the mask. My throat closed. Despite the perfect environment controls, I felt cold.

I made myself move closer. In pictures, the ones that weren't artificially enhanced by the tabloids, haemophiles resembled people—people who perhaps hadn't seen much sun and with something about the depths of their eyes and the fine lines of their faces and bodies that wasn't *quite* right. But this living skeleton seemed like nothing that could be real, nothing possibly alive. Every slope and angle of its skull was evident through the paper-white skin. Its hands were curled rigid like birds' talons. Its fingernails were neat, perfect, translucent and sharp as claws. Its hair was impossibly fine. Even in its matted and dirty state, it looked like it would be soft to touch. A ripped and stained jumper and jeans hung off the wasted frame, looking utterly surreal, like someone had dressed a skeleton in cast-offs from a charity bin.

The machines hummed and bleeped. With growing alarm, I became aware that the creature's ragged breathing was getting shallower. The pulse meter on the machine was barely registering a heartbeat. I stood frozen, not knowing whether I should do anything or whether I could, even as I realized Olivia was right and it was surely dying.

The head rolled toward me. The eyelids flickered then opened a slit. I caught the tiniest glimpse of large pupils, blacker than night, before they fluttered closed again. Its hands trembled. A harsh noise came from behind the mask. Its chest rattled as it pulled in another breath then made the noise again. It was trying to speak. My hands trembled but I reached out, fumbled the fastening of the mask open and gently pulled it free. The creature gagged as a blood-stained tube slipped from its throat. It took a huge breath, opening a very red mouth filled with teeth, surely more than any human had, wickedly sharp and white. I stared, unable to look away and, for the first time, felt fear. It opened its eyes. The whites were bloodshot. The pupils were so large and so black that they were like holes into space. The irises were shrunk to next to nothing, but I could still see they were a luminescent shade of silver unlike anything I'd ever seen in any living creature.

"Kill…me…" Its voice was raw, cracked, but I heard the words loud and clear. Its gaze flickered to the handgun on the wall. I couldn't move. Icy water flowed through my veins. "Please…" it rasped. The bloodshot eyes bored into mine. The terrifying mouth hung open as it struggled to breathe. Then its deep, pained eyes slid closed again. The hands went slack.

I looked around hopelessly. The pathetic bleep of the pulse meter petered to nothing and was replaced by a whining alarm. I froze, waiting for someone to open the security door and come running, but nothing happened.

The alarm whined on. I retrieved a pouch of blood before I had time to think.

"Will this help?" I asked in a shaky voice. The haemophile didn't answer. It hadn't moved again. I stared at the bag of blood in my hand for a long moment, only coming back to reality when I registered that the haemo was no longer breathing. I swore, twisted the plastic release on the blood bag and held the opening to its mouth. A small amount spilled across its cracked lips, looking very red against the pallid skin. I started to shake, feeling very unwell. Nothing happened.

A powerful mix of terror, revulsion and humiliation churned in my gut, but then the creature's mouth opened. Swallowing a bad taste in my mouth, I tipped the bag to let the blood flow. It swallowed. Color suffused its face. Its whole body shuddered. It drank deep, long swallows, the muscles of its throat moving sinuously. The alarm stopped and the pulse meter started bleeping again. The pale eyelids flickered. It rattled its restraints.

I watched the pulse indicator grow stronger and heard its breathing steady. I stepped back, realizing, too late, that the bag was empty. I held my breath, but the creature just lay there, its tension and pain visibly eased. I couldn't decide if it was a trick of the light or whether its appearance had altered. It was still pale, but now it had the coloring of someone naturally fair, rather than the sickly gray of someone close to death. It looked — he, I suddenly realized with a shock — looked more real.

I was hunting for somewhere to hide the depleted pouch when the haemophile shifted, straining against the restraints so hard that they creaked. The bottom dropped out of my stomach. I was backing away when I heard the door open and footsteps on the stairs.

"I knew you'd change your mind," Brody said as he joined me, his smile wide, hair mussed and pupils huge, until his glance slid to the trolley and the empty blood bag on the floor. All the color drained from his cheeks.

"Shit," he swore. "What did you do?" One of the restraints snapped. Brody wore again and pushed me toward the stairs. "For fuck's sake, run."

It all happened so quickly. One second I was making for the stairs, my heart in my mouth. The next there was the groan of protesting metal, a blood-chilling cry and Brody was screaming.

I froze with my hand on the bannister. Brody was on the ground, the haemophile on top of him, hands digging into his arms so hard that the fingernails were slicing through his shirt and into his flesh. Its face was buried in his neck, just under his ear. Its white hair was stained red. Brody was yelling, choking as blood bubbled from his mouth. It pooled on the floor. He slipped in it trying to scrabble backward. His screams grew weaker and his struggles slowed. His body stiffened then went limp.

I tasted bile in my mouth. I still couldn't move. The haemophile straightened, its mouth wide open, taking the deep breaths of a drowning man breaching the surface. Blood stained its face and throat and blackened the front of its clothing. Its eyes were closed in ecstasy, the lines of its face slack with pleasure. It was gripping Brody's body so hard that I heard bone crack.

It opened its eyes. There was a horrible, confused moment when it took in the sight of Brody in its grip, blood-soaked and unmoving, a gaping wound oozing in his neck. Horror filled its face. Then its gaze fell on me.

I tried to run but my muscles had no strength. I couldn't breathe, couldn't think. I could smell Brody's blood. I could smell his terror and my own. I could smell his urine. Silver-gray eyes, clear, pale and sharper than knives, pinned me to the wall.

The muted sound of laughter through the ceiling broke the spell. The haemophile shoved Brody's body away and reached for me. Adrenaline finally released my limbs. I dashed for the stairs, but it was too fast. Hands like vises closed on my arm and neck, the grip so tight it choked off my attempts to yell. Nails dug into my skin. Hot breath smelling like copper brushed over my face.

"Struggle and I'll have to kill you." The voice was low. Smooth. It was a young man's voice, lilting with a Scandinavian accent, sharpened with an edge of something powerful and barely contained. "Move. Slowly."

I blinked until I could focus. I took a step. Then another. The haemophile's body pressed against my back, his hands bruisingly strong. My breath dragged in and out of my restricted throat with a noise like someone gasping out their last.

The corridor was empty. I tried to call out but the haemophile tightened his grip, his nails breaking the skin. Blood trickled down my neck and I couldn't breathe. He let me choke until the world started to go gray, then moved me onward.

Ogdell, Olivia and her husband emerged from the sitting room just as we reached the front door. They froze, their eyes widening, the smiles fleeing their faces quicker than the lightning flashing through the windows.

"Stay back." The haemophile's voice wasn't loud, but everyone winced. Matthew Ogdell-Paige swore under his breath. Olivia pressed a thin hand to her suddenly bloodless mouth. Karlsson appeared behind Olivia, took in the scene and turned white.

"Stanley!" Ogdell called. "Stanley, the shotgun!"

The haemophile snarled and wrenched open the door. I yelled and tried to break away, but it was too strong, nearly yanking my arm from its socket as it dragged me into the night.

"Follow and he dies." His shout was almost lost in the rushing wind as we bowled into the blizzard. I was blinded, bruised and dizzied, sliding in the snow. He tumbled me into the passenger seat of Meg's Mazda and slammed the door. There was a snap as he broke off the handle. The driver's door opened, allowing another gust of freezing wind to blast in, then he was pulling the dash apart with his bare hands.

I rattled the interior handle uselessly. I tried elbowing the glass but there was a cough and sputter, the engine roared and we were speeding off into the dark with no headlights. The sports car slid and scudded over the icy road, already a foot-deep in snow. The gale-force wind caught the side and buffeted it toward the ditch. The haemophile heaved the wheel over and we skidded back onto the road. I fought down vomit as we raced blindly into the storm.

He had a death-grip on the wheel, his knuckles standing out white, flooring the accelerator. His face was a grisly mask in the blue light from the dash, smeared in blood, his black eyes hollow and huge.

"Stop," I yelled the second I had breath. "*Stop*." He bared his carnivore teeth and jerked the wheel. We skidded around a corner, the back wheel crunching into the stones at the side of the road. "You'll kill us both."

He made a low noise like a growl and jerked the wheel over to skid around another corner. I was flung against the car door with bruising force. I clutched the overhead handle so hard it hurt.

"If you're going to kill me, do it now. Get it over with."

The haemophile screamed. It started a low grumble in the back of his throat then rose to a keening cry. He whipped the wheel over. The car groaned and crunched, climbing the verge and ramming something with head-snapping force. My vision swam and I tasted blood in my mouth. By the time I could see straight, the driver's door was hanging open and the haemophile was gone. I fought down vomit and clutched my head, trying to make it stop spinning.

Slowly, I became aware of a sound over the wind. Someone crying out. Great, long, mournful cries like an animal being tortured rent the air, stabbing ice to the center of my soul. I fumbled for the headlight control. Ten feet away, at the edge of the pool of light, the bent form of the haemophile knelt in the snow, head in his hands, swaying back and forth. A painful mix of emotions tightened my chest.

I shook my head, knowing I wouldn't get another chance, and clambered over the gearbox and out of the driver's door. My heart clamored behind my ribs and the freezing air burned in my lungs. I tried to run but stumbled onto my hands and knees in the freezing snow and vomited copiously. When there was nothing left, my head was pounding, my hands stinging and every inch of me shuddering violently.

"Get back in."

I blinked in the stinging wind. The haemophile stood over me, skin and hair glowing white in the headlights, making his blood-blackened clothing seem even darker. I scrambled away, but I was pained and dizzy and the haemophile had no trouble heaving me up by the armpits and crushing me back into the car. I cursed him, struck out, kicked, but he sshoved me into the passenger seat like I was nothing more than a toddler having a tantrum.

"Bastard," I swore. "Sick bastard. You better let me go or —"

He flung the car into reverse. It crunched free of the damaged wall, engine emitting pained coughs, screaming when he pressed the accelerator. He'd wiped his face and hands clean with snow. The ends of his long, pale hair dripped with melt. His flesh had filled into the normal, smooth lines of a healthy, if slim, adult. The eyes were no longer sunken. His hands were less like claws, even if he did grip the steering wheel tight enough for the bones to stand out like cables under his skin.

If he hadn't been wearing the torn sweatshirt still soaked in Brody's blood, I would have sworn it was a different man — a wild-looking, terrifying and dangerous man, but a man nonetheless.

My body shook from cold and coursing adrenaline. I forced my voice to be level. "If you don't want to eat me, what the hell do you want with me?"

He didn't answer. Something inside me snapped and I snarled and grabbed for him. I had no idea what I was planning, but it wouldn't have mattered anyway. He seized my wrist and twisted it. I strained against the grip, felt something give and cried out.

"Don't," was all he said, then he released me.

I clutched my pounding wrist to my chest and doubled over. I rested my forehead on the dash and did something I hadn't done since I was a child. I prayed.

The storm worsened as we climbed higher into the hills. He was forced to slow then stop entirely when the wheels skidded in the slush and the wind drove the snow at the screen too forcefully for the wipers to clear it. When I raised my head, he was staring out at a snow-obscured road sign. At that moment, the engine spluttered and died, plunging us into almost total blackness.

"Where are we?" he asked.

I kept myself very still and didn't answer.

"Tell me where we are." There was no obvious threat in the voice, but my whole body went stiff. I clutched my sore wrist, breathed in and out through my mouth and continued to pray for it to be over.

The haemophile made an impatient noise and opened his door, letting in snow and the heaving roar of tortured trees. There was a moment of fraught silence, then the passenger door was torn open and he was dragging me out. The wind cut through my dinner suit and drove snow into my face. I staggered in the deep drifts as he pulled me along. I clamped my hands into my armpits but they still pulsed with cold. My face stung. My lungs burned. Every time I stumbled, he hauled me upright again with seemingly unending strength.

I choose not to remember that blind, freezing journey through the storm. I'd grown up in those mountains. I knew what exposure could do and how quickly it could do it. I was never able to decide whether I survived only because we weren't out in it for as long as it felt or if I was just too stubborn to give him the satisfaction of killing two of us in one night.

Probably a little of both.

My legs were giving out by the time the haemophile halted, propping me against a solid surface. I heard the sound of wood groaning and splintering, then I was being dragged out of the wind.

I tumbled onto a stone floor, shuddering in my soaked clothes, teeth chattering, muscles convulsing. I was vaguely aware of the sound of something heavy being dragged across the stone, then the world was filled with bright light. I cried out, rubbing my eyes until they stopped watering. I raised myself on one elbow and stared. I recognized the stone-flagged passage. Familiar faces smiled down at me from the photos on the wall.

I got shakily to my feet. The haemophile had hauled an ancient armoire in front of the ruined door. He himself was nowhere to be seen. I leaned against the wall until I could trust my legs to hold me. I moved through the dark and drafty house until I felt a warm breeze sweep around my frozen feet. The clank of someone shutting the door of the iron stove in the kitchen echoed in the stillness.

I picked up my pace, grabbing at the furniture to keep upright. The light was on in the kitchen. I reached the door just in time to see the haemophile pull the phone cable out of the wall.

"You…You…"

"Don't get warm too quickly," he said, pocketing my mobile and grabbing the radio off the windowsill.

"God help me, I'll kill you," I croaked, staggering forward and falling to my knees. He passed me without a glance and I heard him hunting through my bedroom. He emerged holding my emergency radio and left without a word, taking the keys from the inside of the kitchen door. I got to my feet just as he slammed it shut and I heard the key turn in the lock.

I ranted and raved, hammering on the wood. I tried to heave a chair at it but my strength gave out and I slid to the floor, panting—and the world went black. When I woke a bit later, curled in a ball on the hard linoleum, the room was warmer but I was shuddering from my wet clothes. I groaned, easing myself off the floor stiffly, and limped to the stove. I built the fire back up, absorbing the heat through my pores until my shivering eased. My teeth were still chattering as I shed my wet clothes and pulled on warm fleece trousers and shirt, a jumper and thick socks. I sat on the bed, wrapping the duvet around myself, trembling and aching.

My mind ran in circles. I heard Brody scream, smelled his blood and piss, felt the wrench of the haemophile twisting my wrist, the ice of the wind on my face. My arms and neck were scratched, bruised and sticky with dried blood. But still, none of it seemed like it could be real.

I padded around, unable to sit still. The storm continued to rattle window frames and made the very bones of the house creak, but it was nothing compared to my inner tumult. I made some hot chocolate and forced myself to drink it. It warmed me through and the sugar helped calm the trembling, but it did nothing to ease the surging in my brain.

I hunted half-heartedly for my laptop or any other means of communication, but he'd taken everything. I was just trying to find a tool or engine part heavy enough to use on the door when the light fizzed and went out.

My watch told me it was close to dawn, but the raging storm and the snow piled high against the kitchen window kept the place black as night. I shambled back to the bedroom, not knowing what else to do, collapsed on the bed and let exhaustion steal me away.

* * * *

I opened my eyes onto meager gray light. I guessed it must be early morning, but my watch told me it was close to noon. I rose stiffly from the bed. The room had gone cold. I went to the kitchen window and raised the blind. A solid wall of snow greeted me. I stared at it until I started shivering, then hurried to the stove. My strained muscles ached and my head pounded, but my fingers and toes no longer stung and had returned to a normal color. When I'd built the fire up again using nearly all the remaining stock of firewood, I tried the light. It didn't respond. The fridge was off too.

I tried the door, without much hope. Finding it still locked, I hunted again for something to break it down with but couldn't find anything that would make a dent in the thick, ancient oak. I contemplated taking the hinges off, but the screwdriver on my penknife wasn't big enough and my spare tools were missing from their drawer.

"Bastard."

My voice sounded raspy and strange in the cold, still air. I stood helplessly in the middle of the kitchen, trying not to think about why I was still alive. My eyes slid to the window. I rejected the idea before it fully formed. Even if I could break enough of the glass to avoid slicing myself to ribbons, there was no telling how deep the snow was. Muffled roars and groans also indicated that the storm was still in full force. Even if I made it to the workshop, there was nothing to say it would have power or a working phone line. As for making it as far as the garages, there would be no getting a vehicle out in this weather. The only place that could be reasonably gotten to on foot was Clem's cottage, over ten miles north. Even in full snow gear, it would be dangerous. And all my heavy-weather gear was in a cupboard in the hall.

I sat on the edge of my bed and stared at nothing. My wrist was still throbbing and had blackened, but I could clench and unclench my fist, so I reassured myself nothing was broken. I fingered the scratches on my neck in a dumb sort of disbelief. The vision of the haemophile clutching Brody hard enough to snap bone and the ecstasy that had slackened his face as Brody died rose before my eyes. I made it to the toilet, just, and threw up what little was left in my belly. I woke again, hours later, to darkness and the sound of someone going through the kitchen cupboards.

I stepped to the bedroom door. The haemophile was opening and closing cupboards, moving things aside, putting them back. His hair and skin glowed amber in the low light from the newly-rekindled fire.

The kitchen door was open. Slowly and silently, I grabbed a pair of boots and padded to the door. He bent to peer under the sink. I ran.

It was pitch black, but I knew my way around the house blindfolded. I grabbed a heavy coat from the hall cupboard and made for the side door, remembering too late that he'd blocked that way. No amount of straining would shift the armoire. I swore bitterly and ran for the front door, my pulse thundering in my throat. I fumbled blindly for the bolts and heaved at the key. I swore still more bitterly when the cold metal didn't move.

"The lock's frozen."

I spun. The haemophile stood silhouetted in the light from the kitchen door. After a long moment in which I could feel his eyes on me, he turned away.

Something exploded inside me. I stormed through to the drawing room and scrabbled on top of the gun cabinet for the key. I loaded dusty cartridges into the barrels of a shotgun with shaking hands and returned to the kitchen. The haemophile was looking in the fridge. I thumbed the hammer back and raised the gun. The haemophile glanced over his shoulder and shut the fridge door slowly.

"That would be a mistake."

The gun began to shake. Red waves pulsed through my head. Brody's screams filled my ears.

I stared at him down the barrel. He gazed impassively back. He'd changed into an old jersey and a battered pair of winter work trousers I recognized from one of the trunks in the cellar. He must have found the garden room, the only other room in the house with running water, because he'd washed the remains of the gore and dirt from his face and hair. His skin was a warm gold color in the light from the fire. His white hair was tucked neatly behind his ears, brushing lightly against the smooth skin of his neck. It curled slightly where it was still damp. He was taller than I'd thought, almost on an eye-level with me. His fingers were long, like a woman's, tipped with those wickedly-sharp fingernails. His eyes were an impossible shade of gold and silver in the changeable light, fringed with thick, pale lashes that caught the firelight like frost in the sunrise. They were so deep and dark they set my nerves on edge, but I couldn't look away.

"Why are you still here?" My voice shook.

"I'm stuck here. Like you." He turned his back on me and opened the larder.

I took a step forward. He selected a bottle of merlot from the wine rack. "Corkscrew?"

"I said I'd kill you."

"I heard you." I clenched the gun tighter. The corner of his mouth twitched, but whether it was the beginning of a smile or a grimace I couldn't tell. "The shot wouldn't kill me."

"I don't believe you."

"If you shoot me, you'll die."

Rage and terror somersaulted around the inside of my skull. I clenched my eyes shut. When I opened them again, I'd lowered the gun and my chest hurt. "I can't just stand here and let you…" My voice petered away.

He found my penknife and opened the wine, his thick eyelashes lowered. "We're stuck here until either your friends find you or my friends find me. We might at least find a way to be civil." He poured some wine into one of my father's whisky tumblers and held it out to me. I didn't move.

"If my friends get here first—"

"We'd better hope they don't," he said in a low voice, placing the wine on the table with deliberate care.

"Or you'll rip them apart too?"

Something shifted in his eyes. "You should eat."

"What?"

"Your blood sugar. It's low. You've been in shock."

"And what are *you* going to *eat*?" I said between clenched teeth.

He lifted the bottle with a heavy-lidded look. When I didn't move, he reached out and pulled the gun out of my hands as easily as someone pulling a toy from a child. "It's for your own good."

He vanished into the shadows of the house, taking the gun and wine bottle with him. After a stunned moment, I retrieved a storm lantern and searched the ground floor but couldn't find any trace of him. He'd emptied the gun cabinet.

I didn't dare chance the stairs in the dark. I strained my ears above the storm hammering at the boarded windows on the gallery. The whole house seemed to be moaning in pain, but I couldn't hear footsteps or doors closing or any indication of anyone else in the building.

It was then I spotted an arc in the dust on the floor by the cellar door. I stared at it for a long moment then tried the handle, but it was locked from the inside. I scowled at the warped wood, clenching and unclenching my fist, then a wave of lightheadedness went through me. I clutched the doorframe, hanging my head until it passed.

I retreated to the warmth of the kitchen, slammed the door and collapsed into a chair, burying my face in my hands. I felt nauseous, dizzy and sore, but what was going on in my head was far more unpleasant.

I made myself heat some canned macaroni on the stove and swallow it with some bread, though I could taste nothing. The painful knot of emptiness eased in my belly, but my head continued to throb and whirl. I watched the clock over the stove, the hands approaching midnight. I'd slept most of what had passed for the day but still had to prop myself up in a kitchen chair to stop myself from drifting off. When I wasn't watching the clock, I was watching the door. The hours stretched on and nothing happened.

The night had a surreal quality, like one of those dreams that leave a person uneasy once they wake, even though the imagery is lost in fog. The silence, the darkness and the storm continued. I shifted in the chair, startled by the realization that I wished he'd come back. Anything was better than sitting and waiting for him to kill me.

I stared at the tumbler of wine for over an hour before I drank it.

Despite my best efforts and the cold threads of tension that were strung through my muscles like wire, I fell asleep. My dreams were fractured and violent. But waking from them to the cold, empty silence of the kitchen was not as much of a relief as it should have been.

I belatedly turned off the dimming lantern to save the batteries and could just make out my surroundings in the wan light of the new day. The clock told me it was a little after nine. I tried the lights again but the switch was still unresponsive. My breath misted in the gray air.

It took me more time than I care to admit, even now, to walk over and try the door. It opened with its customary low creak. I peered out into the shadowed dining room beyond, my breathing loud in the empty air. I met nothing but dust sheets, silence and cobwebs. I swallowed. My hatred, anger and panic had deserted me sometime in the last twenty-four hours, leaving behind nothing but a naked, acute disquiet.

The dusty rooms had taken on a ghostly quality in the muted light from the snow-blocked windows. I made myself check every one of them and both the doors again, but there was still no way out on this level.

I approached the staircase, my pulse throbbing in my ears. The cellar door was firmly shut. I crept up the rotting stairs, skipping the ones I knew creaked the most. A watery, white light spilled onto the landing from an empty window frame, the boards that had blocked it lying in a drift of snow across the moldering carpet. I approached the window and peered out.

I couldn't see far. The wind had eased but it was still snowing, curtaining the view of the glen in swirls of white and gray. I shivered violently in the skin-biting chill but leaned out to see if there was a way down. The snow was drifted almost ten feet deep against the walls, though I still didn't trust it to be deep enough to break my fall if I jumped. Even if I found a way to climb down, there was still nowhere to go.

I shivered and hurried back to the clinging shadows of the ground floor. I filled my arms from the scullery wood store and hurried back to the kitchen, not looking at the cellar door as I passed. I was making my second trip when a sound halted me in the hall. I listened. I had just convinced myself it was a trick of the wind when I heard it again...

"*Alec*? Alec, are you in there?"

I dumped the firewood and hurried to the front door. "Meg?" I called through the thick wood. "Meg, is that you?"

"Alec, thank God!" Her voice was muffled and came from above my head where she must have been perched on the drifted snow. "Matthew Ogdell-Paige found the car. There was blood. I thought it must...that you must..."

"I'm fine," I called.

"*How*? How are you fine?"

I glanced behind me at the cellar door and swallowed. "It's a long story. What about you?"

She made a strained noise. "We've been trapped in that fucking horrible house for a day and a night." Her voice was high, like she'd been fighting panic for too long. "The storm's cut us off from everything. We lost power, phones, everything. We've been stuck there with…with…oh God."

"What? What is it?"

Silence for a long time. "It killed Brody, Alec. Somehow it got free and before it grabbed you, it must have…Christ. He… The body's still in the basement. Everyone's been fighting over what to do."

I clenched my eyes shut. "How did you get away?" I called.

"Jon and Matthew went out on snowmobiles as soon as the wind dropped, to find you, they said…but they took guns. I think they were hunting for the thing. They found my car but nothing else. I made them lend me a snowmobile. I had to see if I could find you. This was the only place I could think of to check. They all said you were done for, that it would have taken you off somewhere to…"

"I'm not hurt, Meg," I insisted, keeping my voice level. "I promise I'm fine."

"How do I get in? All the doors are blocked."

A low creaking noise echoed across the hall. My throat closed. I turned. The cellar door was open a crack. White fingers clutched the edge, sharp fingernails digging into the wood. In the shadows beyond was the suggestion of a pale face, a very red mouth wide open, a single eye, impossibly dark, fixed on me.

"Don't come in."

"What?" she called.

I swallowed to steady my voice. "There's no way in. And I can't get out. But I promise I'm okay."

"What the hell happened, Alec?" I stood pinned in place, my ragged breath misting in the air. Slowly, painfully slowly, the cellar door closed again. "Alec?"

I shook my head. "He crashed the car. Then he disappeared."

"'He?"

"It," I corrected. "The haemophile. The storm was… We couldn't see. We went off the road. It ran off. I don't know where."

"And you made it all the way here?"

"I'm not sure how…"

"It didn't hurt you?"

I blinked at the frozen lock. "No."

"Why did it take you with it if it didn't want to… If you weren't—"

"I was just for leverage, in case anyone followed. It didn't want to hurt me." A pause whilst the wind picked up, prohibiting conversation, during which I realized what I'd said and that I believed it. "What's happening at the lodge?"

Her voice, when it came, was thin. "It's bad. Jon Ogdell won't go to the police."

"What?"

"He's said no one's to say anything—about Brody, about anything. He knows he'd go down for the donor. He says if anyone talks, he'll take us all down with him."

I clenched my teeth, anger flickering in the pit of my stomach. "Listen, Meg," I said firmly. "Get away, okay? Take that snowmobile and get the hell away."

"I can't," she said. "It's still raging out here. I wouldn't get more than a few miles. Besides, if I run, they'll think I've gone to the police. They know where I live. And that Hans Karlsson? He's dangerous, Alec. They're all dangerous."

"Okay, plan B…" I said, rubbing my temples and thinking furiously. "Go back to the lodge and stay calm. Tell them I'm here, that I'm okay and that the haemophile took off but I don't know to where."

"What will you do?"

I slid a glance back at the cellar, feeling a numb hollow where I thought my terror should be. "As soon as the weather clears, I'll come find you and we'll figure this out."

A pause. "It's supposed to turn by the end of the week, I think. We got that much from the TV before the power went."

"Get back and play along. But leave the minute you can. Okay?"

"All right. Just promise me that you're okay."

I nodded, even though she couldn't see me. "I promise."

Chapter Four

I stood by the front door for a long time after the roar of Meg's snowmobile engine had died away. The cellar door stayed shut. It was several moments before I could make myself move. I retrieved the wood and built up the kitchen fire and went through the cupboards. I tried to focus on anything other than what might be going on at the lodge or in the cellar.

The image of the long fingers curled around the edge of the door and the empty, black eye watching me made my stomach plunge. But then I remembered those same eyes looking down the gun barrel at me, unfathomable but calm. Patient. Even a little sad.

It was only when I caught myself watching the clock that I realized I was waiting for nightfall. I tried to make my throbbing head get in line. I didn't even know if the daylight thing was something I'd read about haemophiles or in *Dracula*. I scrabbled through the old magazines and newspapers that were scattered across the kitchen and piled in the kindling basket. The only article I found was a report on protests in London the day the courts decided to grant haemophiles human rights.

Human rights.

I frowned at the angry expressions in the photos and their placards plastered with the face of Shelly Morris, the nine-year-old girl found dead in Hyde Park over a year ago, covered in bite marks and drained of blood. I scoured the article, but it only reported on the protest, the court decision and details about the girl.

I screwed up the newspaper and threw it into the fire.

It was a shock to be woken hours later, in near-darkness, never having intended to fall asleep. I was sitting at the kitchen table with my head pillowed on my arms. The smell of frying bacon was rich in the air. I jerked up, knocking the chair back against the counter in my attempt to scramble away.

The haemophile was at the stove with a frying pan on its flat top. He was just pouring a mix of beaten egg over fried bacon pieces and mushrooms. The egg mix sizzled as it hit the hot oil. The smell filled the room and made my knotted stomach clench.

"What are you doing?" I said, edging away.

"You need to eat." He shook the pan, bent and threw another piece of wood onto the fire. Incredulous, I watched him cook the omelet, plate it up and set it on the table. He finally met my eyes, unabashed and almost curious. He stood statue-still, motionless in a way no human ever could be. He didn't appear to blink. His face was a shifting mass of soft shadows and amber highlights in the fire's glow. It lit gold threads in his ice-white hair and sent electricity through my skin in a way that both excited and terrified me.

"I scared you today."

"What?"

"In the hall. I'm sorry."

"You're *sorry*?"

"I am."

My fear flagged. Anger rose in its place. "Stop pretending."

His eyes flickered. "Pretending?"

"That you're normal."

Now, he blinked. "What's 'normal'?"

"Not ripping someone's throat out with your teeth."

I expected anger or indignity. Anything. But all he did was meet my eyes without expression. "What about tying someone to a table, starving them, drugging them, bleeding them and drinking it?"

I clenched and unclenched my fists. "You killed my friend."

His gaze slid away from mine. "That wasn't me. It was the Blood. It...protects itself."

"Don't bullshit me."

"I don't expect you to understand," he said, dropping the frying pan into the sink.

"I want you out of my house."

"I can't leave any more than you can."

"Move that damn armoire and go."

He nodded to the food. "It's going cold." I glared at him. He raised one pale eyebrow a fraction. "If I wanted to kill you, I wouldn't need to poison you."

"Then what's this in aid of? Do we taste better when we're well-fed?"

"Your blood sugar is still low. You've been exposed to extreme temperature and shock. Your body needs food."

"How do you know?"

"I can smell it."

I gritted my teeth against the uneasiness that surged up my spine. "Why do you *care*?"

He held my gaze a moment longer then looked away. "If I make you uncomfortable, I'll leave. I only came through to get warm."

He moved to the door. I shifted the other way, keeping the table between us. I could smell the omelet. My stomach clenched but I didn't sit until he'd left the kitchen and shut the door behind him. I stared at the food then grabbed a fork and tasted it carefully. It was fluffy, stuffed with the last of my fresh bacon and just the right amount of salt. I examined it a moment longer, my mouth watering. I took another bite. Then another. Before I knew it, the plate was wiped clean. My stomach eased and my muscles relaxed. I felt more awake.

The wind still howled somewhere above the cocoon of snow. The fire crackled. I searched for my anger. Before I realized I was moving, I'd grabbed the lantern and left the kitchen.

I found him in the drawing room. He was staring at the landscape painting over the marble fireplace. The only light in the room was the one I'd brought, but he stood examining the painting, quietly rapt, like it was on display in an expertly lit gallery.

"This is a Jacob More, isn't it?" I didn't answer, but he nodded to himself anyway. "He always painted Scottish landscapes the best."

"Knew him, did you?"

He seemed almost on the point of smiling before saying, "You've read too much Anne Rice."

"Not immortal, then?" I asked, keeping my words clipped.

"Of course not."

"So how old are you?"

He raised an eyebrow. "Why do you want to know?"

"I..." I struggled for words. "Just tell me."

He contemplated me again with that faintly curious air, giving his unfathomable eyes a human warmth. "I'll tell you anything you want to know," he said, leaning his hip against a covered sofa with the ease of someone so used to their body that they were graceful without trying. "We're supposed to answer questions to help people understand us better. But people rarely listen to the answers — or don't believe them if they do."

"I am the very definition of a captive audience."

"You really want to know?"

"Yes." His silver eyes flickered to the empty gun rack then back to me. "I don't..." I swallowed. My throat was dry, my palms a little damp. I rubbed my wrist, which was still aching dully. "We both know I can't hurt you."

"That's true. But I need you to understand I'm not going to hurt you, either."

I blinked at him. His accent and level voice made him sound like someone out of a film or a radio play. He didn't sound real. He didn't look real. "You hurt Brody."

He pressed his lips together. "I did. But I didn't want to." I found myself wanting to believe him. The realization shocked me and I scowled to cover my reaction. "I won't hurt you," he repeated, firmly, "as long as you don't try to hurt me. I have no control over what might happen if you do." I searched his face but couldn't figure out what I was seeing. Eventually, I nodded. He gestured into the shadows. "Shall we go back to the kitchen?"

"You feel the cold?"

"I feel the cold."

I let him lead the way, still not quite able to turn my back on him. He walked sedately, with that same ease of movement, but I had to hurry to keep up. His breath didn't fog in the cold air like mine. I shut the kitchen door and put the lantern on the table, then fed the fire. I could feel him watching me. I dragged a chair closer to the stove. He took another bottle from the wine rack and two tumblers from the draining board.

"You have questions." He sat and uncorked the bottle. The electric lantern made his pale skin glow. It shone off his high cheekbones and the lines of his neck. His mouth was soft, his lips slightly curved, even at rest. I remembered it open, redder than blood, the teeth shockingly white and sharp. I remembered his hands, strong enough to crack the wood of the basement door, strong enough to break Brody's bones. But now he sat easily in my kitchen chair, regarding me steadily with calm, entrancing eyes. He was terrifying, but he was beautiful, like a freezing winter morning in the very heart of the mountains. I bridled at the thought and dropped my gaze to the tabletop.

"How old are you?" I heard myself ask.

"Not old enough to have known Jacob More," he said, with something like amusement in his voice.

"That's not an answer."

He still didn't smile but something like humor flickered in the dark depths of his eyes. "I don't know exactly. Over eighty, less than a hundred."

"How do you not know how old you are?"

He lifted a shoulder in a half-shrug. "You stop counting after a while." I narrowed my eyes and his mouth twitched. "And, well...at the time, it wasn't considered important where I'm from." His brow creased slightly, his eyes far away. "I remember the Second World War but not the first. Do I get to ask a question now?"

I chewed on the inside of my cheek, regarding him closely and trying not to think about the fluttering in my belly. "What question?"

"Is this really your home?"

"Why?"

He tilted his chin slightly. "I knew you must live here when we arrived. I could smell it. But the place looks like it belongs to someone else."

Something prickled over the skin of my back. "Again, why do you care?"

"Just curious, like you."

"I'm not *curious* about you," I said in tight voice. "That's not what this is."

He inclined his head. "Very well. You don't have to answer. Next question?"

I picked at a splinter on the table, not looking at him. "Daylight…"

"What about it?"

"Does it kill you?"

"No."

"Then why —?"

"The cellar?" He sipped his wine. His mouth was stained slightly pink. I hurriedly lifted my gaze. "We have to sleep, just like you do."

"During the day?"

"We're sensitive to sunlight," he said slowly, factually. "We don't produce melanin in the same way, so we burn easily. And it's hard to see."

"So you just…sleep?"

He frowned at his glass. "Not the way you sleep. The Blood requires us to...offline. Recharge."

"Could you stay awake if you wanted? During the day?"

"Yes, though it's hard. But the Blood wakes us if there's a threat. Is it my turn now?"

I hesitated and reached for the other glass. "I thought you said you were supposed to answer my questions."

"Polite conversation normally goes both ways."

I fought a scowl. "We're not exactly meeting at a dinner party here."

"No," he said softly, looking into the fire. "But that's not my fault, is it?"

I took a long drink. It was one of the last bottles of good wine I had bought after a couple of lucrative summer jobs. The taste warmed me all the way down and I found myself relaxing a fraction, despite everything. "What's your question?"

"Do you know who kidnapped me?"

"You call it kidnapped?"

"What else do you call it when someone takes you away and holds you against your will?"

I took a swallow to buy time. "I think so."

"I'd like to know." His voice was different. Cold.

I hesitated less than I probably should have. "The dealer was someone called Hans Karlsson. The buyer was Jon Ogdell, a property developer."

"Friends of yours?"

I watched him carefully but he was looking into his drink and not at me. "No."

"But you were at his house?"

I scowled. "I went with a friend. We thought it was just going to be dinner."

"That's all you know?"

"It was only the second time I'd met them."

He took a drink. I watched the muscles in his throat move as he swallowed. It sent a different sort of shiver over my skin that had me clenching my glass tight. "Your turn."

The alcohol ghosted through my brain. When I spoke, my voice shook. "Why did you kill him?" He held my gaze steadily but didn't speak. "If this is you," I managed, gesturing at him. "If haemophiles are happy to sit and chat over omelets and insist they don't want to hurt anyone...why'd you do it?"

I couldn't put my finger on what exactly had changed in his face, but he looked older, his eyes blacker. "I told you. The Blood protects itself."

"What does that mean?"

The tendons stood out on the back of his hand as his fingers curled into a fist. "Our Blood heals us, protects us from disease, from ageing. But its first priority is its own longevity. If it detects a threat, it will react. If it is starved of nutrition, deprived of its rest or its host is endangered, it responds."

"You're talking about it like it's a living thing."

"It is a living thing."

"I don't understand."

He swirled his wine for such a long time that I didn't think he was going to answer. When he did, his voice was so soft that it was like he was talking to himself. "Neither do we. We've only submitted ourselves to research recently. No one has answers yet. I don't know if they ever will. All we have are stories passed down from our own kind."

"So...you're saying it wasn't really *you* that killed Brody? You didn't *mean* to...?"

He took a deep breath in and let it out through slightly parted lips. The fine lines of his face were strained. "I haven't hurt anyone like that in a very long time."

The words were weighted. I heard pain. I didn't like the confusion it stirred in me. I chased after the anger, but it was retreating like water swilling down a plughole. "Are you trying to claim that haemophiles don't kill people?"

"Some do," he said, without intonation. "But my commune is registered. Legal. It lives off donations. Has for years."

I drank. I watched him, trying to make out if he was waiting for me to say something more. "It's your turn for a question," I murmured.

I wondered if I read surprise in his eyes. "What's your name?"

I stilled, something quivering behind my ribs. "Alec. What's yours?"

"Terje." The word sounded soft and hard at the same time, rolling off his tongue like sweet sherry pouring into a fine goblet.

"Scandinavian?"

He inclined his head. "Norwegian."

I finished my wine, welcoming the way it singed off the edges of my nerves. "The dealer is Scandinavian, too."

"Yes. A lot of them are."

"Why?"

He gazed into the fire. "Many of my kind are from that part of the world, originally, where it's dark a lot of the year. The biggest dealers usually have connections there."

I nodded whilst my mind wrestled with taking it all in. "So what happens when your people find you?"

He topped up my glass then his own. "I leave."

"That's it?"

He raised his silver-fringed eyes. "I just want to go home."

The image of his skeletal form strapped to the trolley rose in my mind. We sat in silence for some time, the only sounds the snapping of the fire and the low moan of the storm.

"Do you eat?" I asked softly.

He shook his head.

"But you drink wine?"

He stared into his glass. "It helps…a little."

"Helps with what?"

"The hunger," he said. I fought a sudden chill. "How long have you lived here?"

"I was a boy here, before boarding school. But I only moved back recently."

"Why?"

"It's complicated."

"I'm the very definition of a captive audience."

I could almost swear that dark humor was back in his eyes. I sighed, swallowed more wine and felt something inside me loosen. "This is my father's house."

"Where is your father?"

"Dead."

"And your mother?"

"Gone."

"No siblings?"

"No."

He tapped a fingernail on the glass. "And yet you don't see the house as yours?"

I looked around at the cluttered, cheaply-furnished kitchen, the drifts of magazines and papers, the piled engine parts, the dirty crockery. "Not really."

"It's quite a place," he said softly. "If you don't like it, you could sell it." I didn't answer, just ran my finger around the rim of my glass. "I'm guessing this is where it gets complicated."

"I hate it," I heard myself grating out. "I hate every stone of the damn place."

"But?"

"How do you know there's a 'but'?"

He shrugged. It made the shapeless jersey shift and reveal the smooth sweep of his collar bone. "You're still here."

I put the glass down carefully on the table. "If I sell, it will prove him right." I blinked at the wine. I felt gutted, hollow. I could no longer hear the wind over the rushing in my ears. I had never formed those words out loud to anyone, not even Meg. Not even to myself. No living being had enabled me to admit it before.

I raised my eyes. He was watching me, those deep eyes, unknowable and impossibly beautiful, fixed on my face. It was as exquisite and painful as looking directly into the sun, but I refused to look away.

When he spoke again, it was so quiet that his words were almost drowned in the groaning of the storm. "You can't always escape your demons. But you can accept they're real. They'll have less power over you."

"Why are you doing this?" I whispered.

"Doing what?"

"Sitting here, like this. Drinking wine. Talking to me."

"Is it not allowed?"

It was my turn to raise an eyebrow. "After what's happened?"

"It feels..." he said softly after a long moment. "It feels like you can understand."

"*Understand*?" The word came out harsh but he didn't react.

"I don't think you want to, but I think you can."

"Why?"

"You didn't drink."

I searched myself, trying to find where I'd buried my fear. But it was gone, like a frost in a thaw, taking the remaining anger with it. It left a welling spring of guilt in its place. I could still hear Brody dying, but I was finding it harder to hear over the soft crackling of the fire and the warm silence in the kitchen.

"You like old cars?" he said, breaking the spell. He was gazing around rather dreamily at the magazines.

"Fixing them. Yeah."

"Why?"

I shrugged, looking away. "I'm good at it."

"It's hard to be good at something you don't enjoy."

I gazed into the flickering flames. "Taking something old...making it new again. Bringing it back to life." I shrugged again. "I can lose myself in it."

"That sounds good." His voice was soft. "You could do the same with the house, you know. Turn it into something new, something you're proud of, instead of a monument to something you hated." His eyes were heavy. In the fading firelight, he seemed impossibly young and unfathomably old all at once. "You'd feel better."

"It wouldn't work."

"Why not?"

"He'd still be here."

"Only if you let him stay."

I didn't answer. I felt raw, hot and cold all at once.

"You're an interesting man, Alec," he said softly after another heavy silence.

"How am I interesting?"

"You're different." He stood.

"Most people consider that a bad thing."

"All this time alone up here," he said softly, like he was musing to himself. "I think it's let you figure out who you really are. That normally takes more than one human lifetime." He drifted past me, close enough to brush against my legs. I fought an urge to reach out for him that shocked me.

"You don't have to go."

He glanced back. "I think I should. You need to sleep." He opened the door, letting in a gust of icy air that made the fire flicker, then closed it softly behind him. I sat for a long time watching the snow-blocked window gradually lighten to storm-cloud gray as dawn approached.

I built up the fire and made myself go to bed. My belly was full. The wine slugged in my veins, fogging my head. I felt like the calm flat of a beach after a storm tide has retreated. I was asleep in minutes.

It took a while for the dream to form.

It started off with just a sense of warmth, of safety. Of being home. The warm air was filled with the smells of varnished wood and fresh linen. I became aware of dark-painted walls, a black marble fireplace with a blazing fire in the grate. The light flickered off the gold-framed paintings on the walls. More landscapes. Dad had liked landscapes. The bleaker the better. The drapes were thick russet-colored velvet and drawn over the balcony windows, blocking out the dark night. The firelight warmed the mahogany frame of a huge bed that dominated the room. The Glenroe master bed, loaded with coverlets and quilts, piled high with snow-white pillows, looked more inviting than it ever had in my lifetime.

Some part of me knew this room in reality to be a damp and moldering mess, the bed stripped long ago, the fine wood dulled with mildew, the massive grate empty but for dust and debris from the unswept chimney. But in the dream it was more magnificent even than when Dad had been at the height of his career.

Terje stood near the fire, his back to it so his face was in shadow. I could see the lean lines of his torso through the thin shirt he wore. Tight trousers hugged his slim, toned legs. He stood stiller than stone but I felt the heat of his gaze stronger than the flames. After a breathless minute, he stepped into the light. His mouth was open slightly, the lips soft, pale, enticing. The deep darkness of his eyes was lit with a slow flame. His fine hair hung about his face, one strand hanging over his eyes. He held out a hand to me.

"What do you want?" I didn't speak out loud, but he heard me.

"What we both want."

"I don't..." I looked around at the fire-lit room, the large, luxurious bed. My blood thundered. "I can't."

"It's okay." He stepped up to me. "Come," he added in a breathy whisper, running a hand over my chest, down my belly to my waistband. I took a shuddering breath. He took hold of my belt and pulled me to the bed. He pressed me into the soft covers and climbed on top of me. His shirt was open. I could see his collarbone, part of his shoulder, the pulse beating softly at the base of his neck. His hair hung about his face, looking softer than thistledown. He let me run a hand through it, his eyes growing hungry.

"Why are you doing this?"

"Don't you want me?" he asked softly, leaning down.

"You're not human," I rasped.

"That's why you like me," he breathed in my ear, lips brushing flesh, and my whole body quivered.

"You're a killer…"

He ran a hand down my side to my thigh. "You want me anyway."

"I don't know anything about you."

"You don't have to." He smiled in a way I'd never seen him do in reality. It lit his cool, ageless face, making him suddenly warm flesh and hot impulse and thoroughly irresistible. I kissed him. The blood surged into my groin. I pressed against him, desperate for the feel of his lithe firmness, my body flaring when he ground his arousal against mine.

I was brought short by the sharp taste of something metallic. Something cloying and coppery poured into my mouth. I choked and pushed him back. I wiped my mouth and my hand came away bloody. His face had changed. He grinned, showing teeth like razors. Blood dripped from his lips and down his chin, stained his fine, white shirt and ran in rivulets down the toned, white flesh of his chest and belly.

I spat red onto the coverlet and scrambled back. He smiled again, but now his eyes were dead and black. I froze, registering something in the corner of my eye. I turned, stiffly, to look down at the floor. Firelight flickered over the twisted figure of Brody, lying bent and broken on the rich, blue hearthrug, a gaping wound in his neck oozing blood into a spreading puddle on the floor. His clothes were soaked red. His stricken eyes were turned toward me.

I tried to get away but Terje clamped a hand stronger than iron onto my wrist. The bruised bone pulsed. I fought but he was too strong. His fingernails dug into my skin and his teeth sunk into my shoulder. I screamed.

I sat up sweating, my throat raw with yelling. The room, lit by thin morning light, was cold, empty and silent, but I still felt the heat of the fire, the cool steel of his grip. I smelled copper, tasted blood in my mouth.

I shoved the sweat-drenched covers away. I rushed to the hall cupboard, pulling out fleeces, gloves and overcoats. My chest was tight and my head spun. My breath misted in the frigid air but I was still sweating. I pulled on snow boots with trembling hands.

The only sound in the main hall was the moaning wind in the rafters and my own panicked breathing. The cellar door was firmly shut. I rattled at the front door, tugged and pushed until my muscles burned. It still didn't move. I rushed up the staircase, stumbling on the uneven treads, swearing when my foot went right through a decaying stair.

I reached the first floor and broke into a run, kicking through the snow that had blown in through the empty windows. I checked each one, leaning out dangerously far, frantically searching for somewhere the snow was drifted deep enough for me to jump.

I hesitated outside the master bedroom. Nausea uncurled in my belly. My whole body had gone stiff but I knew the balcony was my only shot. I took a breath, shouldered the door open and rushed to the window, not looking around at the rotting bedstead or down at the remains of the blue hearthrug. Glass from the broken windowpanes frosted the moldering carpet. I wrestled the catch open and staggered out onto the snow-laden balcony. The wind stole my breath. I couldn't see the mountains, the glen or the outbuildings for the curtains of swirling white. The wind hammered against the sides of the house. It dug claws into the skin around my eyes. I fumbled through my pockets for snow goggles but realized, too late, that I'd left them behind.

I stepped to where a drainpipe leaned drunkenly against the wall below. I glanced back, fighting myself, caught sight of the corner of the bedstead, shuddered and clambered over.

I didn't think. I could barely breathe. I just kept moving. I had to keep moving. I had to get away. The drainpipe groaned and lurched and I let go, dropping into the drifted snow. The cold enveloped me like shock. I scrambled to more solid ground, wrestling through shoulder-deep drifts. I couldn't see more than three feet ahead. When the shadow of Glenroe had been swallowed by the storm, I was heading roughly north. I turned myself a little west.

I told myself if I could just make it to the road, I would be okay. I could follow it to Clem's cottage, the lodge, anywhere — anywhere but there with *him*. The killer. The murderer. The monster I so badly wanted to touch.

I slogged on, heart thundering, breath heaving, desperate to leave the dream behind. The rational part of me told me to stop, to turn back, that this was suicide. I ignored it.

The panic shifted when I started to slow and shuddering set into my limbs. My fingers and toes started to tingle. It hurt to breathe. I still hadn't hit the road. I squinted around the snow-blasted wilderness and realized that I had no idea where I was. The dial of my compass blurred in and out of focus when I tried to read it. I knew I shouldn't stop. I had to get to the road. I had to keep moving. But the exhaustion was sucking at me in draining waves. Everything hurt.

Don't sleep, I told myself fiercely, my split lips moving but no sound coming out. *Don't sleep.*

I staggered a few more paces before I sank to my knees. My body was beyond shivering. I gave up trying to stand, dragged myself to a crumbling section of drystone wall and curled myself into its lee. It was getting dark — or my vision was failing.

Part of my mind was still fighting. The rest of it was dull, dark, and I welcomed the spreading nothingness. Finally, I thought, the pain would leave me.

Everything that hurt fell away.

Blackness.

Time became unreal. Darkness cocooned me. Awareness came in waves then mercifully faded again. I caught glimpses of the paleness of moonlight on snow. I could hear the shuffling of limbs forcing a path through the frozen blanket. I could hear someone other than me breathing and feel arms stronger than iron around my body. I tried to protest, to fight, to take my own weight, but my body wouldn't respond.

The temperature changing made my skin tingle. I was lying on something soft. My wet clothes were stripped away, making my muscles convulse. My hands and feet pulsed painfully, my injured wrist screaming. I murmured protests and pushed at the hands on me, but they were strong, and I was weak and I could barely see or breathe.

"Alec, you must eat."

A hot mug was being held close to my face. I smelled the richness of soup. The mug was held by a smooth, white hand. I knocked it away, hearing a crash, willing the blackness to return. Finally, I was allowed to collapse into the tangled bed clothes. The blackness rose, tempting me away, offering me an empty, quiet place where nothing hurt any more.

"Alec..."

I was racing away from all feeling, then became aware of a smell—a rich, heavy smell. Autumn fruit and syrup, bonfires and the best, darkest wines threaded through with sharpness of hot metal. It sent threads of sensitivity shooting through me. When it touched my tongue, sensation flooded my body.

I couldn't fight. I swallowed. Heat and pleasure rolled through my flesh like waves of a warm, tropical sea. My extremities throbbed just on the edge of pain. Every cell in my body seemed to be set alight. My nerves were wires sparking with electricity. My brain and groin pulsed with every beat of my suddenly-powerful heart.

I blinked, my eyes watering, the rich smell filling my senses. Through a dizzying mist, I watched Terje rise from the edge of my bed, holding an empty tumbler. Thick residue, a red so dark it was almost black, stained the glass. He pulled his sleeve down to cover a small cut in his wrist, which was already healing.

I searched for horror, for anger, for bitterness and fear. But my consciousness wavered and I faded into warmth and comfort and the feeling that every inch of my body was filled with light.

"Sleep, Alec."

My eyes closed. I slept.

Dreams came—senseless, formless but loaded with sensation, filled with heat and a burning need I'd never known, not even at the dawn of adolescence when my hand and my imagination had first opened a new and entrancing world to me.

I woke with my heart racing, my skin on fire, my breath heaving. Every inch of me buzzed and begged to be touched. My pulse pounded in my neck, my chest, my groin. I was painfully hard. Even the feel of the sheets against my skin was overwhelming. I pushed them back.

The air was warm. The stove in the next room was blazing. My skin prickled in the heat. I was in nothing but my underwear. I reached for myself, gasping at the contact, and I brought myself off in seconds. I groaned as I came, hot seed spilling into my hands as waves ran up my body like rays of an autumn sun. But when the blaze of the orgasm faded, I was left with simmering heat that had only been stoked by my climax.

I closed my eyes and tried to visualize hands on me — David's...or Brody's. But my mind skidded away from thoughts of them both. Instead, it was a pale face with a fall of white-blond hair that rose before me. I saw burnished silver eyes, deeper than wells, ageless and heavy but filled to the brim with knowing, looking at me like they knew and understood me better than I did. I groped for the nightmare that had made me run or the memory of Brody being ripped apart that had dampened and confused my desires the day before. But the images wouldn't form.

All I could think of was Terje touching me. I grew agonizingly hard once again. I lay, panting, my blood thundering in my veins, staring at the ceiling as I pumped my cock, but it wasn't enough. I sat up. I was trembling, but not with cold. I moved through the kitchen in a sort of dream. The feel of the linoleum against my bare feet sent shivers through my over-sensitized skin.

Pulling open the door to the main house let in a rush of frigid air. My skin quivered but the fire underneath it was stoked still hotter. I padded out into the dining room. I could smell the dust, smell the dead leaves on the floor, smell the very age of the darkened room like some kind of heady perfume. There was a low, warm light and the smell of a wood fire and good wine. It threaded through my flesh and pulled me forward. I drifted through the hall, past the stairs, feeling the drafts play against my skin like sighs. The hairs on my arms and legs stood up like a cool hand had been run over the skin. I swallowed thickly, blinking heavy eyes.

I padded to the drawing room. The heat from a huge fire in the dusty grate wrapped itself around me like lambswool blankets. A sofa had been shifted close to the hearth, its dust sheet a heap on the floor. There was a silver candelabra bristling with points of golden light on a table, flickering as the heat from the fire battled with the cold of the room, making the air shimmer and sway.

Terje sat in the pool of light and heat, a book open in one hand, a tumbler of wine in the other. I could smell it mixed with autumnal scent of his skin, the snow-fresh smell of his hair. The warm light played in the white strands and gilded his long eyelashes gold.

He knew I was there but sat so still that it was like he was carved from marble. I knew the strength in those casually draped limbs. I knew the sharpness of the teeth hidden behind the slightly curved lips, the deep, bright red of the mouth. I remembered the way the muscles in his throat moved when he swallowed human blood. Just looking at him, I could tell he was dangerous, that he'd killed people, that he'd seen and done things I couldn't even guess.

And yet my breath caught. My groin throbbed. My mouth watered.

He raised his eyes. My heart skittered about behind my ribs as his gaze met mine. I could tell he knew what

I was feeling, that he was seeing into the deepest, darkest corners of my mind.

I hovered by the sofa for an eternal moment that was filled with the smell of the fire and the sight of his face turned up to me. I sank to my knees. I could trace a hundred thoughts behind the heavy silver curtains of his eyes but wouldn't ever be able to understand even one. I was shaking. I felt a fight in me, bitter and bloody, being lost.

I reached out a hand. It shook slightly. He didn't move, smile or frown. He didn't react at all. I touched him. I ran my thumb down his face, over his lips. His skin, warmed by the fire, was softer than I'd thought. There was a slight rasp along his jaw from stubble so fine it couldn't be seen. He watched me as I traced my fingertips down the smooth curve of his neck to brush over his exposed collar bone.

"You don't want this."

He didn't speak loudly, but the words filled and overlapped inside me. The richness of his voice that I'd never fully noticed before—heavy with something ageless and alien—swelled and swept through me like an ocean tide. It made me shudder with a potent mix of fear and lust. I shifted closer, my hand still on his neck. He didn't move but something slammed down, closing off his eyes.

"This is the Blood, Alec. It's not real."

I leaned over him. He could have pushed me away but didn't. I hesitated, my mouth an inch from his. The dream tried to return, the smell and taste of clotting blood heavy in the back of my throat. It battled at the wall of my thumping desire but couldn't break through.

I leaned in and captured his mouth. He tasted like campfires and pinot noir, like the smell of heather in the foothills when warmed by the early autumn sun, like the whiskies from the islands, heavy with peat and history. He wasn't responsive, but he didn't resist. He let me taste and explore. He allowed his head to be tilted back and opened his mouth so I could deepen the contact. The feel, taste and smell of him blazed through my skin and bones. The sharpness of his teeth was like the bite of winter wind through a late-summer day. I pressed myself against the couch, desperate for friction, feeling my body pulse and tremble on the edge of release.

He made a low noise, like someone letting something go, then he was easing me onto the faded cushions. He ran his hands down my chest and I gasped. He pressed his face into my hair and breathed in my smell. I sensed him holding back the strength in his hands as he trailed his lips down my face. He opened his mouth at the joint of my neck and shoulder. A hot tongue flicked over my sensitive skin. Something sharp grazed against my flesh and a cold spike of fear thrust through me, but he just breathed me in, tasted me with his tongue then continued down. Heat swamped the cold like an icicle held to a flame.

He pulled back my underwear and took me into his mouth, right to the hilt. I gasped. His mouth was hot, hotter than a human's. My breath caught and my chest felt like it was about to burst. I dug my hands into the coarse fabric of the sofa. Everything around me — the heat from the fire, the smell from the wine, the scent of his skin and hair, the feel of his mouth on me, his strong hands on my thighs — poured a sensory deluge down on me so strong I thought I might drown.

In that instant I knew why people drank Blood. Killed for it. Died for it.

He only had to move slightly to bring me crashing into an orgasm like a wooden raft plunging over a waterfall. Light and fire danced over my skin. My life and soul poured through my limbs, out of my cock and into him. It would have knocked me to the ground had I not been sitting.

Even if it killed me—and for a moment it felt like it would—it would have been worth it.

Slowly, the mist cleared. The feelings ebbed. Instead of the stupefying dullness that usually descended on me after sex, I knew a feeling of warmth and completion. Invigoration. I felt I could go climb a mountain or swim a river, storm or no storm. But the drafty room caused me to shiver. I was suddenly very aware that I was naked in Glenroe's drawing room with a stranger—and not a human stranger.

I blinked until my focus came back. Terje was sitting on the end of the sofa watching me.

"I..." I started, stumbling, couldn't bring to mind any words that felt right. "Thank you?"

"The least I could do under the circumstances."

I manhandled my underwear back up, blushing furiously. I would have slunk straight back to the kitchen but I didn't trust my legs to hold me.

"I'm sorry. Did I ruin the moment?"

I stared into the fire, the afterglow dulling to a warm ember somewhere in the center of my core. My hands and feet began to feel cold. "Didn't you feel anything?" I heard the words like they were from far away, in an unfamiliar, slightly high voice. It took me a moment to realize that the voice was my own.

He let out a soft sigh. "Let's not go down this road."

"Tell me."

He hesitated. "We're...different."

"But...the way the Blood made that feel...the way this feels," I ran my fingers up and down my arms, reigniting flickers of feeling. "Is it always like that? For you?"

"For us?" He raised one eyebrow. "It can be. Yes. And more. Though...not the same as it is for you."

"How?" The word hung in the air between us. I was aware of the huskiness of my voice, the barely contained intensity. His eyes searched my face and the low fire in my gut gathered heat again.

"We're...slow burners," he said.

A shiver rippled through my skin. I made myself stand to stop visualizing what he might mean. I padded back to my room, dressed in some warm trousers and a jersey, debated for a long minute then grabbed another bottle of wine and a glass and returned to the drawing room. He sat staring into the fire. The book was in his hand again but he hadn't opened it.

I held out the bottle. His eyes went from me to the bottle, then he lifted his glass. I filled it then filled my own and sat by his feet.

"I was dying, wasn't I?" I said quietly after a long time of drinking in the heavy silence. "Hypothermia. But the Blood saved me. *You* saved me."

"You saved me too. Now we're even." I sipped at the wine, reveling in the new depths I could taste. "You ran." He said it so softly that I barely heard it. The dream fogged again at the edges of my mind. I found I couldn't look at him, especially not now, with the hot feel of his hands still on my skin.

"I…" The words didn't come. "How long will this last?" I murmured instead, my skin goose-pimpling against the soft fabric of my clothing.

He shrugged a shoulder. "Not long. You were asleep for the most intense part."

"It gets more intense than…than that?"

"So I've been told."

The low burn in my gut flared, my sated groin stirring yet again. I drank more wine hurriedly. "But not for you?" I managed to keep it neutral…almost.

"Why do you ask?"

I tried to decide if there was something in his eyes or if I just wanted there to be. "Do you even like men?"

He tapped a fingernail on his glass. "*Human* men?"

"Any…men," I fumbled. I tried to decide if amusement was back in his eyes.

"You're overthinking this."

"I just want to know. Did you…?"

"Did I want to?" he finished for me after a pause. His eyes were on me. His glass was resting on his knee. He looked so beautiful that I ached. I managed a nod. He dropped his eyes. "I wanted to, Alec. It was a thank you…and an apology."

I hated the fact that I'd wanted a different answer. I leaned my elbows on knees and glared into the fire.

"Being horny and angry and scared all at once? It's, well…" He smiled. Actually smiled. It wasn't like in the dream. If anything, it made his face seem more unearthly. I wasn't sure I liked it. "It's human, Alec. And Blood just intensifies what's already there."

"Okay," I replied flatly.

"I won't be offended if you want to go back to the kitchen."

I tried to unpick his tone. "What if I don't want to go back to the kitchen?"

"That's okay too."

The tide started to rise again, urging me to get closer to him, bend over him, press him into the couch and see if I could coax a reaction out of him—any reaction. I swallowed wine, ignoring the more unpleasant note of sourness that I could now sense lurking just beyond the taste of fruit and oak.

"The storm is easing," he said a short time later, his head tilted like he was listening.

"That means you'll be able to leave soon."

"It does."

"What will happen then?"

"To what?"

To me. I stared at the fire. "To the Ogdells. To Karlsson." His eyes went a shade blacker and I had to fight the urge to move away. "You're not going to answer?"

"Do you really care about what happens to them?"

"No."

"Then that's all the answer you need."

I finished my drink. It burned in my belly. I was ravenously hungry but I still didn't want to move. Terje opened his book again. We sat in silence. I watched the fire dance in the wind. The Blood pulsed in my veins, warming the very fibers of my being in a way even the best whiskies and wines in my dad's collection never had. I cautiously marveled at how different this room felt when I wasn't thinking about what it was like when Dad had been alive. How different it felt with Terje in it.

* * * *

115

I woke to the ashy smell of the dead fire and a crick in my neck. The blankets from my bed had been thrown over me, but with the fire gone, it was still very cold. I blinked into the dull light of early morning. I was alone in the shadowy drawing room. It was quiet. The wind had finally dropped.

My eyes were grainy. My mouth tasted sour. My head pounded like I'd spent the night on hard liquor.

The evening came back in a rush. The memory of Terje's hands, the taste of him and the feel of his mouth on me caused hot blood to rush around my body. I clenched my eyes shut. I tasted his Blood on my tongue. I pushed the covers away angrily. My limbs ached and it took an alarming amount of effort to sit up. My hands were white. I pulled myself upright with a hand on the arm of the sofa.

A noise cut through the silence...a distant throb, getting louder and louder.

I stood dumb, trying to make my muzzy head process what I was hearing. Then there was the groan of something heavy being dragged across stone. I hurried to the side corridor. The armoire was back against the wall and Terje had opened the broken door, spilling mounds of snow and weak sunlight into the passageway. He was bundled in more clothing from the cellar — scarves, gloves, a peaked cap and tinted ski-goggles, his skin completely hidden. The storm was over, but the thunder of the landing helicopter drowned out any attempt either of us made to speak. It touched down on the other side of the outbuildings, looking very black against the blanket of snow. The wind from the blades scattered flakes in every direction and I lifted my arm to shield my face.

I tried to think of something to say, but I couldn't untangle what I wanted to feel, let alone what words would make sense of it. I felt his eyes on me through the darkness of the ski-goggles. A door in the side of the helicopter opened and a figure in a balaclava and a dark visor leaned out, calling out in another language. Terje laid a hand on my arm briefly, then turned and waded out into the drifted snow. He climbed into the helicopter and the blades sped up. With a roar and a whine, it lifted into the iron-colored sky.

I stood shivering in the doorway for much longer than was wise. Only when the trembling started to set in again, reminding me of the close call I'd had the day before, did I retreat back to the relative warmth of the kitchen.

I found my mobile phone, the landline handset and emergency radio laid out on the table. I tried them but the batteries were dead, of course. I plugged the landline into the wall. No dial tone. I stared at the blank screen of the mobile like it was an object from another lifetime, another planet.

I ate mechanically, tinned soup heated on the stove with some stale bread. It tasted dull, like I'd lost the ability to experience flavor. But I must have needed it, because after finishing, I felt revitalized enough to get dressed in proper snow gear and face the prospect of going outside. I fought my way around the house and down to the workshop, trying to stay focused on the state of the estate rather than the spot over the mountains where Terje's helicopter had disappeared.

I couldn't see any significant damage to the buildings, besides a few new holes in the roof of the house. The snow had stopped falling but was frozen solid and still too deep to get any vehicle out of the garages, even the Jeep. The glen was deathly silent and surreally unfamiliar under its meters-deep shroud of white. It must have been the worst storm to hit the Cairngorms in years, certainly the worst I'd ever known. The house perched on its rocky outcrop above it all, looking for all the world like it didn't recognize where it was either.

I tried to decide if the house, too, appeared different because of the snow or because something had changed in me. When I stood still, I could feel the faint frisson under my skin, a heightened awareness of the blood pulsing in my veins. It made things stir in my gut and a thirst dry my mouth. I remembered the taste of autumn fruit and bonfires, and my fingers curled with craving.

I shook my head. Too much had happened in too short a space of time. That was all. I suddenly loathed this frozen limbo. My fingers itched for the steering wheel of my Jeep. I visualized racing toward Auchallater Keep, confronting Jon Ogdell and making him answer — answer for Brody, answer for my nearly dying, twice. He needed to answer for me being unable to blame Terje, unable to hate Terje, unable to stop thinking about Terje.

I brought myself off that night with just the memory of him and the thrum of his Blood rushing through my own. The darkness that crashed in in the wake of the retreating orgasm filled me with thoughts that stopped me from falling asleep until the kitchen fire had burned out.

I found myself standing in the drawing room staring at the sofa and the table next to it, on which still stood Terje's wineglass and the book he'd been reading. I picked it up and opened it to the title page.

Paradise Lost.

Of course.

I was using a torch to try to find where in the library to return it so I wouldn't have to look at it, when there was a flicker and a buzz and all the lights came on. I hurried to the kitchen, the strip light now showing up the increased level of dirt and clutter with startling clarity. I tried the landline, but the phone lines were still down, so I plugged in all my devices and paced impatiently whilst they charged.

My mobile finally flickered to life. I resisted the urge to grab it and immediately run down to the spot by the workshop where it received signal, knowing the battery wouldn't last the time it would take me to get there until it had more power, and instead fired up the transistor radio.

I managed to get Clem, the only other person I knew with a receiver, on the second try. The signal was crackly and muffled, but he gruffly informed me that he was fine and that power had just been restored to his cottage. He confirmed the roads were still impassable.

"Two more days, tops," he said. "We're due a thaw, radio news said."

I agreed to open the workshop again as soon as possible, dodged questions about the last few days then commenced my pacing until my mobile had enough charge to cope with the slog to the workshop.

I reached the signal spot by the front door and my screen was flooded with notifications of emails, texts and voicemails. My heart began to thud. Most were from Meg.

Ring me when you can.

I'm back in Glasgow. Ring me.

Are you alive?

Alec this isn't funny. Ring me.

The phone rang only twice before Meg answered. "Alec?"

"Hey."

"Thank God. Are you okay?"

"I'm fine." I managed to sound normal. "I've only just got power back. I'm still snowed in."

"But you're okay?"

"Yeah," I said, tightly.

"Has something happened? You sound strange."

"I'm fine," I insisted. "What about you? You're home? How did you get away?"

"As soon as the storm blew out, Ogdell sent one of his staff out on a snowmobile. They managed to find somewhere to rent a plow. Once a way was cleared to the A9, he threw everyone out."

"But your car?"

"One of the guys gave me a lift. That actor guy, don't ask me his name. I don't remember. I just wanted to get away."

"What happened after you left me?"

She took a shuddering breath. "Nothing. Nothing's happened, Alec. They didn't find the haemophile and Brody is dead and nothing has happened. I don't even know what they did with the body." I clenched my jaw. "They're going to get away with it."

I stared into the sky, looking heavy and white and far too low. "I'll do it."

"You'll do what?"

"I'll go to the police."

"Alec, no—"

"This can't be allowed to happen."

"No," Meg said again, firmer this time. "I told you what they said."

"I don't care," I said bitterly. "Jon Ogdell can't be allowed—"

"It won't be just you, Alec," Meg cut in. "It'll be all of us. Me included."

"We didn't do anything," I argued.

"Ogdell will find a way to make it look like we did."

"Meg, we can't let them get away with this."

"I'm working on it," she insisted. "Please, Alec." I chewed on the inside of my cheek. My pulse beat in my temples. "Promise me you won't do anything yet."

I made an impatient noise. "Okay."

"Thank you. I'll think of something. Trust me. In the meantime, we must play it cool. No messages about it, no emails, okay?"

"Okay."

"Come through and see me when you can," she said, sounding defeated. "We'll talk more. And be careful. Please."

I stared at the mobile screen for a long time after she'd hung up. I stood staring at the workshop forecourt, the road, the entire glen lost under its coating of white, the suffocating silence filling the frigid air, until the cold drove me back to the kitchen.

It took another three days for the promised thaw to loosen the stranglehold of snow. Rivers of icy water trickled off the mountains, washing dirty slush in rivulets down the paths and gullies around the house. The sound of the burns swelled with meltwater echoed loudly, bouncing off the mountainside and filling the air with an eerie rushing noise. The sky refused to lighten from its low, leaden glower.

It took almost that amount of time for me to regain my strength. I'd avoided frostbite, somehow, but I still tired easily, and now that the Blood had worn off, my muscles and bones ached even in the warmth of my bed. I'd gotten off lightly and knew I should have been grateful. But it just didn't feel as simple as that.

By the fourth day I was finally able to lift a spade and spent two hours shoveling slush away from the garage doors. I climbed into my Jeep and roared it down the drive and onto the road, pushing Meg's entreaties to the back of my mind. Melting snow flew up in sprays around my wheels. I kept my hand on the gear stick and wrestled it along the winding, pot-holed tarmac, skidding in meltwater. I reached the crossroads and turned toward Auchallater Keep.

It seemed to take forever, even at my ill-advised speed. Part of me marveled at how Terje had managed to get us most of the distance on foot in a storm. I pulled up in front of the lodge in just over an hour. The door was shut. The blinds were drawn. I hammered on the door, still wondering what I would do or say if someone answered it. Nothing happened. I circled the building, blood pulsing in my ears, peering in at windows, but all was dark and silent.

I stood on the front steps, staring up at the stone, the neat, new-cut blocks crowding in on the uneven walls from the original keep, trying to decide if I was disappointed or relieved. I thought about the basement beneath my feet and my skin crawled.

When I got back to Glenroe, there was a missed call from an unknown number on my mobile. They hadn't left a message.

* * * *

I nodded distractedly whilst Clem moaned that we were going to be late getting the supply order in. The smell of oil was heavy in my nostrils. I maneuvered tools on autopilot. I was up to my elbows in a 1963 Corvette Stingray, its innards exposed like the spilled guts of a hunted animal, working hard enough to sweat despite the freezing air, but everything seemed to be held at a distance. We were lucky that another job had come in—I couldn't bring myself to work on Ogdell's Jaguar, so that had fallen entirely to Clem—but I didn't feel lucky. It was like a mesh curtain hung between me and the real world. If I thought about it too long, my mouth would go dry and I'd have to close my eyes and breathe until the feeling passed.

Clem had thrown himself into getting back to normal the moment the workshop had become accessible. I could sense the storm had unsettled him and his routine, his precious form of normalcy. I wasn't even sure what normal was anymore.

At night I dreamed of a hot mouth and strong hands. Of eyes holding several lifetimes' worth of secrets, lips that had smiled once but hardly spoke. I dreamed of lying in a blanket of snow with those hands on me and my skin on fire.

And I dreamed of blood—dark rivers of it pooling on a concrete basement floor. Brody's blood, thick and rapidly cooling, viscous on my hands, staining my clothes, filling the air with the smell of metal. And Terje's haemophile Blood, hotter and sweeter than melted chocolate laced with cognac, richer than the finest liquor I'd ever had, restoring my life and lighting fires along my veins, waking me aching with need.

It was only Clem's rough bark from the kitchen doorway that made me realize I had been staring at the engine for several minutes without moving. I blinked at him but he was nodding past me toward the window.

I turned just in time to see Hans Karlsson climbing out of a black Ferrari on the forecourt. He stared around with a faintly disparaging expression. His silver hair was combed back from his high forehead, immaculately styled and resisting the gusting wind. He wore a suit and dark wool overcoat that I could tell cost more than our profit margin for the entire year. A large man in anonymous black got out of the driver's side and stood to attention by the car.

I opened the door just as the older man reached it, stepped out and purposefully shut it behind me. The other man gave a smile that didn't reach his ice-blue eyes. "Lord Aviemore."

"What the hell do you want?"

One of his white eyebrows twitched slightly. "Good to see that you are quite recovered from your ordeal."

I narrowed my eyes. "Either tell me what you want this second or get that piece of Italian crap off my forecourt before I get my gun."

Karlsson shook his head regretfully. "Such hostility? After everything we've done to protect you?"

"*Protect* me?"

"Of course. You must realize how quickly this would turn nasty for all of us if the truth of what happened at Auchallater Keep got out."

"There is no 'us', Karlsson."

"Oh, but there is, my lord. We're all in this together."

"I've got nothing to do with —"

"Please, sir. We must be frank. Mr. Harris died, after all."

"Because of you."

"Not the way I see it."

"Whose fault was it then?"

"First and foremost? The haemo, of course. They're so strong, you see…and unpredictable. Keeping them sedated is a very delicate balance. I've always been hesitant about donors in the hands of private citizens."

"And yet you arranged it all."

"It's true." He tilted his head to one side. "I am a businessman, after all. You understand business?"

"Blood is business?" I shook my head. "Leave. Leave now —"

"The creature is still out there somewhere," he cut in. "It would be irresponsible for me to not at least check in on you. You had a very lucky escape, Lord Aviemore."

"Don't call me that."

"As you wish. But I regret I cannot leave until important matters have been settled."

"If you've come to do Ogdell's dirty work —"

"Jon?" Karlsson let out a laugh. "Jon Ogdell is a good client. He's also an upstart and a fool, an indulgent fool."

"Who wants to hush up a murder," I muttered, glancing again at the man-mountain by the Ferrari, who hadn't seemed to have blinked since he arrived.

Karlsson nodded toward the path to the house. "Shall we walk?"

"Why?"

"I have a proposal that it would be in your best interest to listen to in private." His gaze slid over my shoulder and I glanced back to see Clem hovering at the window. I turned on my heel and crunched up the path. Once the workshop was out of earshot, I faced him, folding my arms. Karlsson stood gazing at Glenroe with a quiet smile on his lined face.

"You've got two minutes," I stated.

His eyes drifted to mine. "Okay, MacCarthy. Time to be frank. Brody Harris was killed. You were there."

"So were you."

"Not in the basement."

I kept my face blank. "Your donor went berserk."

"That is what the wounds would suggest."

A slow churning starting in my belly. "What else is there to suggest?"

"By me? Nothing. Right now."

"I'm not going to the police, if that's what you're scared of."

"Scared?" His smile could cut glass. "I'm not scared."

I shifted in the snow, my face suddenly hot. "Spit it out, old man."

"It really is a very impressive home you have here," he said, gazing up at the house. "You really should reconsider your position on selling, you know. The possibilities of this place in the hands of a developer…"

"Like Ogdell?"

He smiled, showing all his teeth, shining white but blunt, with a gap at the front. "We have the means to make the place great again, like you would never even dream."

I narrowed my eyes. "*You* want it?"

He put his hands in his pockets, gazing at Glenroe like he was selecting a wine from a rack. "Pictures don't do it justice. It's astonishing but wasted, decaying.

Can't you see it's dying?" His eyes were suddenly bright. "I could make your legacy *worth* something."

Realization dawned. "The caves..." His eyes flickered. "You want it for storing donors, for Blood dealing..."

He shrugged his slim shoulders. "Business is business. Business means money. Money means the restoration of your heritage."

"My heritage is *my* business."

He shook his head sadly. "Oh, but it's not, Mr. MacCarthy. Not anymore." He produced a phone from his pocket. The screen displayed a photo of me and Brody, snorting coke at Lure. He swiped. Another one of us in the Glasgow restaurant, his hand pressing mine on the table. There were two more—us arriving at his hotel, him leaning in to talk into my ear. Then, lastly, one of us sitting together at the dining table at Auchallater Keep, heads bent close, smiling knowingly.

"You were obviously very fond of young Mr. Harris," Karlsson purred, putting the phone back in his pocket. "It really is a great tragedy that he died so horrifically, with you standing right by. And given your obvious connection, the police will be very keen to know more."

"The haemophile—"

"We know you fed it, MacCarthy." His voice and face had lost their veneer of charm. His pale eyes were like ice. "Several of the guests saw you leave the sitting room. We found the empty blood bag in the basement. We know you gave it the strength to break loose, kill Mr. Harris and flee."

"He was going to die. You bastards had starved it to the point—"

"So it's okay that Brody Harris died instead?"

"I didn't *know*—"

"The death was a tragic accident, so long as you sell me Glenroe. If you refuse, well..." His brow creased. "It would be an even greater tragedy if these pictures were to show up just as his body was discovered."

"Those pictures prove nothing."

He raised his eyebrows. "Oh, but the police like connections like this. Love them, in fact. In the current climate, they also love avoiding trouble involving haemos. They will want to believe another human killed Harris. And with your record..." I went cold as his eyes narrowed. "Assault... Battery... Who would have thought?" He shook his head rather sadly. "It doesn't look good, my lord."

"That was years ago," I bit out. "After university. I...I had a rough patch."

"Criminal records don't list extenuating circumstances, I'm afraid."

I groped after some semblance of calm. "If you go to the police, what's to stop me telling them everything?"

"You could, of course. Though Mr. Ogdell has much better lawyers than your friend Miss Carlisle on his books. And Miss Carlisle? Well...she's in a very vulnerable position, close to you as she is. Sadly, it would be all too believable that she would want to help cover up your mess." I bristled. The blood rushed up my neck and pounded in my temples. I stared at him. He didn't even blink. "You have two days to think it over," he continued, holding out a business card. "If there is no deal by then, well...Jon and I will be forced to take matters into our own hands."

I took the card with numb fingers. I stared at it, navy blue with white lettering. "This was the plan all along, wasn't it? With the club opening, Brody, the Blood

Party. It was to bribe me to sell. And if that didn't work, blackmail."

Karlsson adjusted the cuffs of his suit. "Have a good day, Lord Aviemore. Do pass my regards on to Miss Carlisle when you speak to her." He turned on his patent-leather heel and trudged back down the path.

"Tell Ogdell the Jaguar deal's off," I yelled after him. "If he doesn't send someone to pick up his scrapheap, I'll burn what's left of it."

He didn't look back. The wind moaned in my ears and tried to yank the business card out of my grip. I nearly let it go, but after a moment, I crumpled it in my fist and shoved it into my pocket. The Ferrari's toothy roar was fading into the distance as I reached the forecourt.

"We're going to fall even more behind if you keep slacking off for visitors," Clem barked from the workshop door.

"Stop work on the Jaguar."

"What?"

"I said no more work on the Jag," I gritted, glaring at the dissipating exhaust trail from the Ferrari. "Dump it out here and leave it."

I didn't listen to his answer. The workshop door slammed. It felt like the earth was shifting under my feet. I pulled out my phone and paced about until I found a signal.

My already-racing heart lurched in my chest when the messages and voicemails began to ping through.

Alec, ring me, please.

Meg didn't pick up. I swore, tried again, and it went to answerphone. I tried to think what I could possibly put in a voice message, swore again, hung up. I was just about to head back to the workshop when the thing buzzed in my pocket.

"Meg?"

"Alec…" Her voice was choked.

"Meg, what's wrong?"

She drew a shaking breath. "I'm sorry. I had to get somewhere I wouldn't be heard."

My chest clenched. "Did Karlsson come to you too?"

"Karlsson?" She sounded bewildered.

"Ogdell's dealer?"

"No. It's Matthew Ogdell-Paige."

"Who?"

"Olivia's husband."

"What about him?" I asked, feeling something inside me sink.

"He's disappeared."

"What do you mean?" I made myself ask when the pause had stretched on.

"I mean that he's vanished."

"Done a runner, more like," I muttered, looking at the crumpled card in my hand.

"No, you don't understand. He was…taken."

My mouth dried out. "Taken?"

"In the middle of the night two days ago. Olivia woke up and he was gone. She'd taken a pill, so she heard nothing. All the doors and windows were locked, but there was blood on the bedroom carpet."

I stared at the swollen burns cutting gullies in the drifts of melting snow. I took a slow breath, trying to make sense of what I was hearing. "How do you know this?"

"The actor guy who gave me the lift… He rang me. He's scared."

"Scared?"

"That's not everything."

"Go on," I managed.

"Another guest from the party, the MP. She's vanished too."

"What?"

"Last week. Apparently, there's some scandal about to break in her personal life. Everyone assumed she'd skipped town to avoid the heat. But now Matthew too…"

"What are you suggesting, Meg? Ogdell's taking everyone out to stop them talking?"

"It's not Jon," Meg said. "He came to the firm for a meeting this morning. He looks like death. He's scared shitless."

"But if it's not him…" The silence hung between us. I could hear her breathing. "You think it's the haemophile?"

"It must be," she said, voice high. "Out for revenge. Working its way through everyone who was at the party."

"No," I said, though my throat was closing.

"What else could it be?"

"I just…" I started, then lost the words.

"Alec, I'm scared."

I clenched my eyes shut and pinched the bridge of my nose. My body was throbbing, my mind swirling. She was speaking again, but I couldn't hear the words.

"I'll come through," I said eventually. "Sit tight. I'll come to you."

"Then what?" Her tone was harsh, but I could hear her fear.

"Stay calm," I said in a flat, lifeless voice of my own. "I'll be there soon."

"Get here before dark," she said. "Please."

* * * *

The X-Trail ate the miles, despite the slush and driving sleet. Other drivers swerved and beeped their horns, but I was racing the night. I rang Meg as I got into Glasgow, told her to come meet me rather than lose precious minutes battling through city center traffic. I heard her reluctance to venture out in the gathering dusk, but the sense of it won out. I parked and waited, watching the sky. Eventually I spotted her light-colored coat among the crowds. She hurried toward the car, wrestling with a black umbrella and small, wheeled suitcase. She opened the back door, hesitated when she saw the shotgun lying across the seat and shoved her suitcase into the footwell. She was shaking when she climbed into the passenger seat. I pulled her into my arms. We clung to each other. We didn't speak for several long moments.

"I don't understand, Alec," she said into my coat. "How can this be happening?"

"It's fine," I said pulling back to meet her eyes. "It's going to be fine."

"How can you be so sure?"

"We'll figure it out."

She must have heard something in my voice because the lines of her face eased and she looked more like herself again. "Where are we going?"

"Somewhere safe."

I steered into the traffic, checking every car around us despite myself. I took a round-about route back out of town, toward the outskirts. The buildings got dingier, the roads quieter. Meg peered out of the window as we drew up to a tall, exhaust-stained building with boarded-up windows and large, barricaded doors plastered in shredded flyposters.

She got out into the sleet and stood staring at the rain-slicked stone with a dazed expression. "I didn't know you still had this place."

"No one does," I said, grabbing her suitcase, my backpack, our shopping bags and the gun from the back seat. She followed me down an alley cluttered with rubbish, sticking so close that she was almost treading on my heels. We made our way up the rusted metal staircase at the rear of the building, overlooking an abandoned carpark, rampant with weeds and litter. I punched a code in a keypad on the door at the top and slipped an ancient key into the Yale with a prayer. It was stiff with years of disuse, but it turned.

We slipped into the echoing, dusty chill of a large, empty building. It smelled of dampness and rotten malt. I fumbled for the light switch and let out a sigh of relief when the luminescent bar flickered then flooded the sparse, dusty space with harsh, white light. The old sofa and armchair were still drawn up to an electric heater. An ancient television set perched on a coffee table in the corner. There was a kitchen counter against one wall, several dusty mugs on the draining board and a bowl catching water from the dripping tap in the sink. I followed Meg to the bank of windows and gazed into the dark warehouse below. I could just make out the large metal tuns and vats lurking silently in the shadows, like sleeping giants.

"I can't believe this is still here," she said softly. "Wasn't it condemned?"

"The accountant had to do some juggling. It's under another name now, but it's still technically mine. No one will find us here."

"You could have sold it," she said, looking around the improvised apartment space with a mixed expression. "People might not want a derelict distillery with a squat in the office space, but the land could fetch something."

I dumped the bags and turned on the heater. "I thought I might need it again one day." She stood staring out over the distillery floor, not speaking. I pottered about, gathering crisp packets and empty paper coffee cups, and stuffed them in a bin bag. When I came back from making the bedrooms as habitable as possible, she was checking the lock on the door. "We're safe here, Meg. Trust me."

She nodded stiffly. "I trust you."

The words sent a pang through me. There was real fear in her face. She picked up her case and drifted to the hall. I heard the bathroom door shut and the groaning of the water pipes. I stared around the place that had once felt more like home than anywhere else in the world. But now all I could think of was the roaring fire in the Glenroe drawing room, a space I had previously hated, now filled with the memory of heated skin, silver eyes, the feel of warm breath, the smell of clean, fine hair and a mouth filled with banked passion and sharp teeth.

I couldn't marry the feelings the memory generated with the reality of Meg's revelations. I searched again for any news articles on my phone. The fact that Matthew Ogdell-Paige hadn't shown up to a public event the previous day had generated a stir of interest, along with his wife's and brother-in-law's refusal to comment, but otherwise there was nothing.

"It's coming for us, isn't it?" Meg was stood in the doorway, looking wan, shadows under her eyes. She'd changed into pajamas and a hooded top. Her shoulders were slightly slumped. She looked very young. I was suddenly reminded of the only sleepover I'd ever been to as a child. I'd told ghost stories that had frightened everyone, even David, and Meg was the only one who'd talked to me at school the next day.

"We don't know that."

"What else could it be?" she said, speaking in a low voice like we were going to be overheard. "First that politician and now Matthew?"

"You said yourself that Karlsson is dangerous."

She frowned. "The dealer?"

I ran a hand through my hair. "He came to see me this morning. He and Ogdell are going to pin Brody's death on me unless I sell them Glenroe."

Her face flattened. "He said that?"

"In so many words."

She shook her head. "It can't...no. The disappearances aren't them, Alec. I told you, Jon's just as terrified as us."

"Karlsson wasn't scared."

"Maybe he doesn't know," she snapped. "Why aren't you taking this seriously? You've heard what's been happening in London…"

"It can't be—"

"This is *real*," she cut me off, voice high. "Don't you get it, Alec? If the police don't get us, the vampire will."

I put a hand on her face without thinking. She drew in a breath sharply and I wondered if I'd made a mistake. Her eyes were very large and very brown, the rich color of sun-warmed earth. "I don't believe he would hurt us."

"He?" She stepped back out of my reach. "You called it that before."

I hesitated. "You didn't see him, Meg."

"It killed Brody —"

"I *know*." I hadn't meant to snap, but I couldn't keep the emotion in check. "I know," I continued in a softer voice. "I was there."

"You were?" she said, her eyes widening.

"Yes." I lifted a hand to touch her again, saw the look on her face and dropped it. "I watched him kill Brody and I'll never forget it. But you didn't see him after."

I remembered him crying out into the storm, that lost, desolate sound like a wounded animal. I remembered him bathed in firelight, impenetrable but tinged with sadness. The way his hands had moved on me, the way his mouth had felt against my skin. The sound he'd made when he started to kiss me back. He was closed and distant, like an ancient book in some lost language, but when I remembered how that had felt, how *he'd* felt... Blood or no Blood, he couldn't have made me feel like that unless he knew what it was to need, to want release, comfort, the touch of another living thing.

"He wouldn't hurt us," I said with conviction.

"How do you know?" she asked, her dark eyes wary.

"I just know."

"What aren't you telling me?"

"He didn't hurt me," I insisted.

"Did he do anything *else* to you?" Blood flooded my face but kept my mouth shut. "Alec?" I turned away and set about filling a saucepan with water and rummaging in the carrier bags of supplies. "Oh my God..."

"It's not what you think."

"What exactly do you think I'm thinking? Because you can't possibly be thinking what I'm thinking because what I'm thinking is... It can't... *You* can't..." I put the pan on the hotplate with a clang. "Alec," she snapped, "tell me you didn't *fuck the vampire*."

I dropped pasta into the water. "I didn't fuck the vampire, Meg."

"Look me in the eye and tell me that."

I met her look squarely. "First, vampires don't exist—"

"For Christ's sake, Alec—"

"Second," I went on firmly as the pasta started to bubble. "We didn't... I didn't... No, we didn't do *that*."

"But you did do *something*."

I glared at the wall, feeling something between us start to crumble. "Yes."

Her face creased. "How...? Why...?" She shook her head and made an inarticulate noise. "He *killed* someone, Alec."

"I *know*—"

"Do you?"

"Yes, Meg. I was *there*."

"Then how could you...?"

"You don't understand."

"You're fucking right I don't."

I came forward again but she took a step back and folded her arms. "You're scared. I get it."

"I'm not scared. I'm bloody terrified—"

"*I get it*," I repeated in what I hoped was a soothing voice. "I'm scared too. Something's happening here. I just don't think it's what it looks like."

"What else could it be?"

I dropped my gaze. "I don't know."

"They're dangerous, Alec. Whatever the legislators say, they're dangerous. They *kill people*. And *eat* them."

"They don't eat people, Meg."

"Drink from them, whatever. Alec, you can't be serious about this. Tell me you're not serious."

She was searching for something in my face, but I didn't know what I could say that would make it better. I wasn't even sure I *wanted* to make it better. The thought gave me a stab of guilt but didn't make the feeling go away.

"We'll lie low here until we've figured something out," I said again, hoping the repetition would make it true. The pasta was boiling. I turned the plate off and drained the water. She stood by the sofa, arms wrapped around herself, glaring at the wall.

"He didn't run off like you said?" she asked quietly.

"No," I said, stirring sauce and grated cheese into the pasta.

"He was there...at Glenroe...with you?"

"Yes." She was chewing her manicured fingernail. Holding the bowl out to her broke the spell. She took it stiffly, not looking at me. "He's not going to hurt us, Meg."

"You don't know what you're talking about, Alec. You can't understand them. No one can understand them." Emotion swept through me but she continued before I could speak. "Besides, even if it really does have a weird inter-species crush on you—and sorry, Alec, I know you're cute, but cute enough to raise the dead?" I made a disparaging noise but she raised a hand to cut me off. "Just listen to me. Let's say for the sake of argument that you're right and it *wouldn't* hurt you. And, for your sake, let's say, that maybe it wouldn't even hurt me…" She was quiet for a while. When she raised her eyes to meet mine, they were dark and loaded. "Say it kills everyone else who was at that party, but not us. Is that really okay? Could you live with that?"

I pronged some pasta. I couldn't find an answer. We ate in silence.

"How long can you get out of work?" I murmured as we were clearing up.

"You think that's necessary?" Her voice was deliberately flat as she dried the bowls, but I could see the tension in her shoulders.

"Until we know more, it might be best for neither of us to be where anyone would expect us to be."

She nodded stiffly. "I can make arrangements for a week at least, maybe two."

"Okay. Clem can manage without me for —"

"Goodnight, Alec." She headed for the bedrooms. I heard one of the doors shut, then silence descended. I looked around at the threadbare sofa, the windows looking out onto the distilling floor, the worn but familiar rugs and posters of cars on the wall. I'd lived here alone during Sixth Form then for years after Cambridge, but it had never felt this empty before.

Chapter Five

I lay awake listening to the distant noise of the city just on the edge of my hearing, like a storm out at sea. The streetlight shone between the ill-fitting curtains to cast a beam of white across the tiled ceiling. This room, this bed, held some very good and very private memories. This was where David and I had first discovered what we really felt for each other. I had always slept well here. But tonight, sleep wouldn't take me.

I wrestled with my mind. It was like trying to strip myself of burning clothing without scorching my hands. Every time I even came close to being objective about what might be happening, a taste ghosted across my tongue, like the afterburn of whisky, filling my mouth with saliva and making my pulse quicken.

I turned over to stare at the wall. Old pop punk and F1 posters were familiar shapes in the gloom. It started to rain. The steady drum on the window reminded me of Glenroe and finally allowed me drift away.

The dreams came, as usual. I floated through them, sensing the new layer of unease in the background, tainting them, turning the sweet tastes bitter and lacing the heated feelings with fear and guilt. I dreamed that someone was at the window, but when I drew the curtain aside, there was nothing but freezing rain and blurred streetlight.

It was late morning when I woke, groggy, unrested and with a familiar ache in my groin that I wasn't able to enjoy. I padded through to the sitting room, thinking of coffee, but paused in the doorway.

Meg was curled on the end of the sofa, her legs tucked under her like a child. Her face was drawn, lines showing that I'd never noticed before. Her phone lay limp in her hand and she was staring at the TV. I blinked at the screen. She had the volume off but the subtitles on. There was a reporter stood outside the glass doors of the Glasgow Hilton.

"Staff raised concerns this morning when Olivia Ogdell-Paige didn't place her regular breakfast order. The socialite has been staying at the Hilton whilst the police investigation of her home after the abduction of her husband continues. No signs of a struggle were found and both the door and windows were secured, but the hotel have confirmed all her belongs are still in situ and there is nothing on CCTV to show her leaving the premises. Police are concerned."

Meg turned it off. Her brown eyes were asking me for something I didn't know how to give.

"We're safe here," I stated. I spooned instant coffee into two mugs and fetched the milk from the otherwise-empty fridge. She came and stood at my shoulder in silence until I turned around.

"David called me."

I stared at her. "Why?"

"He's seen the news. He's worried."

"How much does he know?" I asked, my voice tight.

"I had to talk to someone, Alec. You were cut off for days. I was scared."

"You told him?"

"Yes." I ran both hands through my hair as the kettle spewed steam. "We have to trust someone," she continued, her eyes pleading. "And he knows things. Living in London, he has some idea —"

"*David*?" It came out sharper than I intended.

Her face hardened. "Put away your bruised ego for a second and remember he's my brother — and your oldest friend."

We're not friends. I managed not to stay it out loud. She pressed her lips together and poured the hot water into the mugs. "He's coming up."

"He's *what*?"

"Stop talking to me like I'm the enemy," she said in a very level voice, stirring the coffee.

"I told you I could keep us safe."

"You don't know *how* to keep us safe. Neither of us do."

"And David does?"

"I don't know, Alec," she said, her tone measured and firm, like someone keeping their temper in check with an effort. "But I, for one, would feel happier not being alone."

"You're not alone, Meg."

She gave me a long look, part accusing, part regretful, then took her mug toward the bedrooms. "I'm going out."

"Out?"

"Yes. I need some air, some headspace."

"You're safer here."

"It's daytime," she pointed out mildly, then sighed. "I am grateful to you, Alec. And I trust you, I do. But we're in over our heads. And if I stay in this place, staring at the wall until nighttime, I'll…" She closed her eyes and took a deep breath. When she opened them again, she seemed steadier. "And I'll be damned if we're having pasta and sauce for dinner again."

She went to her bedroom and shut the door. I sipped the coffee, wondering if it was really as bitter as it tasted. I hesitated then flicked the TV back on. The news had moved on to a terrorist attack in Paris. I sat on the edge of the sofa, watching a different newsreader outside a different hotel with an equally grim expression.

Meg re-emerged, dressed in her overcoat, designer jeans and boots. Her expression was warmer but her face was still drawn. She kissed me on cheek then disappeared out into the rain. I finished the coffee but couldn't summon the energy or inclination to eat. I showered and dressed in a sort of fog, paced the cluttered living space for a period that could have been anything from ten minutes to an hour, then caved in and grabbed my coat and keys.

I took the subway to a part of the city I didn't know well, found a corner in an anonymous cafe and ordered a much stronger coffee. It was rich and filled my head with the rush of heat and caffeine. I ordered another and a bacon roll, took out my phone and began scanning the news. The doom-mongers were already out in force. No one had, so far, mentioned anything about donors or revenge kidnappings, but speculation about the Glasgow disappearances was rife and the haemophile spokesman Ivor Novák was being pressed for a statement.

I thought of Meg's drawn face and the punch I'd felt in my gut when I'd learned she'd reached out to David. I stopped myself twice from phoning Karlsson. I didn't know if I was going to demand answers or beg for help. I left the cafe and drank spiced tea from a street vendor to try to calm my tumultuous anxiety. The rain soaked the streets and buildings. It dripped from the hood of my waterproof jacket, splashed up and soaked my jeans. The air smelled like car fumes and wet rubbish. The day wore on. I switched from tea to whisky. I avoided bars with TV screens, deciding I didn't want to know any more.

It was only when they turned the lights on in the dingy pub I'd ended up in that I realized the shadows had started to lengthen. I also remembered that I had the only key to the distillery flat in my pocket. I hurried to the nearest subway, cursing myself under my breath. The rain had turned into sleet, stinging and cold. I reached the distillery just as a nearby church bell chimed four. It was already dim and shadowy in the alley.

I almost didn't see the slim figure leaning against the wall. It was the smell from his cigarette I noticed before anything else. I stopped. He watched me in grim silence. His hair had grown out and was standing in a dark cloud around his head, pinpricked with droplets of rain. He was thinner and there were smudges under his eyes. Stubble blackened the hard lines of his jaw. His clothes were drab, worn and wet. It should have made him appear wasted, scruffy, but it worked on him. Everything that shouldn't work on anyone worked on him.

The sight of him there, real, not in my mind's eye, sent a jolt through me like electricity from a faulty socket. He leveled a dark look at me with eyes the color of good coffee and dropped his cigarette stub to the ground.

"What are you doing here?" I was proud my voice stayed level when I finally found it.

"Meg called me."

"No, she didn't. You called her."

He laughed softly. "You always did like to think you were closer to her than me. And closer to me than she was, come to think of it."

"What do you want, David?"

"I'm taking her away."

"Don't be stupid," I retorted, pushing past him and stomping up the stairs.

"And staying here is the smart choice?"

I banged the door open. He got himself in behind me before I could slam it shut again. "We're safe here," I insisted, forcing the words to be steady.

"Are you drunk?" I kept my back to him, filled the kettle, fetched the instant coffee. "Where is she?" I glared at him. "*Where is she*, Alec?"

"You should leave," I said.

"If I found you, they will too."

"And what are you going to do?" I bit out. "You can't even look after yourself."

His brow clouded. "I knew you'd be this way."

"Get out, David," I growled, sloshing hot water onto the coffee grounds. My heart was thumping, my skin itching. I swallowed some, burning my mouth but desperate for something to still my swirling head.

"You've got no right to be judging anyone's life choices, Alec MacCarthy."

"I said get out."

"Not without Megan." He'd folded his arms in a gesture so similar to his sister's that my heart ached. "And this is the last time I'm gonna ask where she is."

"She went out," I muttered.

"You let her go out?"

"'Let her'?" I said. "She's not my prisoner."

"If they see her, smell her —"

"*Smell* her?"

He shouldered his way out of his coat. His shirt shifted, allowing a glimpse of the gun in his waistband, and I went cold. "You really don't know anything, do you?"

"I know you can only make things worse," I said, eyes fixed on the shape under his shirt.

He stepped up to me. "I'm not the one who's put her in the path of some vengeful haemo —"

"You think this is *my* fault?"

"I know it is."

"*She* invited *me* to that damn club opening —"

"And why do you think the hotshot property developer got himself in with her in the first place, huh? It couldn't be so that he had a way in with you, Lord Aviemore, could it?" I stared at him. My stomach felt like it had filled with concrete. He smiled unpleasantly. "Yeah, *now* you see."

I strode to the window and glared into the empty distillery.

"I just want to make sure she's safe." His tone wasn't exactly conciliatory, but it held a fraction less antagonism. I didn't answer. I watched his reflection in the glass as he scanned the room. Something in his face made my chest hurt.

"You shouldn't have come," I said in a low voice.

"You can't blame me for everything, Alec."

"You'd be surprised."

"Okay, since we're fucking skirting the subject... How was what happened between us my fault?"

"The fact that you don't know just proves my point."

"*You're* the one that gave up on us."

"You left...without a word."

"Only after you said we had no future."

I spun to face him. My chest hurt. My head hurt. The words tumbled out of me like an avalanche. "I had to pick you up from the hospital. *Again*. I was...so angry." I balled my fists. "I still am. I didn't..." I scowled at the floor. "I couldn't stand by and watch you kill yourself."

"So now you're fucking something that doesn't die?"

My blood ran cold. "What?"

His face twisted. "That's right. Meg told me. I knew your dad had fucked you up, but Jesus Christ, Alec."

"You have no idea what you're talking about."

"Don't I?"

"Clearly not, if you think they don't die."

"Oh, I've read the Public Health articles too," he said with a sneer. "But you forget that I've *seen* shit go down with these things." His face clouded, his dark eyebrows drawn together. "Nasty shit. You'd be amazed what can be kept off social media when someone important enough wants it buried. You want the truth? The only way to put one down? Shoot them right here"—he pressed a finger between his eyebrows—"at close range. Get them anywhere else, even point blank, and you just make them angry. Have ever you seen a haemo angry?" Silence hung between us like wet fog. There was a nasty taste in my mouth and Brody's screams filled my ears again. "You know what I'm talking about." His voice was low and he was watching me closely.

A knock on the door made us both jump. He got to it before me.

"David." Meg dropped her shopping bags and threw her arms around him. He held her close, talking softly in her ear. I hung back near the window, not moving even when she broke the hug to smile at me. Her face fell when she took in my expression. "I see you've had your reunion."

"Meg, I don't—" I started.

"I don't want to hear it from either of you." She turned her look on David, who raised his hands in a *not-guilty* gesture.

"We should go," he said.

"Now?" I glared. "It's nearly dark."

"You think you're the only one who can drive like a maniac?"

"I *said*," Meg cut in, "I don't want to hear it."

"Meg—"

"No." She cut off her brother. "Alec's right. It's too late to try to get anywhere tonight." David shot me a black look. Meg started unpacking the bags. "This place is as safe as we're gonna get, for now," she went on, laying steak on a board and starting to chop.

"Meg, if you've had Blood, they can smell it for miles—"

She stiffened, the hand gripping the knife going white at the knuckles. "Blood? You think we drank Blood?"

David looked startled. He glanced at me then back at her. "You said—"

"We didn't *know* it was a Blood Party until it was too late." She continued to chop, a little more forcefully. "But we didn't drink, David. We're not stupid."

David assessed me and I met his scrutiny with a level stare. Eventually his eyes slid away. "Good. That's an advantage to us. But you still need to get away from this city."

"Tomorrow," she said, heating sesame oil in a new frying pan and tossing in the steak with some green peppers and garlic. She glanced at me over her shoulder then back to her brother. "We'll go tomorrow. I promise."

* * * *

I'd never known anything more uncomfortable than that meal with David and Meg. Her stir-fry was excellent, fragrant and rich, but it sat like stone in my belly. The TV was on in the corner, tuned to some movie channel whilst they kept up a flow of stilted conversation. I couldn't tell if the elephant in the room was David or me. I gave short, one-word answers until Meg gave up trying to include me. I tried to figure out whether they expected me to leave with them or whether I wanted to if they did.

I tried not to look at David. I'd made myself not think about him for years. I remembered his branded sportswear, expensive shoes and overpriced, ugly watches. I remembered watching it all disappear as his drug habit worsened. Now he sat with his legs crossed on my faded second-hand couch in non-branded jeans, a plain black T-shirt, no watch, un-groomed and thin but smiling…at Meg, not at me…talking easily, calmly. There was no twitchiness from withdrawal, none of the nervous energy I remembered from when he would be coming down. He had apparently had the same job in a South London Starbucks for the last two years and was on his way to becoming store manager. I couldn't decide if it was the truth or whether he was just saying it for Meg's benefit…or mine.

I desperately wanted to go to my room and shut the door on them, but I couldn't leave. I kept watching the door, the windows. David's gun was like a fourth person in the room. Eventually Meg patted her brother's knee a little stiffly and rose. She gave me an apologetic glance and wished me goodnight. When we heard her door shut, David's face changed.

"Say whatever you want to say."

I chewed over several things, rejected all of them and left the room. I leaned against my bedroom door, kneading my temples. The ache didn't leave. I got into bed, leaving the curtains open, and made sure the shotgun was in reach. I listened to David move around the sitting room, turning off the TV, rooting in the cupboard for spare blankets. I listened to everything fall silent.

The only sound was the low growl of Glasgow in the distance. Physical and mental exhaustion wrestled with the caffeine and fear. I waited for the dreams.

Terje appeared in the corner of the room. The light from the streetlight shone in his white-blond hair and glinted in the sliver of his eyes. He stood motionless, hands in the pockets of a long, black overcoat. His eyes were on me, darker than night, deeper than space. A strand of hair had become untucked from behind his ear. I wanted to reach out and brush it back. My skin and veins started to thrum whilst the chill of fear spread slowly through my insides.

I reached out. Sometimes in the dreams, he came to me. Sometimes I had to go to him. This time nothing happened. It was only when my hand dropped and I felt the worn, old sheet under my fingers that I realized I wasn't asleep.

I scrabbled for the gun, heart climbing up my throat. I leveled it at him, panting, palms sweating.

"I think we've been through this." His voice wasn't loud but it filled my head and flesh with electricity.

"You can't bite me if I blow your head off." My own voice was thin.

"Do you want to blow my head off?"

I didn't dare blink. My hands were shaking. Silence stretched on. His eyes were like points of starlight in a black night. I'd forgotten how completely unreal he looked. And how completely entrancing.

"How did you get in here?" I quavered, thinking of Meg and David sleeping a few feet away.

"Your friends are fine," he said, as if reading my thoughts on my face. He took his hands out of his pockets. They were so long, so fine, the nails sharper than cut glass.

"Don't move."

He raised an eyebrow. "We're to stay like this all night then?"

"Stay back."

"I'm nowhere near you, Alec."

"Don't call me that."

"You're panicking."

"Did you kill —?"

"Alec," he cut me off, stepping closer. I gripped the gun tighter. "I'm not going to hurt you."

"I don't believe you." *Not anymore.*

He came closer. My finger trembled on the trigger. He drifted to the bed. The barrel quivered an inch from his face, which was as cool and distant as snow on the mountaintops. Cold sweat stood out on my face and back.

"I've come to help you." His voice was like coffee laced with liquor. I wanted so badly to swallow it and feel comforted, but I didn't dare.

"*Help* me?"

"Yes."

"The way you helped that politician? And Olivia Ogdell-Paige? Her husband?"

Something shifted in the backs of his eyes. "They are not my concern."

I drew breath in and out through my teeth. "They're dead, aren't they?" He didn't speak. "Did you kill them?"

"Alec—"

"They were right," I gritted. "The Ogdells. The anti-haemos. The protest groups. You're monsters, all of you." In a movement too quick to see, he'd taken the gun. I scrambled out of the bed and stood against the wall. "Just leave Meg alone. Please. She didn't do anything. She didn't—"

"Alec," he said softly, propping the gun against the wall. "You need to listen."

"I don't want to hear anything from you."

"I've not hurt anyone."

"You didn't?" I wanted to believe, so badly, but I didn't trust myself to spot a lie. "Where are they, then?"

Something dark ghosted in his eyes. "I don't know."

"I don't believe you," I ground out.

He gave a small sigh. "You don't have to, but you'd be safer if you did."

I clenched my fists to stop my hands shaking. "If you didn't take them, who did?" His glance slid away. "*Who*, Terje?" His name felt strange in my mouth. I'd said it so many times in dreams or in the safe cage of night in my bed at Glenroe. I'd never thought I'd say it to his face again. It felt weighty, like an overladen water pail. He still didn't speak. "You're going to tell me what's going on, or..."

"Or what?"

I held his gaze with some effort. "I don't think you want to hurt me," I ventured, watching him closely. "But the Blood will fight if I'm a threat, right? So tell me. Tell me what's going on or I'll go for the gun—"

"That wouldn't be wise."

"*Tell me.*"

His eyes flickered. "It's my Magister."

"Your *what*?"

"The head of my commune. My..." His glance slid to the wall again. "I can't tell you more, but you must believe me when I say that it wasn't me that took those people."

My mouth was dry. "Then why are you here?"

"I told you. To help you."

"Why?"

He blinked again, slowly. "I don't want you to get hurt."

"This Magister... He wants to hurt me?"

"*She* wants to hurt everyone," he said slowly. "Everyone who was there that night."

"Meg and I didn't do anything—"

"We don't have much time." He stepped toward me. "I can protect you, but we must leave. *Now*."

"I can't leave Meg."

"She can't come, Alec. She won't understand."

"I won't leave her on her own whilst—"

"She's safe. I promise. She's the only one who is."

I frowned. "Why?"

"It doesn't matter."

"*Terje.*"

He huffed out a breath through his nose, the first sign of impatience I'd seen him display. "She didn't drink?"

"No."

"Then my Magister won't find her."

That taste rose in the back of my throat again. I could smell burning leaves, sun-warmed heather. My heart skittered about. My fingertips pulsed. Blood rushed into my face. He was watching me realize. "I didn't ask to drink."

"That won't matter to her."

Anger warred with fear over an echoing pit of something deep and dark in the back of my mind. He was so close that if I reached out, I could touch him. For real this time, not a dream. I wondered if he'd want me to…if he'd let me. I wondered why that was all I could think about right now.

He moved close. His breath brushed my jaw. I could smell his hair, clean and cool like mountain wind. "Please, Alec, let me help you."

I let out a shuddering breath, fighting for control over the feelings battling in my chest. I finally nodded and watched something that might have been relief warm his face.

"Get dressed," he ordered. "Quietly."

I obeyed in a daze then stuffed what little I'd brought with me into my rucksack and followed him down the darkened corridor. I stopped outside Meg's room, but he urged me on with a firm hold on my elbow.

He opened the door into the sitting area silently and ghosted through, making no more noise than fog. We were halfway to the front door when a lamp snapped on. David stood by the sofa, his pistol raised.

"Don't move," he bit out, but whether he was talking to me or Terje I couldn't tell. His face was a rigid mask. Sweat shone on his forehead.

"David, put it down," I said.

"Step away."

"David—"

"*Step away*, Alec."

"It's not what you think."

"If you've even touched Meg—"

"She's fine," I said, stepping between them. David's forehead was twisted, his jaw bulging. The gun didn't waver. "David, she will be fine. She's not in danger."

"Who's told you that? *Him*?" He jerked the gun over my shoulder to where Terje stood by the door, unmoving, eyes locked unblinking on David.

"I trust him."

"Christ," David breathed, his eyes widening. "I didn't want to believe it. But it's true, isn't it?"

"What is?"

"You've got Bloodlust. I saw it in your face. I didn't want to believe but—*don't move*."

Terje had put his hand on the door handle. "We must leave, Alec. *Now*."

"You have no idea what you've done," David breathed, words addressed to me even though his eyes were fixed on Terje. "You'll end up doing anything that thing asks, just for a sniff of the stuff."

"That's not true—"

"Bullshit," he snapped. "He owns you now."

"No—"

"How do you think he found you, Alec? He can *smell* it. They can sniff out anyone who's drank Blood." I stared at Terje, but he was as readable as carved marble. "*You* brought this down on us," David said, looking at me for the first time, his eyes jet black with pain. "You put Meg in danger. And for what? A Blood hit? After all the self-righteous shit you spewed at me the day I left?"

"It's not like that," I said, willing it to be the truth.

"Isn't it? Just you wait, Alec. You think me on crack was bad? You have no idea—" David jerked his head up. Meg was moving around in her room.

A gust of cold night air made me jump. The door was open and Terje had vanished.

"*Alec!*"

David's desperate plea was lost in the noise of me rattling down the steps. I braced myself for the sound of a shot, but it didn't come. I skidded out onto the deserted road and stared around dumbly, jumping at the sound of an engine starting. A black Mitsubishi SUV roared up to the pavement, Terje in the driver's seat. I hesitated then climbed in. He pressed the accelerator before I'd shut the door. I watched the dim shape of the distillery disappear in the wing mirror.

"Phone." He was holding out a long-fingered hand.

"Why?"

He wound down his window. "Give it to me."

"I'm not giving up my phone. What if Meg—"

"You can't be of any more help to her," he cut me off. "And someone may use it to track you."

"I'm not giving you my phone," I said firmly.

He sent me a sideways glance but dropped his hand. "I won't make you. But this will have all been for nothing if you don't turn it off and leave it off."

"If this Magister can find me by smell, why would she need to trace my phone?"

"She doesn't. But it's only a matter of time before someone makes the connection between you all. Then she won't be the only one hunting you."

I took out my phone and stared at the screen. There were two missed calls from Meg already. Another from an unknown number. I swallowed, then switched it off.

Terje drove fast. I watched warehouses and factories skid by, trying to wrestle my mind into order. My heart rate slowed as we left the city behind, but my chest didn't loosen. I realized I was clutching the seat and made myself ease off.

"You're right to be scared," Terje murmured, "but not of me."

The buildings thinned out, then we were on the motorway. The streetlights whizzed by overhead, arching blackness between, before they gave out entirely.

"Where are we going?" I asked into the chill silence.

"Somewhere safe."

"If she can track me by smell…"

"She has to be in range for that. We have to get you far enough away that she can't detect you."

Silence descended. I snuck glances of him out the corner of my eye. He didn't use the mirrors. He barely blinked. I simultaneously longed for him to speak whilst praying he wouldn't, afraid of what else I might learn.

We barreled on into the night. Fatigue raked claws down the backs of my eyes but I clutched my knees and sat ramrod straight in the seat, unable to relax. My shoulders ached. My head pounded. David's words rang in my ears. But under all that, more persistent and more unnerving, was the now-vivid remembered sensation of Terje's hands and mouth on my skin. I shut my eyes against it, against the sight of him sitting so close with an infinite gulf of fear and danger between us.

It started to snow. Pinhead-sized flakes whisked up the windscreen. The wind picked up and the flakes fattened, became the size of coins and swirled thickly in the headlights until the road was barely visible. Terje didn't ease up on the speed.

Despite everything, I was starting to nod, then the car turning off-road jerked me awake. He'd turned the headlights off. All I could make out was the star-studded arch of the sky over black nothingness ahead. We bumped over uneven ground for more than two hours. The sky grew lighter and I could finally make out the rough track we were following, barely more than a lip jutting from a scrubby hillside, nothingness yawning on the other. The snow was already a foot deep — or else we were so far into the mountains that we were where it had never melted. Terje had put on a pair of sunglasses, rendering him even more unreadable.

When he finally stopped the car and turned off the engine, I was bone-weary and aching with tiredness. I blinked out at a small stone cottage that was built so tightly into the mountainside it was like it had just sprung from the ground. The sloping roof was covered in a thick blanket of white. The windows were dark, masked by blinds.

"Where are we?" My voice was creaky with fatigue.

Terje pulled up his hood and climbed out into the snow. He waded through the snow and put a key in the lock of the heavy wooden front door. I climbed out and stared around. It was deathly silent. The snow-covered mountainside rose sharply above the cottage. On my right, the sloping land ended in a straight line about five feet from the car. Beyond that was a yawning, unseen glen. More snowbound peaks towered on the other side.

There was something vaguely familiar about the rocky outcrop sticking out of the snow like the rigid hand of a corpse on the mountaintop high above the cottage. At another time of year I might have recognized where we were, but the snow had stolen the land, turning it into an alien wilderness. There was no other living thing in sight, no traffic or background noise, no animal tracks, no trees. I clutched my phone in my pocket, realizing it would be useless out here anyway, then waded through the snow to the open cottage door.

The interior of the building smelled of furniture polish and new upholstery. It was pitch black, all the windows made dark by blackout blinds. Terje switched on lamps, flooding the space with a warm orange light. There was a top-of-the-range wood-burning stove against one wall and a deep charcoal carpet underfoot. Simple, comfortable-looking chairs and sofas were arranged around the stove. There was a flatscreen TV on the wall over the mantlepiece. Against the far wall was a modern kitchen unit with surfaces of varnished wood, dominated by a massive, industrial-sized refrigeration unit. It took me a couple of glances to realize that there was no oven.

The walls were plastered and whitewashed. There was no decoration apart from a large, framed map of the Cairngorms next to the door. It was all anonymous, blank, simple. It was shining new but…empty.

"Close the door. Lock it."

Terje was passing through an inner door, closing it behind him. Numb, I closed the heavy front door, shutting away the sight of the snow, the naked cliffs, the white sky and the perfect silence that came from being miles away from anywhere. I heard the sound of electronic locks slamming home. There were also two large iron bolts. I heaved them over with a heavy feeling.

I stood by the door, unsure what to do, until Terje returned. He'd shed his coat and sunglasses. There was a heaviness to his eyes. My watch told me it was a little after eight in the morning.

"I have to sleep," he said, voice thick. "There's wood for the fire and food in the cupboards."

"There's no oven," I said stupidly.

"Stay inside," he continued. "Don't turn your phone on."

"What is this place?"

"I have to sleep," he said, slurring. His eyelids were heavy. He straightened with visible effort and went back through the door, and I heard it lock. Then there was silence.

I lit the wood-burner with the supply of logs and kindling neatly stacked alongside. The warmth began to permeate the air and I hung my coat on a hook by the door, dumped my bag and shed my boots. I double-checked my pockets, but all I found was my phone and my penknife.

The new carpet was deep and soft under my stockinged feet. I found a set of stairs behind a narrow door on the other side of the kitchen that led to a small, windowless bathroom. It didn't look like it had ever been used. The fittings were plain and very white. I found a towel in one of the cupboards and washed in an attempt to normalize the situation. The water was only just above freezing, I guessed due to the newly-lit fire. One of the kitchen cupboards contained coffee, cereal, long-life milk, canned soup, tinned fish and jars of pickled vegetables. There was one bowl, a plastic spoon and a paper cup. The rest of the cupboards were empty. There were no plates and no other cutlery. I opened the fridge. Dozens of bottles of red liquid filled the shelves. I shut it hurriedly.

I opened a tin of fish with my penknife, ate some cereal and sat in front of the fire. The TV didn't receive any signal. It had a DVD-Blu-ray player built in, but there were no discs anywhere. The stove gradually warmed the room to a comfortable temperature. I dozed. The wind groaned around the cottage. The windows didn't rattle and the door didn't wheeze in its fittings. It was like I was walled away from the world, buried out of reach. I thought about Glenroe, how the weather had barely been held back by the crumbling stone, how there I'd felt like part of the storm but safe from it.

I turned my face into the sofa cushions and let myself drift. I tried not to think of Meg...or of David. I tried to believe they were safe. I turned my phone over and over in my hands but didn't turn it on.

As night approached, I pulled a blind back from one of the windows and watched the sky darken. It seemed the sun had been set for hours by the time I heard the inner door being unlocked and Terje came through. He was in black jeans and a gray jumper, the muted tones making his skin and hair seem luminescent. His feet were bare.

"Did you sleep?"

I nodded stiffly, hovering near the window.

"You're still scared."

"I'm not scared."

His eyes slid to the bowl next to the sink. "Sorry. This place isn't really set up for your kind."

"What is it?"

"A hide," he said quietly, moving to the fridge and taking out a bottle of blood. "A safe space."

"For haemophiles?"

He nodded. "It's not quite finished yet. But the location is isolated, the energy provided by solar power, heat and hot water from the fire. And there are caves in the cliffs farther up the mountain, a bolt hole from the sun should anything happen. Evgeniya was thinking of setting up a branch of our commune out here. At least, that's what she told me."

"Evgeniya?"

"My Magister. The hide is the reason I was in Scotland in the first place. I'd come to oversee the final stages."

"It's a bit…spartan," I mumbled, looking around at the plain walls, the new but functional furniture.

His mouth twitched and I wondered if he was fighting a smile. "I'm afraid I don't have much imagination when it comes to interior design. That's what happens when you don't need much in the way of physical comforts."

"This is why you were this far north?" He nodded. "And Karlsson found you?" I heard myself ask when the question had hung in the air too long unasked.

"It was my own fault," he said, moving toward the stove. "It's dangerous to venture far on your own, especially away from your commune. But I wanted to see more of the National Park. This place…" His eyes went far away. "It's so alive. So…it's hard to say in English. Honest, I suppose. Real. Like your house with its ancient stones and secret caves. It's all like it's from another time…a harsher but more natural time." His eyes were far away. "But I was spotted in the hills above Aviemore."

"You carried me for miles unconscious in a snowstorm. You moved that armoire with your bare hands. How did anyone manage to capture you?"

"They were professionals — stun guns, real guns, nets."

I chewed on the inside of my cheek. "How long were you in that basement?"

He didn't answer for a long time. His long fingers turned the bottle round and round. "I don't know, exactly. Weeks, at least."

"Christ."

"I knew I'd been seen. I shouldn't have risked walking that way again. Evgeniya warned me. They all did. But I really thought things were different now."

I shook my head, trying to make sense of it all. "And now your Magister is out for revenge?"

His face changed. "That's a very 'Hollywood' way of putting it."

"How would you put it?"

"She's dispensing justice."

Something uncomfortable worked its way up my spine. "She must care about you a lot."

He raised his eyes, slightly narrowed. "That's not what it is, not in the way you mean it, anyway."

"Then what is it?"

"A commune is... Well, there's no word for it in English. It's more than family. We depend on each other. We protect each other. And we obey our leaders. It's how we survive. How we've always survived."

"So, when someone gets hurt...this *family* steps in?"

He stared at the fire. "A member of the commune was abused. The wrong must be righted."

"If she really has killed all those people, it will set people's attitudes back years."

"I know," he said, seating himself on the sofa in a slow, lithe movement.

"Why didn't you stop her?"

He frowned at me, a delicate line creasing between his fair eyebrows. "Stop her?"

"Yes," I insisted. "You could have reported Karlsson to the police — and the Ogdells. You could have let the authorities handle it...lawfully, without any killing."

He raised his eyebrows, open incredulity flattening his expression. "Evgeniya is my Magister," he said calmly. "I report to her. She is the only authority over me."

"What about the police? The law?"

He looked vaguely bewildered. "What about them?"

"*They* are the authorities."

"Not over us."

"But you're part of this world now. That was the whole point. All the campaigning —"

"Those institutions want us to turn to them. And in an ideal world, one I had hoped we'd reached, we would. But all the human establishment has done so far is make matters worse."

"That can't be true."

He regarded me levelly. "The last member of my commune that reported human-perpetrated abuse to the authorities vanished. We've not seen or heard from her in months. Even the Magister hasn't been able to track her down. She thinks she's dead."

I shook my head, bewildered. "No...no, that can't be right. There are laws—"

"There are," he said calmly. "And I still hope—within my lifetime, though probably not yours—that those laws might one day mean something. But right now?" He shook his head without looking at me.

"It can't be true," I repeated.

"Alec, think about the way your kind treats different strains of its own species, even after generations of attempts at change. How long do you think it will take them to accept a new species they don't even understand yet?"

"But, what's his name, Ivor Novák?"

"Novák's doing what he can. But you are aware of the sort of people who can afford a donor, Alec." His voice tightened and I wondered if I was seeing pain flickering in the back of his eyes. "They're not the sort of people your *authorities* go after if they can avoid it. So, until the world Novák wants to create becomes a reality, we'll protect our own, as we always have done."

I felt slightly unwell.

"Do I wish things were different?" he said softly after another long moment. "Of course I do. I was foolish enough to hope they already were. And look what happened."

"So you gave her names, the names I'd given you, knowing what she'd do?"

"What she does is her business."

"Did you even *try* to stop her?"

A bitter smile turned up one corner of his mouth. "This is not something you can understand, Alec. She's my mother, my leader, my master…all those things, none of those things. I don't have any say in what she does or in what she tells me to do. And I can't hide things from her. I wouldn't, even if I could."

My palms prickled. "So what would she think of you hiding me like this? Of us being together here, now?"

His eyes slid away. "She won't find out."

"This isn't the first place she'll look when she doesn't find me at Glenroe?"

"No."

"Why not?"

His jaw tightened. "Because the only way you'd be here is if I brought you. And it would never occur to her that I'd defy her like this."

I put more wood on the fire simply to fill the silence. I was very aware of his eyes following me and wondered what it meant.

"If you want to drink that, don't let me stop you," I said, sitting in an armchair. I heard him open the bottle, then the sound of him drinking. I tried not to watch. I failed. His eyes were closed. He drank in long, smooth swallows. He tilted his head. His hair moved against his neck. The bottle emptied. When he lowered it, his face was slack with such an intense expression of pleasure that it made my blood start to thump, even whilst chills ran up the skin on my back. I looked away.

"How long do you think I'll have to stay here?"

He put the empty bottle out of sight beside the sofa. His cheeks and lips had warmed to the color of new cream and a light danced in his eyes. "Until she's done," he said, voice slightly drowsy.

I shifted in the chair. "Done *killing* everyone?" He didn't answer. I was ashamed that I didn't have the courage to ask again. "How long will that take?" I asked instead, in a quiet voice.

"I don't know," he said again. "But you're safe here, Alec. I promise." He spoke slowly, staring into the fire, then his eyes slid to mine. My heart danced sideways, a familiar throb starting deep in my gut, a hot awareness of every blood vessel in my body sparking to life. His eyes flicked between mine, like he was reading my thoughts. "Do you still think about it?" he whispered.

"About...what?"

"The Blood," he said after a pause.

I wrestled with that for a long moment. When I spoke, my voice was harsh with equal parts pleasure and pain. "Yes."

His drew his fine brows together. "I'm sorry I gave it to you, but there was no other way."

"It saved me."

"You'll never forget it," he murmured. "You'll think about it for the rest of your life."

"I think about you more." I heard the words come out of my mouth in a heavy, loaded voice. The tips of my fingers and toes tingled. My belly churned. The smell of red wine and dry leaves came to me, threading through the fresh, cool smell of his hair.

He absently ran his hand over fabric of the sofa, eyes far away, ice-white eyebrows slightly arched. "It's just the Blood, Alec. It's not real."

"You're wrong."

The corner of a sardonic smile played across his lips. "You don't think I maybe have a little more experience in this area than you?"

"Then why am I here? If there's really nothing between us, what difference does it make to you if this woman kills me or not?"

"I'm not a monster, Alec. And neither's Evgeniya. You might not understand her actions, but she is punishing those she believes deserve it. Your society does exactly the same thing." His gaze slid to the fire. "But I know you didn't drink at that house. I know you helped me. And you gave me shelter in your home, even after…after you'd seen me at my worst. Evgeniya won't believe that you had nothing to do with the Blood Party. But I know you didn't."

A long silence fell in which I fought with a hundred things to say. In the end there was only one question that mattered to me. "Is that all this is?"

He blinked, slowly. "What do you mean?"

I shifted to the edge of my seat. "I want you to admit there's something here…between us. I don't understand it…but I know it's there."

"You're mistaken."

I knew a flinty moment of doubt. My hands went cold. I kept my voice level with an effort. "I don't think I am."

With a small sigh, his gaze returned to the fire. "I've already told you, Alec. This is just the Blood. It does this to your kind. You can't let go. Why do you think people get addicted?"

"I felt this way before I drank it."

"I can't see how that's possible."

"Me either, but it's true. It terrified me. Why do you think I ran away?"

His eyes met mine. "You watched me kill someone—someone you cared about."

I pulse flickered in my temples. "I can't explain it."

"You were going to shoot me over it."

"I was angry…and scared." He continued to watch me. I moved cautiously to the other end of the sofa. "But then you saved me. Then when we…" I swallowed thickly. I wondered if more color had crept into his face or if it was just my imagination. "I *felt* something. Something real, between us. It's insane, but I know it was there."

There was a long silence. I heard my own words going round and round in my head and they sounded more stupid with every repetition. My certainty weakened and peeled away. David's disgusted looks and angry words came screaming back, along with Meg's incredulous, disbelieving protests. But I knew, somehow, under it all, that this was something I couldn't deny. I wasn't even sure I wanted to.

That scared me more than anything.

"It's not possible, you know."

His words were like ice down my neck. "What's not?"

He heaved a deep sigh and I thought I saw a suggestion of regret in his face. "Relations…between our kinds. They never work."

"The time on the sofa worked pretty well," I managed.

"For you," he replied coolly.

"You're saying you felt nothing?" I didn't believe it. Couldn't believe it. His eyes flickered but he didn't speak. I shifted closer. He watched me move, wariness clouding the mask of his eyes. "Why, exactly, don't they work?"

"How many answers to that question do you want?"

I shifted closer still. My leg touched his. My arm brushed his elbow. He watched me warily but didn't move away. "If you look me in the eye now and tell me there's nothing here, I'll believe you and I won't mention it again."

He shifted, his forehead creasing. He hesitated, then lifted a long-fingered hand and ran his thumb through the stubble on my jaw with a faintly wistful expression on his face. The touch sent lines of white fire darting along my nerves.

"I'd forgotten how heated your kind can be," he said softly, his fingertips sliding to my hairline, pushing loose strands back. "How you hold everything so close to the surface. It's why it's so easy to fall for you. But it can't happen," he went on, shaking his head and dropping his hand to my chest, like he'd push me back.

"Why not?"

"We're too different."

Outside, the wind sighed and groaned. I could smell the clean, new upholstery of the sofa and the faint thread of icy freshness that was the scent of him. He was so weirdly, impossibly beautiful that it made me ache. I suddenly needed to taste him again so badly that it hurt. I stopped thinking and leaned forward, but he pressed his fingers to my mouth, holding me back.

"You can't understand me, Alec," he breathed. "You have to stop trying."

"I understand you need something," I whispered against his fingers.

"What makes you think that?"

I gently pulled his hand away and leaned closer. "You're still here."

I held his eyes for a long time, watched them stare into mine and almost thought I could see the struggle raging in their depths. Then I kissed him.

He let me lean close, explore his mouth, savor his taste. Maybe he was hoping the feel of his sharpened canines might put me off, but it just heightened the prickle of excitement down my spine. I kissed him deeper, letting myself drink in the alien feel of it, the faint, autumnal flavor of him. It lit bonfires along my veins, and I swore I could smell their smokiness in the air.

I ran my hand up his leg. He put his own hand on top to stop it and broke the kiss. I was breathing heavily. My mouth felt bruised and hot. My lip stung where it had caught on his tooth. I had to blink a few times to bring him back into focus. His breathing was level, calm. There was no heightened color in his cheeks, no parting of his lips. My desire dampened, until I noted that his eyes had lit with a deep, dark fire.

"We can do this...if you want," he said softly. "But it won't be like you expect."

"Do you want to?"

His eyes watched mine. I searched them desperately for what he was thinking. I was a storm battering against a sea wall. After an achingly long minute, he threaded his hand into my hair and drew me to him.

He kissed me. It was slow, deep and strong. He breathed in, inhaling me like the bouquet of a fine wine. He took possession of my mouth like he was entitled to it. He pushed me back into the sofa and climbed on top of me. He was a lot heavier than he looked. The weight of his frame crushed me almost to the point of pain. His kiss became powerful. He licked the cut in my lip and shivered. He gripped my wrist and shoulder. My wrist pulsed where he'd twisted it in Meg's car, what seemed like a lifetime ago. Fear flashed through me. Then I gave myself up to it and lifted my hips so my swelling cock pressed into his thigh whilst I slipped my free hand under his jumper.

His skin was cool and firm. I could feel the raw power in it. He didn't react to the touch or lean into my caress. I was like a light rain on parched land, not enough to nourish what was underneath.

He tightened his hands, digging into me like he was searching for something. His fingernails pricked my skin, but when I winced, he loosened his grip and shifted away. I pulled him close again, fighting back the dampening sense of futility that was rising underneath the burn of my arousal.

I got my leg up and rolled him gently onto the floor. I tugged at his jumper and he allowed me to pull it over his head. His torso was lithe and toned, the muscles moving under the skin like iron beneath silk. His skin was the color of warmed milk, completely unmarked — no scars, not so much as a freckle. It was like he'd been painted or sculpted. I couldn't imagine him being born, being a child or growing up whilst grazing knees and elbows, climbing trees, chasing friends around a play park. I was startled by the realization that I didn't know if he ever had been.

His fine hair pooled on the carpet and his hooded eyes burned into mine. I removed my own shirt and recaptured his mouth, reveling in the feeling of my hot skin cooling against his. As I continued to move against him, it slowly dawned on me that something wasn't right. A tentative fumble at his waistline revealed nothing against my hand except the rough denim of his jeans.

I had no idea what I was doing, no idea what he needed, what he wanted. He'd tried to tell me. I hadn't listened. It was like a bucket of cold water dumped down my back. He must have felt me tense, because his face changed. He watched me for a moment, then he leaned up and brushed his mouth against my ear.

"It takes time," he whispered in a voice loaded with a desire so deep and dark it made me shiver. "Just go slow."

Flames erupted in my belly. I lifted his knee so I could settle more firmly between his legs and buried my face in his neck. I kissed the tender flesh and let my hands run up his legs and along his sides. He eased and, eventually, his breathing began to deepen and he started to move against me. I dared to slide my hand down again and his cock was finally growing firm under his clothing.

"Touch me, Alec," he whispered into my ear.

I swallowed the helpless noise that rose in my throat and fumbled desperately with his fly that suddenly seemed far more complicated than any I had undone before. Finally, I got my hand into his pants and wrapped my fingers around his hardening length. His hands tightened on me and he let out a noise so low that I felt it in his chest.

"So warm," he murmured into my hair. "*Gud*, you're so warm."

I groaned and kissed him again, hard. I started to move my hand, causing him to inhale almost like he was trying to swallow me.

I forced myself to go slow and focus on his smallest reactions. It was like learning to read with my hands. My patience waned and waxed, and my need grew sharp and dulled. I had moments of uncertainty that were like clouds moving between me and a hot sun, but they never quite managed to extinguish the warmth.

The sight of the gradually mounting need in his eyes kept me going, like someone parched who sees an oasis on the horizon. His body slowly came more alive under my ministrations, like a forest fire spreading through dried undergrowth. I pulled his remaining clothing away. He did the same for me, languorously and with low noises, eyes heavy like he was dreaming. He rolled me onto my back, holding his weight off me with an elbow and burying his face in my neck, gliding a hand down to wrap it around mine as I pumped his cock.

He guided me with his touch, his breath and, eventually, his panted words. His voice changed, becoming deeper, slurred, like someone drunk on red wine. I pressed the fingers of my free hand into the tender flesh of his lower back, drinking the sight and smell of him in through my skin, willing him to feel what I was feeling. He gradually sank his weight onto me as his need weakened him.

It was like nothing I'd ever experienced. He brought something to the surface in me that was unfamiliar and a little frightening. He knew exactly how to touch me, look at me, breathe on me to keep me chained to his needs. I grew very aware of just how much older he was, how different, and how little I might ever be able to know about him. I remembered the feel of his Blood in my veins and knew, on a level of myself I didn't want to acknowledge, that if I just had some more, I'd understand. I'd be on his level. This would become even more…real.

He crushed me to him, sinking his fingernails into my skin, pulling everything from me with his body and mouth. I let him, being no more able to stop it than I could stop a landslide with my bare hands.

I finally knew he was close when he slid his other hand between us to grasp my neglected cock. He was gentle, but the strength in that hand jolted fear up my spine. He breathed my name in my ear and worked the sensitive flesh in time with his own, chasing away the doubts. He gained speed and increased the pressure, mumbling something in another language over and over. The powerful muscles in his back and legs started to bunch.

I threw my head back as my climax built, like a bushfire flooding a firebreak. I teetered on the edge of release, and for several tingling, glorious seconds, reveled in it, before hearing him groan deep in his throat. I forced my eyes open so I could watch him come, but he pressed his forehead into mine, arched forward into my hand one more time and let out a low, keening noise, hot and full of relief and a little desperation. Warm fluid spread over both our hands and I let go, coming hard in waves hotter than windblown smoke.

When I was able to focus again, we were both lying on our sides in front of the fire, clutching each other, breathing like we'd run a marathon. I was scratched, aching and every inch of my skin was sensitive as a healing burn. His fingers, still gripping my upper arms, trembled. His face was pressed at the place where my neck met my shoulder. He brushed my skin with his teeth for the briefest moment before he drew away.

Sweat plastered his fine hair to his forehead and jaw. His mouth was open, saliva shining on his lips. He breathed through his mouth like an animal, tasting the air between us. His eyes were dreamy, as though he wasn't really in the room.

Waves of sated desire flagged outward from my middle. I felt the question of whether it had been enough for him hover in my mouth but couldn't find the breath to form it.

His eyes flicked over my face and he leaned in and kissed me again, deeply but chastely. I wasn't sure whether he was telling me something or just trying to reassure me. He prized his fingers away from my arms and stood, slowly, like someone moving through water. I watched, dazed, as he gathered his clothes and disappeared into the other room, closing the door gently behind him.

I sat up stiffly, feeling drained, sore. I could feel bruises forming on my arms and wrists. My feet and hands were cold. I fumbled more wood onto the wood-burner then stared at the inner door, fatigue dulling my brain.

I lifted a hand to gingerly finger my neck. The skin was intact, though it felt tender and over-sensitized. I had no idea what to think or feel. I dragged my jeans on then drank greedily from the kitchen tap. I hesitated, went to the inner door and knocked. No answer. I tried the handle. Locked.

I glanced at the clock. A vast amount of time had disappeared, but it was still several hours before dawn. I sat and tried to not think about the locked door or what that last, slightly strained kiss might have meant.

I slept. I woke. Dawn lightened the blinds. I ate a little, drank more water and spent the day keeping the fire going and chasing confused, dulled thoughts around the dark cave of my brain. I must have been more tired than I thought, because one minute I was watching the clock, waiting for nightfall, then I was being woken by the soft sounds of someone moving close by. I blinked the sleepiness away and saw Terje attending to the wood-burner.

"I didn't want to wake you," he said softly.

I shifted on the sofa, trying to find something to say. The hard knot of doubt in the bottom of my belly seemed to block all my senses. Finally, he raised his eyes to mine. They were the color of flint in the low light. His pale hair was neatly tucked behind his ears. He was wearing the same jeans and jumper. I remembered the feel of his skin against my fingertips and the taste of his mouth. But the passionate creature who had given himself up to me on the carpet under my very feet was completely absent from the blank, otherworldly face now turned my toward me.

I couldn't think of what to say. I knew what I wanted to ask, but the words wouldn't come.

"Are you all right?"

"I'm fine." He raised his eyebrows slightly. I dropped my gaze. "You left rather quickly last night." He watched me closely but didn't answer. I clenched my hands together. "I don't understand," I said softly, finally admitting it to myself.

He stood perfectly still, his gaze unwavering. "It's okay that you don't know what to feel," he said in a voice devoid of any intonation. "Our kinds don't fit together easily. And this? Well..." He glanced around the room. "This is an unusual situation as it is."

"I'm sorry I don't know what to do for you...to make it good."

His gaze came back to mine. "You're overthinking this."

"Am I?"

Something lightened the impenetrable darkness of his eyes. "Thinking doesn't come into this. Understanding does. And you understand better than you think you do. More than most. That in itself is…refreshing."

Something lifted inside me. "I do?"

A smile twitched up the corner of his mouth. "Don't you?"

I stood and went to him. His face, impassive and blank, was turned up to mine. My hands tingled at my sides, longing to touch him.

"You should eat," he said softly after a long moment. "Your blood sugar's low again."

I swallowed. "And then?"

One pale eyebrow arched. "Then?"

I lifted a hand and ran a thumb over his slightly parted lips. "I want to do it again."

"It wasn't what you thought," he said softly after a heavy silence.

"No."

"It takes a long time."

"It does."

"And I hurt you."

"A little."

He narrowed his eyes slightly. "So why…?"

I leaned in and ran my lips over his ear. I brushed my fingers over his neck, feeling the life pulsing there. "I like to learn."

"Why learn this?"

I chewed on that for a moment. "Life hasn't felt…real for a long time. Feeling something, *anything*, real is a relief. It's…good, even if I don't fully understand it." He let out a long, controlled breath. I pressed my lips to the skin just below his jaw, just soft enough to touch, a half-taste. The smell of leaves and wine rose in my mind. The taste of sweet darkness at the back of my throat. The bruises on my arms throbbed.

"I'm not giving you any Blood."

I ignored the slight chill of disappointment that ghosted through my chest. "I'm not asking for any."

He guided my head back with a firm grip on my chin. "You can't pretend you don't want it."

I opened my mouth to protest but couldn't. The thought of feeling what he felt, burning as he burned, of tasting and feeling him all through me when we came together, made my mouth water and my heart pound. He traced the thoughts on my face, and I sensed that I was on the brink of failing some monumental test.

"It was good with the Blood," I said in a low voice. "Very good. But it's you I want."

"You know nothing about me."

"I know how you make me feel."

He held himself very still. Slowly the memory formed in my mind of his face pressed to my neck, his mouth open, the hunger in his gaze, the way he'd licked the cut on my mouth. I took a shuddering breath.

"What about *my* blood? Would that make it…?"

His face shifted. "Alec—"

"But…would it make it better—?"

"No," he cut me off, voice suddenly firm, an iron curtain slamming down behind his eyes.

"But it's what you want…?"

"You don't know what you're talking about," he said, breaking away and pacing into the kitchen.

"I…I don't mind," I said in a thick voice. "If it's what you want…I think I could —"

"Stop." The word resounded louder than a bullet into body armor. "Stop talking about it. You don't know what you're offering."

"Surely it's my choice —"

"*You don't know what you're offering,*" he repeated. His eyes were very black, barely a trace of the silver iris showing. "Don't ever mention it again."

"I've offended you."

He opened the fridge and took out a bottle without looking at me.

"How can you expect me to get things right if you don't explain —"

"I've tried to explain —"

"Try again," I insisted, my own voice hardening. He turned a set, blank face toward me. I was very aware of the bottle of human blood in his hand. The way he held it slightly behind himself told me he was too.

"I'm not drinking from you, Alec," he said in a voice with an edge fine enough to slice metal. "Don't ask me to again."

"But I've heard that for your kind, it can be —"

"I don't care what you've heard."

"You said I could understand. Help me understand."

I thought for a minute he was going to hit me, but he remained deathly still, unblinking eyes fixed on mine. He only spoke again after a moment long enough for me to begin to wonder whether I'd ruined everything.

"It's true that some of us find human partners for that. And, yes, the act, the taste… It…heightens things." The way his eyes flashed lit a fire in my insides but his mouth remained a hard, unforgiving line. "But it's dangerous and wrong. And I find it distasteful. Kindly do not mention it again."

A roll of emotion that was equal parts relief and disappointment tumbled from my brain down to my belly and back again. "Okay, Okay," I repeated, stronger this time, putting a hand on his arm. "I won't." I stepped closer, bent my face close to his. "Help me find other ways to please you, then."

His eyes, so close to mine, glinted. "Being stranded here is not good for you," he murmured. "You wouldn't be so fixated on this if we were back in the real world."

"The real world is overrated," I replied and closed the gap between us, opening my mouth to his. Like last time, he let me in, let me drink in his taste and smell, not responding but not resisting either. He was cooler than the previous night, the taste of him like a fresh, light wine. I tried not to think about the bottle of blood in his hand and how consuming it might change the taste and feel of him. I tried not to imagine what it might feel like if right at the moment he came, his teeth sank into my neck.

I firmly shelved the thought and backed him against the kitchen counter, trying to speak to him through the kiss, desperately seeking a way to reach him. After a few minutes, he dropped the bottle and ran his long fingers up my neck into my hair. He tilted his head back to allow me to deepen the kiss. I sensed him letting me coax him, tease a response from him like one would do to draw a wild animal from its lair.

I reined myself in from pressing too hard, instead easing him up onto the countertop. Again, I was surprised at his weight, but he moved with me, sitting back and pulling me to him. I leaned in between his knees, ground myself into his groin, needing the contact but stopping myself from being demanding with an effort. I was used to leading, taking control and setting the pace. Holding back was hard, but as the kiss continued, his grip on my hair tightened. His long eyelashes fluttered against my face.

I moved along his jaw to his neck, breathing him in, mouthing the throb of his pulse. His breath was hot against my ear. I was unable to stop myself from tasting him, even though it reawakened the yearning for his Blood. The thought was dizzying but I didn't let it show, instead hurriedly moving on from his throat to tug at the neckline of his jumper and lavish attention on his collarbone. His chest was flush against mine as he inhaled. Trembling threatened to take over my limbs and I repressed it, focusing intently on what made him push against me or caused his breath to catch, making myself take it slower than the night before.

I was rewarded by him tugging at my clothes, more feverishly this time. We stripped our tops away then his mouth was hot against my jaw, my shoulder. He spread his fingers wide against my back, pressing his skin to mine as though he could drink in my heat through his pores.

My control took a hammering when his long fingers went for the button of my jeans. I dropped to my knees to keep out of his reach, instead undoing his buttons and taking his gradually hardening length into my mouth. He gasped, his whole body going rigid. I heard him make a noise low in his throat that was almost enough to send me tumbling off the edge on its own. I adjusted the way I knelt to relieve some of the pressure on my own arousal and sank myself into the taste and feel of him in my mouth.

I was slow and meticulous. His breathing got heavier as he grew harder. He arched off the counter. After a few long moments, he threaded his fingers through my hair. His grip grew almost painful. He muttered something in his own language. His voice was low, guttural, coming from somewhere deep inside him. I resisted undoing my jeans with a force of will I'd never known myself to possess before.

I knew I was good at oral. I'd been able to reduce David to a quivering mess in a matter of minutes whenever we'd done this together. But Terje burned slower but hotter, like a furnace gathering power. I was generous with my mouth and hands, keeping the rhythm steady and intense. It was no longer a case of staying patient. Every second was better than the last, just listening to him. His voice became ragged, his breathing hitched. I shifted when my knees began ache, but I didn't allow myself to pause.

He started to pant. The noises he made were of a higher pitch. The foreign words took on the tone of desperate prayer. He leaned back on the counter, gripping the edge, his knuckles standing out white.

"*Alec.*"

The wood splintered in his grip with a dull crack. His back arched. The sound of him saying my name was all it took to finish me off. My whole body shivered, trembled, gathered itself just under my gut and poured out in waves against the restraining fabric of my clothing. Despite my body and mind reeling over themselves, I didn't stop until warm, smoky fluid spilled into the back of my mouth as he let out a series of high-pitched whimpers.

I rose, shakily, to my feet, the heavy taste of autumn fruit on my tongue. I didn't have time to wonder at the alien nature of it. He grabbed me by the hair and pulled me in for a fierce, wild kiss, bruising me, his sharp teeth catching my tongue. He panted against my mouth, murmuring nonsense syllables, swallowing desperately.

"I need more," he said, one hand on my back, fingers digging into my flesh, the other sliding down the front of my jeans. "I want more, Alec."

The sated embers of my desire rekindled and a low groan escaped my throat. He crushed me to him, fingernails digging into my skin, but the pricks of pain were like candle wicks igniting in deep, swirling darkness. He kneaded at my slowly reawakening erection. His own was stiff against my stomach.

"What do you want?" I breathed into his neck. "Tell me."

"I want you in me," he panted into my hair, his voice so low and loaded that it no longer sounded like his own. "I want you to take me, like you would one of your own. Make me feel human again, Alec."

I moaned, reclaimed his mouth and leaned into him, like I could do what he asked just by crushing us both against the kitchen counter so hard that we might sink into each other. He pushed at me, not exactly gently, tearing at my remaining clothing as we stumbled back to the sofa. The heat from the fire flushed my naked skin, but it was nothing compared to the heat now radiating off his flesh. It was like he had stepped out of a scorching shower or was running a fever.

We fell onto the sofa and he rolled me on top, arching up into me and moaning in the back of his throat. His calm and composure had evaporated, transforming him before my eyes. I knew a moment of fear when I took in the naked hunger in the deep, dark eyes and open, tooth-filled mouth. But then he tightened his fingers in my hair and kissed me hard, wrapping a leg around my waist to draw me closer, and I closed my eyes and willed the fear away.

I sucked on two of my fingers whilst a thunderstorm built in my lower belly. He watched me do it with something dangerous burning in his eyes. I kept my eyes locked on his as I slid my hand down and began to press against the tight ring of muscle at his entrance. He breathed in sharply.

"Is this right?" I whispered, heart skipping around as I slowly worked in a finger. "Is this really what you want?"

"*Gud*, Alec," he panted, closing his eyes. "Go slow."

I made myself obey, preparing him with one, then two and finally three fingers. My own neglected cock quivered and ached where it pressed into his leg. I took deep breaths and buried my face in his neck, breathing in his bright, fresh scent, and I shut my eyes to listen to his gasped words and incoherent sounds, which stoked the storm in my belly to a crescendo.

"Terje," I breathed. "I'm gonna... I mean...Christ."

He wasn't listening. He was moaning in Norwegian, pushing against my fingers with his head thrown back into the cushions.

"Now, Alec," he said. "Now."

I gritted my teeth to still the trembling climax and slid into him. I moaned into his shoulder, the hot tightness enveloping me with a completeness so exquisite that it nearly undid me. I took a long moment to lie there, revel in the feeling and fight back the tidal wave that threatened to have me coming hard at the slightest movement.

"You have no idea how this feels," Terje breathed into my ear. He slid his hands down my back almost reverently, like he was handling something precious but delicate. "I wish I could show you…"

"I don't know how long I'll…" He pushed against me and I groaned aloud.

"Breathe," he whispered, his lips against my face. "Breathe deep, Alec. Make it last."

I drew a breath right into my belly and started to move. Heat sparked along every nerve and vein. The thick, smoky-sweet taste of his Blood filled my mouth again, and the memory of how it had made me feel flooded me. I couldn't fight it, didn't want to fight it. It slowed everything down, even as it dialed every sensation up to an almost unbearable ferocity. Knowing that must be how he was feeling now caused my mind and body to explode like a match dropped into dry kindling.

I thrust hard, reveling in the feel, the sound, the entire all-encompassing absolution of it all. He met my movements with his own, murmuring my name over and over, running his tongue over the skin of my neck and shoulders. When he was no longer able to form words, he just keened into my ear, holding onto me with an almost palpable desperation, and I could only guess at the power of what might be building in him.

David had been my first. Being with him had been like a much-anticipated spring after a hard, lonely winter. Everything had been new, bright and exciting, even when it was sometimes clouded with uncertainty. I never knew when a cold day might follow a bright one. But it had been a time of hope and discovery and, whatever I had said to myself, to Meg or even to him, it was a time in my life I still mourned the loss of.

Brody had been a summer holiday on some exotic, overseas beach, all dizzying sights and smells, soaring heat and crashing, warm waves that smelled of ocean and city breezes all at once—as refreshing and passionate as it had been fleeting and unsubstantiated.

Terje was the languorous autumn that follows any overheated summer, clinging to the earlier season's sultriness with warm, leisurely winds, heavy with the smell of sun-warmed heather and seasonal fruit. He was like heated, fragrant and enriched days with the prospect of smoky bonfires and fiery sunsets, even though those days inevitably fell into long, cold and sometimes stormy nights.

I sank myself so deeply into the experience that part of me wondered whether I would ever surface again. But even that part of me didn't care. Sweat stood out on my skin and I pressed my forehead to his, taking from him as he took from me, no longer able to think and not needing to.

Eventually, his face changed. His skin was flushed and damp, his eyes hooded and entirely black, no trace of the silver irises remaining. He thrust against me and gripped harder, crushing me deeper. Sensing he was reaching the edge, I reached a hand between us and grasped his trembling length.

He cried out, threw his head back and came in my hand, his entire body shaking and stiffening like he'd been electrocuted. His body tightened around me like a fist, undoing whatever had been keeping me in control. I let everything go and tumbled off the precipice with him, moaning his name into his mouth.

Afterward, we lay tangled on the sofa, for a long time in silence, staring into the flames dancing behind the dull glass of the wood-burner. Our breathing was in time, our pulses gradually slowing and the sweat was cooling on our skin. I was lying on top of him, my head on his chest, one of his hands in my hair, the other still resting on my lower back. I could hear the low, deep thump of his heart, slow but loud, like a distant drum. His sweat smelled like a stream in spate, too fresh to be human.

The skin on my arms and back stung with new scratches. It was a sharp counterpoint to the low, dull throb of tired muscles and the pulse of bruising where he'd held on too hard.

"Tell me about the boy," he said, barely above a whisper.

I blinked, his words penetrating my stupor like stones dropped in a still pond. "Who?"

He took a deep breath. It stirred my hair as he exhaled. It was another minute before he spoke again. "The boy in the basement. The one who died. Tell me about him."

I raised my head. He was gazing into the fire. His skin was pale again, all the color and heat fading as we lay still. The bottle of blood was still where he'd dropped it on the kitchen floor. "Why do you want to know?"

"He was obviously important to you."

I resisted the urge to shift away, the thought of Brody intruding like a sudden, damp fog. "I don't understand what you're asking me."

His face was once again a closed mask. "I want to know what he was like, what you felt for him."

I shifted onto my elbow, taking a moment to marshal my voice. "Why?"

He ran an index finger down the side of my face and along my jaw, his eyes following it like I was a book he was reading. "I hardly remember what it was like to feel the way you feel," he whispered.

I stared at him. "You mean...you did once?"

His eyebrow twitched. "Are you asking if I was once human? Of course I was."

"I don't know anything about..." I stumbled. "I didn't assume anything. No one really knows much about how you..." I trailed off, searching his face, which was unreadable and blank apart from the sparkle in his eyes.

"We don't...reproduce," he said after a long moment, a corner of his mouth twitching. "Not in the way you do."

"So how do you make more..." I fumbled. "Like you?"

Whatever had been warming his eyes vanished like a black blind being drawn over a window. "I can't tell you."

"You can't?"

"It's dangerous for you to know. No humans know. It's part of the agreement."

I took a moment to absorb that, watching him closely. "So what we just did... That's not for reproduction?"

"Even humans would struggle to reproduce, doing what we just did," he said, the glint back in his eye.

"You know what I mean."

"I do," he said, brushing his lips over my cheek, my forehead. "And the answer is no. That is just for the feel of it. Simpler in a lot of ways." He paused. "More complicated in others."

I took a deep breath. "Brody and I hadn't known each other long," I said quietly. "He was part of a plan to force me out of Glenroe. But I didn't know that at the time. I liked him...or thought I did."

"I'm sorry you had to see what you did," he murmured. I glared at the carpet, fighting the images. "I've upset you."

I shifted away. The need to touch him was still unsettlingly strong, but the thought of Brody gave the feeling a sharp, bitter edge. After a moment, he sat up next to me, snaking his arm around my waist and pressing his face into my hair.

"Tell me," he whispered.

I shook my head. "I don't want to talk about it."

He sighed into my hair. "You don't know how wonderful it is," he whispered, "to feel the way you feel. Even your pain is beautiful."

"You feel things," I said, a little bluntly. "You can't pretend you don't. Not now."

"I feel," he said, tilting my chin so I was looking into his face. "Of course I feel. But not the way you do."

"How *do* you feel?"

His eyes glittered. "Haven't I shown you?"

I frowned. "I still don't understand what this is, what I'm doing...who you are."

He ran a hand slowly over my bare chest while brushing the knuckles of his other hand against my cheek. "You can't *know* any of that," he said softly. "Not really. They're things you can feel but not know."

"Tell me. Tell me how you feel."

He tilted his head. "Slowly. Deeply. Strongly," he said in a low, breathy voice that caused my stomach to clench. "There aren't really words for it."

"Do you like being this way?"

"It's all I know. Has been for a long time." His eyes went over my shoulder, gazing into the shadows of the room. "But I like to try to remember what it was like before. Most don't."

"What do you remember? Of being human?"

His eyes narrowed in thought. "Not much. That life...it sort of fades, after a while. I was in love—once, I think. Your sort of love. But I don't remember much about it."

"Was it with a man or a woman?"

His eyes returned to mine, again with that wry glint. "Does it matter?"

I picked at a loose fingernail, trying to figure out if it did. "I didn't feel much for Brody," I murmured. "Nothing real, anyway. But the other man you met. At the distillery..." I could feel his eyes on me. I stared intently into the stove. "David. He was important. Once."

"Once?" I withdrew from his arms to start gathering my clothes. "Did you love him?"

I padded around, pretending to look for my socks. "Yes."

"What was that like?"

He watched me, his arms on the back of the couch, his chin resting on his hands, gazing at me with a soft light in his eyes.

"Wonderful, at the beginning. Terrible at the end."

"What happened?"

I toyed with my shirt, my throat suddenly tight. "He was a drug addict. Still could be, for all I know. It became...difficult."

"Do you find all relationships difficult?"

"If you're so interested in human relationships, why didn't you stay in one?" I regretted the bitterness that leaked into the words, but he only regarded me calmly.

"Would you feel the same way about me if I were a human?"

"Yes," I answered, heat filling my face. "And it would have been a whole lot less complicated."

He watched me a long moment. "You realize if I were human, we would never have met? I'd be an old man slowly wasting away in another country, if I were still alive at all."

"You know what I mean. It would be easier if you weren't…what you are."

"Are you sure?" I looked at him hard. He was regarding me with a mix of expectancy and curiosity. "You're so far removed from your own kind that you find them hard to be around. And, well, I'm the same. Don't you think *that's* what's between us?"

"I would still like you if you were human."

The suggestion of a smile played on his mouth. "You can't know that."

"Why didn't you stay one?" I asked again. "Why did you ever want to become…what you are now?"

He dropped his eyes. "Who says I was given a choice?" I stopped where I stood, trying to let that sink in. He let out a small sigh. "For the record, I'm not particularly interested in human relationships. Just yours."

"Why?"

"You're interesting."

"How?"

"You live in a place you hate, yet refuse to sell it or make it your own. You're a prisoner of your past but still fight it at every turn."

"It's not like that," I said, heat flaring in my face.

"Isn't it?" He was gazing at me, his expression blank. There was no inflection in his tone, no judgement, but it felt like he was seeing right into me.

"What has this to do with anything?"

He stood from the couch in one lithe movement. His lean form outlined by the light from stove was breathtaking, but he seemed as unaware of his beauty as he was of his state of undress. He studied me for a long moment. "You're interesting because you're different."

"Because I hate humans?"

His eyebrow rose. "Is that how you'd describe it?"

I muttered something under my breath and bent to put on my jeans. I didn't hear him move, but he was suddenly next to me and using his strong hands to raise me up to meet his eyes. His intense gaze felt like it could peel layers from my flesh. "Being different doesn't mean being wrong." I held myself very still. He examined me for another long moment then gave my shoulders a gentle squeeze and drifted back toward the sofa. "Eat, Alec," he said. "Then sleep. It's nearly dawn."

He pulled on his jeans then scooped the bottle of blood off the kitchen floor before passing through the inner door and closing it softly behind him.

Chapter Six

I spent most of the following day drifting between fretful sleep and equally fretful wakefulness. I ate a little food but had no appetite for it. I daydreamed about what night would bring and was vaguely angry at myself for wanting it so much. I made myself think about Meg and prayed she was okay. David too. I wondered if Terje's Magister, Evgeniya, had taken anyone else...

I showered, wincing when the hot water washed over the cuts on my arms and torso. Catching sight of myself in the mirror, my flesh pinstriped with hairline cuts and purpled here and there with bruising, I felt slightly nauseated. But that didn't stop my mind from racing right back to when Terje had made those marks, run his mouth over them and shuddered with ecstasy.

I returned to the sofa and held my head in my hands. Then I noticed his jumper was still on the floor. I ran the soft material between my fingers, breathed in his distant, fresh scent, then fell asleep with it pillowing my head.

The dreams were back. I was caught in a snowstorm, the biting wind raking over my exposed skin. My blood was freezing in my veins. There was a voice somewhere in the wind, cool, calm reassuring—but it terrified me.

I woke again, cold but sweating. I had another shower, built up the fire and paced the small room. I peered out of the window to the snow-covered mountainside, which was completely empty of even animal life. I turned my phone over and over in my hands before returning it to my pocket with a curse.

I stood watching the inner door as the darkness gathered outside. My blood stirred and my mouth watered when the handle turned. I briefly wondered what the hell was happening to me. Terje stepped out, clothed in heavy boots, coat, hat and gloves.

"I have to go."

"What?"

He went to the fridge for a bottle. "You need more food. And I need to find out what's happening."

"Now? Tonight?"

A corner of his mouth twitched. "It has to be at night."

"But why tonight?"

His blinked once, slowly. "It's been two days. It might all be over. Don't you want to go home?"

I clenched and unclenched my fists a moment. "Of course I do." *Just not yet.*

His face softened, like he'd heard the unspoken thought. He came forward and gave me a cool, chaste kiss. "Trust me, Alec," he murmured against my skin. "This'll all be done with soon."

"Take me with you."

"You're safer here," he said, unlocking the front door.

"Wait." He paused whilst the frigid night air swept into the room and stirred his hair around his face. I fidgeted, knowing what I wanted to say but instead opting for what I knew I should say. "Will you check on Meg? And tell her I'm okay?"

He studied me and I tried to figure out what he was seeing, but I could just as successfully read the paint on the wall. "I'll be back tomorrow night," he said. "Try to get some rest."

He left without looking back. I heard him lock the door, then his car started, followed by the muted sound of the tires crunching through the snow. I watched from the window, but without headlights, the rapidly shrinking pinpricks of light on the dash were all that could be seen. Soon the only sound was the wind.

I hesitated a moment then tried the inner door, but that too was locked. I sat and thought about why I felt abandoned and foolish. Slowly, I realized that I'd thought about being with him since that first night at Glenroe, even as I'd leveled a gun on him and my gut had roiled with terror and rage. Now I'd gotten everything I wanted. I'd made love to him. I'd tasted his mouth and skin and Blood. I'd possessed him — some of his secrets and all of his body. And yet he'd left me with nothing but a kiss that had felt more like something given out of politeness than attraction or affection. But at the same time, there was no denying the strength of his reactions when we'd been together, even if some were ones I didn't understand.

By the time the next evening came, I was about ready to start throwing things from boredom and frustration. I finished off the pickled vegetables and fish, but my stomach was still a hard knot of hunger. I drank from the tap to try to ease the pangs and smiled a sardonic smile at finding that I missed my larder of budget canned goods at home.

I blinked, realizing I'd thought of Glenroe as home for the first time.

Night fell. He didn't come.

I forced myself to be patient. Midnight came and went and still there was no sound of a car approaching. I paced. I peered out of the window into the blackness. I swore, unlocked the front door and crunched out into the snow. My breath billowed in the spilled light from the cottage door. There was nothing but unbroken night around me, alleviated only by the blanket of stars high above. I stood, watched and listened until shivering set in, then retreated.

I fell asleep around dawn, too exhausted to stay alert, released by the knowledge that it would be at least another day before Terje returned. When I woke, I tried not to think about what might have delayed him.

Nightfall came again. Terje didn't. It was past midnight by the time I could stand it no longer and turned on my phone. It had half its battery left, but no service. I checked for WiFi then 4G without much hope.

No networks detected.

I rattled through the drawers until I found a torch, pulled on my coat and headed out the front door. It would have been a stupid thing to do even in good conditions in an area I was familiar with. Climbing unknown mountains in the dark and the depths of winter was an act so foolhardy that I felt I'd almost deserve to fall and break my neck or leg, die of exposure or lose digits blackened to frostbite at the very least. But something was wrong. I could feel it. And I couldn't just sit and do nothing.

The snow was shin-deep as I plowed uphill. My jeans were soaked through in minutes. Fat, lazy flakes drifted in and out of the torch beam, catching in my hair and eyelashes. I wiped them away impatiently, keeping one eye on my phone as it hunted for signal.

Searching…

My lungs started to burn. The wind got stronger. Scree shifted in the snow under my feet. I stumbled twice, the second time having to scrabble for my dropped phone in the snow. The cottage lights shrank to a dot of yellow far below in the otherwise unending darkness.

I stumbled onto a plateau. The snow was gathered in deep drifts against jutting rocks on either side. The rocky outcrop like stone fingers reached into the night over my head. With a jolt, I realized where I was. I'd done rock-climbing there with David, years ago, when he had still liked sports. There was an overhang and caves, which must be the ones Terje had mentioned, farther along the ridge where we'd practiced free-handing. It had taken hours of hiking to get here. We had come specifically because there was next-to-no chance of tourists.

I shuddered, very uneasy at knowing just how far from civilization I was. I swung the phone about, left then right.

Searching…

When I turned around a third time, despair threatening to swamp me, a bar of phone reception blinked into existence. I held perfectly still, heart jittering. No 4G registered, but the reception bar held. Text messages began pouring in, lists of missed calls, voicemail notifications. There were a number from unknown numbers with no messages left. Had the police finally connected the disappearances to the guests at Ogdell's Blood Party and were trying to track me down? There were texts from David, demanding to know where the hell I was, and a surly text from Clem with no punctuation, wanting to know what I was playing at, disappearing with no word. But the majority were messages from Meg, which became steadily more desperate, finally just pleading with me to let her know I was okay. The last one had come in earlier that morning. Knowing she was still alive flooded me with a relief that was almost palpable. Only then did I finally admit how scared I'd been.

My face and fingers started to sting whilst I queued the voicemails. I stared into the dark, a new cold that was nothing to do with the weather stiffening my limbs as I listened to Meg's second message.

"It's Karlsson, the dealer. He's dead, Alec. Not missing like the others. Dead. Murdered. Butchered in his own home. What's left of him was displayed on the roof garden of his house. They say his head was ripped off. Not chopped off, ripped off." She paused and I could hear her gather herself. *"It's absolute chaos. They know a haemophile's behind it. The anti-haemos are out in force. There are protests in London, Glasgow, Birmingham. There was a riot in Manchester this evening. Three men were shot. People are targeting haemophile communes, their human reps, everyone. It's madness. You have to come back. We have to speak to the police. I know what I said, but it's all gone too far. We have to tell them what we know before this gets any worse."*

The message had come in the first night I'd spent at the cottage with Terje. That had been four days ago. God knew what might have happened since. Her voicemails after that were just her ordering me to let her know I was okay.

There was one voicemail from David.

"Alec, you better be alive because, God help me, I'm going to kill you if you don't let me know you're all right."

I tried to search for Internet again, desperate to read the news, but there was still no coverage. My finger hovered over the *New Message* icon. The low-battery warning flashed.

I typed hurriedly.

I'm okay. I'll ring as soon as I can.

I hesitated over the send button, those calls from unknown numbers sending tendrils of unease creeping through me. But I gritted my teeth and pressed *Send*. The screen blinked and went black. I cursed, holding down the power button, but it was dead.

The wind surged and my jaw ached with the violence of my chattering teeth. I set off back down the mountainside, following my scuffed trail that was already disappearing under fresh snow. By the time I was closing the cottage door behind me, I was stiff with cold. I showered and changed into dry tracksuit pants and a hoodie from my pack, laying my other clothes by the fire to dry. I hunted through the pack for my phone charger, even though I knew it was still plugged into the wall at the distillery, just for the sake of doing something. I drank more water in an attempt to drown the nervous roil of my innards and the increasing demands of my hunger, then I stared out into the night, feeling walled in by cold, clinging fear.

"Where are you, Terje?" My voice was small in the solid silence.

I forced myself to ration the fuel for the wood-burner. I bundled myself in all my layers as soon as they were dry and sat, huddled on the carpet, watching the flames. A dull, confused emptiness stole through me.

I woke, curled in a ball in front of the now-cold wood-burner, to the sound of a vehicle approaching. I sat up, groggy with fatigue and hunger, and hurried to the front door and out into the thin, freezing air. A 4-by-4 was coming up the narrow track. I rushed to meet it squinting to try and make out Terje through the tinted windows. I realized, too late, that it wasn't the SUV and that weak winter sun was flooding the glen.

There was nowhere to run, even if I could have done so. The large, black vehicle stopped a few feet away. The doors opened and out stepped Jon Ogdell, along with three people in black with body armor bulking out their already considerable frames and automatic weapons in their hands. I stared at the guns, then at Ogdell. His round face was drawn and his formerly-bright eyes were sunken, haunted. His skin had the sallow paleness of someone ravaged by sleeplessness and stress. But he was smiling.

He paced forward, brand new snow boots having no trouble on the uneven terrain, taking in my own appearance with obvious, even slightly manic glee. "Lord Aviemore," he drawled, "fancy running into you all the way out here?" He waited for an answer, his smile tightening when I didn't reply. "Shall we go inside?"

"What do you want, Ogdell?" My voice was thin but I kept it steady.

"Just a little chat, Alec," he said. "A brief, friendly chat about some mutual acquaintances."

"How did you find me?"

"Couldn't resist texting your girlfriend, could you?" Ogdell continued. "You managed four days. I'll give you that. But I knew you'd cave. Weak men always do."

"Look... I don't know what you want—"

"Take him inside."

I tried to dodge but the three armed figures, two men and a woman, were all larger than me and weren't weakened with hunger and fatigue. The men grabbed me under the armpits and dragged me along whilst the woman followed with her gun at my back. They marched me into the cottage and dumped me on the sofa. Ogdell scanned the room with an air of bewildered curiosity, his breath misting in the cold air. He opened the cupboards, then the fridge, and froze.

"So where is it?"

"Where is *what*?"

He closed the fridge softly and paced over to stand in front of me. "You know what." I glared at him. "Don't play dumb," he grated, gesturing at the fridge. "You think I don't know what this place is?" When I still didn't answer, he bent his face to mine. I could see the broken capillaries in his nose and the threads of red in the whites of his eyes. "Where's the damn vampire, MacCarthy?" I scowled harder. His frown deepened. "Check the whole place," he ordered. "Tear it apart if you have to."

One of the men hurried up to the bathroom while the other battered at Terje's locked door until it splintered.

"Are the hired thugs really necessary?" I said. "You too afraid to talk to me alone, Ogdell?"

"Don't flatter yourself. They're not here for your benefit."

"Haemo sleeping cells," reported the man returning from the back room, "but they're all empty." The other came back down from the bathroom and shook his head.

"Where. Is. The. Fucking. Vampire?" Ogdell's face was flushed an ugly red. I forced myself to hold his gaze without wavering. His eye twitched. He dragged over a chair and sat close, our knees almost touching. His mouth was a thin, bloodless line. "I know you fed the thing," he said in a low, dangerous voice. "I know you let it escape."

"I didn't—"

"Don't lie to me." He cut me off with a finger at my face. "Karlsson told me everything. Before it massacred him, that is."

"Terje didn't kill—"

"What?" he interrupted, his eyes narrow. "What did you call it?" I clenched my mouth shut, trying to scan the room for any kind of improvised weapon. "You know its name? 'Ter-jah'?" Ogdell drawled, seemingly butchering the pronunciation on purpose. "Do you know what this thing did to Karlsson? To my sister?"

"He didn't—"

"*He*?" He barked a harsh laugh. "Jesus, MacCarthy. I didn't think you were *this* twisted."

"*You* abducted *him*," I growled. "Drugged him. Tied him to a table. Tortured him. You drank his Blood, for fuck's sake, and you call *me* twisted?"

Ogdell's eyes flickered. The manic light in them was snuffed, leaving behind a low, impenetrable darkness. "It's a monster," he breathed. "A demon. A murderer and a degenerate."

"Try looking in the mirror sometime."

I thought he might hit me, but instead he just stared. "I didn't believe it," he breathed, "but it's true, isn't it?"

"What's true?"

He kept staring at me like I was something he'd found rotting under a stone. "Karlsson reckoned you had more than just Bloodlust for this thing. And he was right right, wasn't he? Fuck me. I knew you were bent, but I didn't think you were perverted as well."

"You don't know —"

"There's CCTV of you getting into its car and driving out of Glasgow," Ogdell countered. "Willingly. Leaving your little friends behind. What would make you abandon them like that without a struggle, I wonder? Two people you supposedly care about, leaving them to face what the rest of us are facing alone?"

"You have no idea what you are talking about."

"*You* let that thing loose." His voice rose. "*You*, the Lord of the Manor, King of the Hill, judgmental, self-righteous arsehole, helped it escape to go on a blood-rampage. And now you're *protecting* it for the sake of a Blood-fueled *fuck*?"

I managed to land one punch before a guard wrestled me back. Ogdell was laughing, though his eyes were watering and his nose bled into his mouth, reddening his teeth.

"Like that, do you?" he said, wiping his nose with the back of his hand. "The sight of blood? Turn you on, does it?" He spat in my face. I swore, wiping at my eyes. "You're the degenerate here, MacCarthy."

"At least my degeneracy was consensual."

He grabbed me by the hair, spittle and blood speckling my face as he shouted, "Tell me where that thing is or I will put bullets in your head."

"You don't scare me."

He laughed again. "Then you're even dumber than I thought." He gestured to the woman, who raised her gun.

"You think shooting me will change my mind?"

A slow grin split his face like a wound. "All right. How about I shoot Miss Carlisle?" He put his head over to one side. "Or possibly Mr. Carlisle? Which would be more effective, do you think?"

"You're crazy."

"*You're* crazy if you think I'm going to let you get out of this with anything you care about in one piece. And I'm not just talking about Glenroe. Which I will take, by the way, just to grind to rubble. Karlsson was the one who wanted it standing, but we're way beyond that now." He leaned close, his voice dangerously low. "I'll kill Megan Carlisle *and* her brother. Then I'll make you watch as I kill the haemophile…slowly."

"You're bluffing."

"Am I?"

"You're a self-indulgent narcissist prick with too much money and not enough balls."

His smile didn't falter. "Not seen the news, have you? Riots. Shootings. Haemophiles hunted, humans attacked in the night. All bets are off, Lord Aviemore. It's every man for himself."

"It won't last," I countered. "It can't last."

"Maybe not," he replied. "But I'm going to make the most of it while it does."

"I was wrong," I murmured. "You're not just crazy. You're full-blown criminally insane."

"Says the man who let my family be slaughtered then fucked the monster that butchered them." He narrowed his eyes. "I bet he let you watch. Did you lick their blood off his hands? Or suck it off his—"

"Shut it!" My pulse thundered in my hears. My breath misted in the air, but I was hot, the sweat standing out on my palms. He watched me hungrily, his eyes empty as a shark's.

"You know what you've done," he said quietly. "Help me find the thing and I'll put you out of your misery quickly."

I clenched my teeth shut, fighting back a roll of nausea. My fingers dug into the fabric of the couch, the couch where I'd been with Terje, where I'd given him everything I was, praying only that he'd feel something back, without sparing a thought for what was going on beyond the cottage walls.

He hadn't done these things, but he hadn't stopped them. And I'd wanted him anyway. Still wanted him— and Jon Ogdell knew it.

"Still no answer?" he said after another loaded silence. He shook his head in disappointment. "So that's that. Tie him up." I tried to run but the three guards were too fast. They bound my hands and feet with zip-ties then secured my ankle to the leg of the couch, pulling the plastic loops cruelly tight.

"Those cupboards are empty. But the fridge is full. This would suggest to me," Ogdell said, kneeling to pile the last logs into the stove, "that our toothy friend is planning to return...and soon." He lit the stove and shut its screen, staring into the gathering flames.

"You're wasting your time. He's not coming back."

"It won't let its pet perish from starvation. Not before it had had its fill, that is." He sent me a poisonous look. "So we wait."

"I'm not going to help you do this. You might as well shoot me now."

"And let you miss out on all the fun?" He was no longer smiling. "Oh no, Lord Aviemore. I'm not nearly through with you yet. Very obliging of the haemophile to bring you somewhere without witnesses. I must remember to thank it before I cut its throat."

The wood-burner gradually fought back the chill in the air. The guards paced, taking turns keeping their weapons trained on me and going to the windows to peer out into the falling snow. Ogdell sat in the corner, staring at me. I became very thirsty then even more hungry, but I refused to speak, refused to ask for anything. I schooled my face when I remembered my penknife was in my pocket. But I didn't dare reach for it with the woman's gun aimed at my head.

I prayed for something to distract them, but the day crawled on and nothing happened. No one spoke. They barely moved. For the first time in days, I dreaded night coming. The shadows gathered and the male guards lit a lamp then drew all the blinds but one. They stood watch at the window like hawks. Ogdell, returning from the bathroom, resumed his seat, alternating between watching the guards and watching me. If anything, he'd grown edgier, shifting in the chair, biting his nails, darting his eyes around the room.

I sat in silence whilst my mind reeled through and rejected plan after plan. Night fell. Still nothing happened. As the hours wore on, the guards began to glance amongst themselves, muttering in low voices. Ogdell paced to the window then back to his chair. He ran his hands through his hair, the hundred-quid haircut sticking up in every direction. Blood flamed in his cheeks. He muttered to himself between clenched teeth.

My relief that Terje had stayed away warred with the pain at the knowledge that he'd abandoned me.

Ogdell was growing frenzied when the guard at the window tensed. "Shit," he muttered.

Ogdell's head snapped up. "What is it?"

"Kill the light," he hissed, pulling night-vision goggles from his utility belt. The other man doused the lamp whilst the woman stiffened next to me.

"What is it?" Ogdell repeated, voice tight, blundering toward the window in the darkness.

"Quiet," the man ordered and I heard the clicks of weapons being readied.

"I'm the one paying you. Tell me what the hell is going on."

"There's something out there."

"What?"

There was a series of loud bangs followed by a smashing noise and the banshee screech of tearing metal.

"What the fuck was that?" Fear sharpened the mania in Ogdell's voice.

"Something's gone for the car," murmured the guard. "Burst the tires. Smashed the windscreen."

"*What?*"

"I can't see what," the other continued. His silhouette was black against the paler square of darkness of the window. The small red dots from the guard's communicators jerked about in the blackness.

"I didn't hear a car, did you?"

"There is no car," the other man muttered.

"Bollocks," Ogdell growled. "Nothing could get out here without—"

Someone knocked on the door—three slow, hard knocks. My heart went into my boots.

"Why's it knocking?" the woman breathed. "Surely it has a key?"

Silence filled the room like concrete. I strained at the ties binding my feet and my heart hammered at my ribcage. I prayed the woman was focused on the door and fumbled for my penknife. I hacked at the bindings on my feet, sweat standing out on my face, whilst the others took up positions around the door.

"Don't let it get close," someone muttered. "Shoot first."

"Get it alive," Ogdell hissed. "Hear me? *Alive.*"

"On three. One. Two. *Three.*"

The door slammed open. Cold air rushed in. Boots thundered on the carpet then crunched on snow. The bindings on my feet gave. I sawed through the ties on my wrists and crept toward the door, my pulse thundering in my throat. The air tasted like ice. The guards fanned out, weapons raised, the red lights from their radios bobbing about in the darkness.

"Anything?"

"Negative."

"Where the hell'd it go?"

A scream pulled the air apart, followed by a snap then a hideous tearing noise.

"Depak? *Depak!*"

"What's happening?" Ogdell yelled from somewhere in the darkness. A torch flashed on, flooding the night with white light.

"Shut that off," another guard ordered.

"Like hell…" Ogdell trailed off as the beam swept over a spreading red stain in the snow.

"Depak?" The woman's voice was tight.

The beam revealed a heavy boot, a black-clad leg, a torso. The clothes were soaked with something dark. His gun lay at his side, his fingers still curled around the grip. I couldn't look away, even when the beam swept over the place where his head should be. I had time to make out the remains of his neck, the ocean of blood staining the snow and the jutting white of broken bone before I bent over and vomited.

"Shit, shit, shit," Ogdell swore over and over again. "Shoot. Shoot, you idiots."

"Stay back," ordered one of the remaining guards, panic sharpening the words. "Stay behind us. Don't move."

"Don't move?" Ogdell screamed. "It's out there! Get it! Get it *now*."

"If we miss its head, it'll make it worse — "

The bone-jarring noise of screeching metal silenced them. They spun, Ogdell's torch illuminating the 4x4. Four ragged scratches, like the marks of fingernails, were torn clean through the bonnet.

I ran.

"*MacCarthy!*" Ogdell was nearly shrieking now. "He's getting away."

Bullets thundered into the snow around me. Someone fired in another direction with a wild cry. Then came another sound, above and below all the panicked noises of the humans. A laugh. A high, eerie laugh in the wind.

Adrenaline surged through me. I pelted uphill, wrestling through the snow. Above the sound of my heaving breaths and thundering pulse came the confused sounds of pursuit. Ogdell's torch beam swung drunkenly around me as he shouted hysterical orders. More rounds were fired, but struggling uphill in the snow threw off their aim. I ran, refusing to think about rocks, cliffs, caves. When I stumbled onto the plateau and almost into the jutting rock that marked the start of the ridge, I scrabbled around it and squatted in its lee, out of the wind, making myself as small as possible, trying not to think about the yawning gulf at my side. I heard their labored approach and saw the torch beam sweeping the snow as they got close.

"Follow the trail," Ogdell ordered. "Find him. He's our only leverage—"

A high-pitched scream rent the air, followed by a bowel-churning bubbling noise. Just as suddenly as it started, it was cut off. Someone yelled and opened fire. The air was torn apart by the flash and thunder of gunfire. When it was over, the silence that fell was heavier than lead. I heard their ragged breathing and Ogdell's mumbled curses.

"Where's Willman?"

"She's dead."

"*Fuck.*"

"This is not good," the remaining guard said. "We need to get to a defensible position."

"Defensible my arse," Ogdell spat. "Fucking kill it, already."

"I can't see it," the guard ground out. "I can't hear it. Out in the open like this, we're sitting ducks."

"This is what you *do*," Ogdell cried. "You caught it alive once before. Killing it should be easy."

"That was a planned operation," the guard growled back, "in a known environment. We warned you about trying to ambush it out here when it's on the offensive."

"Just fucking *shoot* it," Ogdell ordered.

"I *can't*—"

"There are caves," I called. The two men swore and jerked around, the torch beam bobbing about the wind-whipped plateau.

"MacCarthy? Show your face, you cowardly shit."

"Kill me and you're both dead," I called. I heard them muttering, the crunch of boots in the snow. "Give me some night-goggles and I'll find the caves. We can defend ourselves better there."

"Don't listen to him," Ogdell ground out. "He's setting us up."

"I'm trying to keep us all alive."

"Bullshit," Ogdell yelled with mounting hysteria. "You're in love with the damn thing."

The words went through me like a knife. I marshalled my strength and called back, "This isn't *Terje*."

"You're lying."

"I'm *not*," I cried. "Listen… Either shoot me and wait for this thing to come tear you apart or give me the goggles, accept my help, and maybe we have a chance."

"I have spare goggles," the guard called over the babbled objections of his employer. "Where are you?"

I took a deep breath of the freezing air and stepped into the beam of the torch. Ogdell barked something incomprehensible but the guard dragged him back with a hand on his elbow. He held out a pair of goggles. "Get us somewhere enclosed," he said. "I'll do the rest."

I put the goggles on, wincing at the sticky substance coating the eyepiece. The guard ordered Ogdell to shut off the torch, which he did only after he, too, was given goggles. I blinked through the lenses at a world washed dull green. Blackness yawned on my left. I shuddered at how close I'd been to the edge before turning and hurrying along the angled, snowy ridge. I tried to dredge up the map of the area in my head, battling to keep my focus in the whipping wind and flurried snow. My feet pulsed with cold, my breathing was shallow and my chest tight. Ogdell had fallen quiet, but he was close enough behind me for me to hear his chattering teeth. When I glanced back, his face, ghostly-green in the goggles, was a rictus of fury and fear. The remaining guard brought up the rear, his weapon ready, sweeping this way and that in the dark.

We froze when low, almost-inaudible laughter was whisked toward us on the wind.

"It's coming," Ogdell whimpered.

"Hurry," was all I managed to get out. I struggled on, scanning for any sign of the rock shelf that marked the way to the caves. I cried out, beyond words, when we scrambled over a rise and I made it out ahead, overhanging the swirling shadows like the beak of some monstrous bird. The snow had obscured the scree slide under its overhang, but I scrambled blindly on, my hands so cold that they were beyond pain. The icy scree shifted. I clung on and kept moving, not letting myself still long enough to be swept away. Ogdell came down behind me, too close, spitting and swearing as the ground gave under his feet.

I grabbed his arm to stop his fall, grunting with the effort. He hung over nothing for an agonizing moment before he got his feet under him again.

"Don't stop moving," I ground out, "and don't get too close to me."

"Get a fucking move on then, MacCarthy."

I scrambled farther and, finally, spotted a jagged black opening, rimmed in snow. My arms, legs and shoulders were all pulsing with the effort, but I gave it one final push, then I was crabbing, stiff-limbed, down into the cave, falling out of reach of the wind with palpable relief. My feet hit level ground and I heard the muffled curses and clatters of the other two men making their way down behind me.

We all stood panting in the dark.

"We need to get deeper," the guard muttered. Too breathless to question, we followed him. The jagged ceiling dropped claustrophobically low overhead. The walls bellied in then fell away in stony folds. We scrambled over scree, rock piles and icy stones. We didn't stop until our way was blocked by a fall of boulders. I wrapped my arms around myself, feeling like I could drop to the cold stone right there, adrenaline the only thing keeping me on my feet.

The guard took up position with his gun aimed at the narrow gap we'd just squeezed through. Our breaths misted in the air, toxic green in the goggles. My heart continued to race. Minutes slid by. Nothing happened. The wind groaned through the cave opening like some long-buried monster waking in pain. The guard stiffened.

"What is it?" I murmured.

"Stay back."

A shadow moved across the entrance to our hiding place. Ogdell swore and pressed himself against the rock. There were muttered curses and the sound of fumbling, and his torch beam flooded the enclosed space, blindingly bright in the goggles. I just had time to make out a tall, white-faced figure staring at us and grinning, when the guard opened fire.

I dropped to the ground, covering my head. Shards of rock rained down and bullets ricocheted off and exploded in the stone. The noise was deafening. It seemed to go on forever. When it stopped, my ears were ringing so loud that I only just made out the sound of him frantically reloading. I raised my head just in time to see a white hand whip out of the shadows, quicker than a snake, and latch on to the man's throat. He let out a strangled yell that spluttered into gasps as the strong fingers and razor-sharp nails crushed into his windpipe and tore open the flesh. Blood fountained into the air. Ogdell dropped his torch to the floor. I heard him scrambling at the rock, gibbering curses and prayers.

I tore off the goggles, now cracked and useless, and reached for the dropped torch. The guard's body, throat a ragged mess of flesh and bubbling blood, crumpled into the circle of light and was still. I couldn't move. I couldn't breathe.

"Sick fuck," Ogdell was screeching. "Psycho *freak*."

"Shut your face," I growled, grabbing the torch and raising the beam.

A woman stood near the wall. She was very tall, taller than me, with limbs so slim that they appeared elongated. She had very black hair, cropped short over a long, bone-white face. Her eyes were burning yellow coals ringed in impossibly thick, dark lashes. They were fixed on Ogdell's and didn't flicker, even when I shone the light on her face. The glass-like smoothness of her skin made it impossible to guess her age. Her mouth was open and butcher-counter-red, the long teeth impossibly white and sharp.

She was dressed smartly — dark trousers, a fashionable coat and flat but stylish shoes, nothing any normal person could survive wearing in this environment. That and the fact that her hands and clothes were soaked black with blood made her the most terrifying thing I'd ever seen.

"And then there were two." She didn't speak loudly, but her cool, rich voice filled the narrow space and echoed off the walls, flooded my head and churned in my belly.

"Stay back," Ogdell growled. "Stay back, bitch. I'm warning you."

"*You're* warning *me*?" Her gaze didn't waver from where Ogdell crouched, trembling, in the shadows.

"Freak," Ogdell spat. "Twisted, blood-sucking freak of nature. We'll hunt you all down, hear me? You're history, all of you. We'll drain you of every last drop of Blood and laugh while we do it."

I didn't see her move. She was just gone from my light, then came the noise of Ogdell choking. I swung the torch around. The haemophile crushed him against the rock by his neck. His feet, dangling a foot of the floor, kicked wildly. He scrabbled at her hand, his round face flushing purple.

"You *dare* talk about Blood?"

"Wait," I called. "Evgeniya, wait." She froze like I'd stabbed her, her yellow gaze turning on and slicing through me. "Please," I breathed. "Terje wouldn't want this."

"How do you know those names?"

I raised my free hand and took a step closer, the light shaking in my grip. "Please. There's been too much death already."

"There you're wrong," she said. Ogdell rasped and spat as her hand tightened.

"He needs to be brought to trial," I continued, raising my voice. "Made a public example of."

Evgeniya dropped him. He landed with a sickening thud and lay groaning on the floor. She turned on me, breathing deep through her nose. Something in her eyes slowly caught fire. "You were there too," she said in a low voice. Her eyes were the color of molten metal. Her nostrils quivered.

I swallowed but resisted backing away. "I was."

"You drank," she said, barely audibly.

I took a breath to keep my voice level. "It's not what you think."

"Isn't it?"

"I want justice for what was done to Terje," I said, not breaking eye contact, "just like you do."

She grabbed my coat and slammed me against the rock, hard enough to knock the breath from me, the pressure strong enough to bend my ribs. "*Justice*," she hissed. "You humans and your pretty words, pretty concepts—all to disguise the filth underneath."

"If you do this," I rasped, struggling to get my breath in, "everything will be ruined. You'll be hated forever. Hunted. Exiled."

"We already are," she said, her face so close that I could feel her hot breath against my jaw. She smelled of blood and snow. Her fingernails cut into my flesh through my coat. "We always have been and always will be. But we protect our own. We know how to survive."

"It doesn't have to be that way."

She smiled, the expression splitting her face like an open wound. "We don't need *you*," she purred. "You're. Just. Food." She leaned in, crushing my ribs, and sank her teeth into my neck. I didn't even have time to yell. I pushed at her uselessly, but it was like trying to halt an avalanche with my bare hands. I felt blood being drawn out through the wound, the pain needling through my veins like lightning. Every muscle cried out in protest. I called to Ogdell but he didn't reply. My vision began to swim.

"Magister." The voice filled the cavern and penetrated the roaring in my ears. The pressure on my neck and chest disappeared. I fell to the cold floor. I lay, gasping, blinking, feeling warmth soak my collar and stabbing agony with every breath.

"Terje." Evgeniya said his name like a curse. With all the strength I had left, I turned my head. Terje was standing at the entrance, snow melting in his fine, wind-swept hair. Fading marks on his face and neck marred his pale skin...scratch and bite marks. He leaned his weight against the rock like he was struggling to stay upright. But his eyes were flashing dark silver, his face blank and dangerous.

Fury tightened Evgeniya's face and she growled something at him in another language.

"No more, Magister," he said, cutting her off.

"You want to speak English? For *them*?" She spat. It hit Ogdell. He whined an obscene retort.

"Their army is coming," Terje continued. "They figured out what this one was planning and followed." He nodded at Ogdell. "It's all over."

"Let them come," Evgeniya returned. "I'll bleed them all dry."

Terje's eyes darted to me then back to Evgeniya. "Novák's with them. You can't win, Magister."

Evgeniya's lip curled, baring one long canine in an animal snarl. "I ordered you back to the commune once. Don't make me do it again."

"This concerns me too."

"Not anymore," she said, pushing him back toward the entrance. "You will answer for your interference. But I will end this tonight. Then I'll deal with Novák."

"Not him," Terje, said, gesturing at me.

Evgeniya looked back over her shoulder, hot eyes drilling holes in my face. "And why not?"

"He wasn't part of this."

Ogdell scrambled for the gun. Evgeniya grabbed him by the collar and pulled him back. He thrashed about in her grip while she stared at me, darkness like winter storms building in her eyes. "He drank, Terje," she murmured. "I know he drank."

Terje's face didn't change but something glinted in his eyes. "Not like the others."

Her fire-yellow gaze slid from me to him. "Then how, exactly?"

"I gave it to him."

Her grip tightened and Ogdell gasped, face flushing red. "Why?"

"He was dying."

"So?"

Terje held her fiery gaze without a flicker. "I couldn't let that happen. He saved my life."

Her face changed, like granite shifting in an earthquake. I got shakily to my feet. "I wasn't lying," I rasped through my bruised throat, gripping the bite wound in my neck, blood oozing between my fingers. My vision was gray at the edges. My head pounded. I fought to keep focus. "Any more killing will only make things worse."

Ogdell writhed, trying to twist himself out of her hold. He flailed his foot at the gun but only managed to kick it farther away. Evgeniya flung him into the corner in disgust. His head bounced off the rock and he collapsed with a low, burbling moan. Her gaze raked over me like claws. "Terje, have you been with this man?"

"That's not—" I began.

"Silence!" The volume of her command made my ears ring. "Terje, answer."

His eyes flickered to me. "Yes."

"A *human*?"

"He's not like the others."

She flew at him and slammed him, hard, against the rock. She grabbed a fistful of his hair and bent his head back, exposing his neck.

"Back off," I yelled, scooping up the gun and aiming it, hands shaking, at her head.

Terje held up a hand. "Don't, Alec—"

"Don't look at *him*," she growled, shoving him harder against the wall. "You answer to *me*." His eyes as they held hers were steady, though his jaw had tightened and his long fingers were curled into fists at his sides. He was scared. "You betray me with a *human*?"

"I'm not bound to you," he said calmly. "Not that way."

"Stray for pleasure, fine," she growled. "With our own. But after the last human, I explicitly forbade you—"

"You can't forbid me this—"

Her hand closed on his throat. He didn't flinch, but she pressed herself hard enough against him that the breath was crushed from his body.

"You're mine," she gritted through clenched teeth. "You belong to me. You will obey *me*."

"Terje, *fight*," I begged.

"He won't," she growled, tightening her grip until he gasped, "because he knows if mutinies, he'll be exiled. Clanless, cut off from donations, hunting in slums, feeding on rats. Chased to the ends of the night by Bloodthirsty humans with no one to protect him."

"Let. Him. Go." The barrel of the gun trembled. I prayed the guard had managed to reload before he'd died.

She turned her face to me. "It never works, you know," she said with a wicked smile. "You'll never be enough for him."

"Step. Back," I ordered.

She laughed, that low, eerie sound that came from the bottom of her lungs and filled the air like the rumble of an approaching storm. "I see he's snared you well and truly. Not that I can blame you," she said, gently brushing the hair back from Terje's face, tender as a lover. "He is one of my finer creations. But you should know"—she stepped away from him in one fluid movement but he stayed against the rock, pinned in place with her look—"that he only beds humans to exasperate me."

Stones dropped in my belly. "It's none of your business."

"Oh, sweet, pliable child," she cooed, stepping close so the gun pressed into her chest. "It's nothing *but* my business. I've never managed to stamp out the revolutionary spirit he gets from his peasant ancestors. It was a mistake, turning him, but, like you, I couldn't resist." She smiled, her needle-sharp teeth whiter than snow against the red of her lips. "But whatever he is, he's mine—his body, his Blood, his mind. He can never be yours."

"He chose me," I forced out between clenched teeth.

She examined me for a long, spine-tingling moment. Terje's eyes were on Evgeniya. I willed him to say something, to deny her. But he stood frozen where she'd put him.

"Did he tell you why he was up here on his own?" she murmured softly. "That it was a punishment? No, of course not. He wouldn't have wanted you to know the truth about himself." I poured all my remaining strength into not looking away from her burning gaze. Her smile widened. "He's ashamed of his nature, you see. Imagine that…being ashamed of the very things that make you what you are. Not that *I* even particularly care about a kill ending up in the papers, but it had recriminations I would rather have avoided."

"I didn't kill that child," Terje finally spoke.

"So one of her own kind pulled her apart and exsanguinated her?" she asked dryly. "Then left her in Hyde Park for the first human of the morning to find?"

"Shelly Morris was *your* victim," Terje stated flatly. "I was trying to help her. Whoever you sent to follow me that night snatched her from her garden. *They* killed her."

She heaved a sigh, looking between us with a disinterested crease to her brow. I lowered the gun, my strength leaving me in floods. I couldn't even feel the wound in my neck or the freezing hardness of the cave wall at my back. Cold had sunk into my bones.

I stared at Terje with Evgeniya's words swirling in my head. I knew at that moment that I should never have touched him, never had let myself be drawn in. Knew it just as certainly as I knew that if I had the chance, I would do it all again.

I breathed his name. I don't know what I was asking for or even if he could give me an answer. He didn't speak and I couldn't read the wild storm of his eyes.

"What a sorry mess this all is," Evgeniya went on in a bored voice. "Another weight for that guilty conscience you treasure so dearly, Terje *elskede*. But my patience is at its end."

She wrenched the gun out of my weakened grip and reached out for me. A monstrous noise, somewhere between a hiss and a roar, filled the air and Terje pounced. He moved too fast for my dazed senses to follow. I was only aware of the noise of tearing clothing and flesh, yelps of pain, animal snarling. I dropped to the floor, curling myself tight, but was still caught by flying feet. Ogdell grunted as they crashed into him where he lay curled in the corner, bleeding heavily from a cut on his head.

I was trying to reach the gun again when the cave was flooded with blinding light. It stabbed into my skull, making my cry out. Screams, almost too high-pitched to hear, split the air. Squinting, I made out Evgeniya and Terje, both bloodied and torn, staggering back, flinging their arms up to shield their faces.

"Stay back," ordered a voice amplified and de-humanized through a megaphone. "Stand against the wall. The daylight flood will be switched off when you have your hands against the rock."

Moving stiffly, Evgeniya and Terje turned, their eyes clenched shut, faces twisted, teeth bared, and placed their shaking hands on the rock. The light dimmed. Both haemophiles sagged with relief. Voices shouted orders over the click of dozens of weapons and the tramp of boots as the cave filled with people in helmets, goggles and body armor. I was hauled onto my feet and bundled out.

"Take it easy with the human casualties," the megaphone said, loud enough to split my head in two. I blinked around, trying to make sense of the crowd of armed people moving briskly and efficiently over the snow-swamped mountainside. They wore crampons, climbing gear, snow boots. I strained my eyes and made out Terje, held firmly by three armored men with three more keeping careful aim at his head, being marched along behind me. Behind him came Evgeniya, similarly accompanied but with a much darker and more deadly expression on her cut-glass features.

They bundled me in extra layers, but the wind bit into my raw skin and made my bones pulse. It was an agonizing age before the ground leveled and I summoned the strength to raise my head to see the cottage, bleached white in the headlights of a number of off-road vehicles crowding the track.

"I'm sorry, Alec." I blinked. Terje was behind me, his guards scanning the milling crowd and chatting into communicators. He looked pale and drawn. Older. There were fresh bite marks in his neck and bloody rips in his clothing. His lip was split, part of his ear torn. Fingernail scratches raked over one eye and onto his cheek. His blue-white hair was matted and stained red-black with Blood.

"Where… Where were you?" I managed.

"I was…detained." His eyes flickered toward Evgeniya, standing just beyond him, her only visible injury a scratch on the forehead. She glared with steady, yellow eyes and Terje seemed to shrink in on himself. He opened his mouth to say something else but a guard poked him with his gun.

"Let's move."

"Wait," I croaked, but the guards marched both the haemophiles toward one of the armored trucks and out of earshot. An impossibly tall man with long, black hair and a sweeping navy-blue coat separated himself from the knot of milling soldiers and strode toward them. He rumbled in a low voice that I felt rather than heard, his wide, statuesque features stern. His skin was an unearthly shade of bronze under the harsh light, dark but with the underlying pale haemophile glow.

Evgeniya scowled at him, her canines bared. Terje stood at her side, meeting his eyes without speaking.

"Over here, mate." One of the soldiers was pulling at my elbow. "Medic's over here."

I reluctantly allowed myself to be steered to a brightly lit truck where a woman in a high-viz snow jacket was opening boxes of medical supplies. She gave me a perfunctory visual assessment before wrapping me in a silver survival blanket and pressing an oxygen mask over my face.

"Breathe normally," she ordered, opening sterile packets. My belly jolted when I saw Ogdell being brought to the med truck by two more soldiers. He was bucking and pulling in their grip.

"Take me back," he yelled. "Let me at the fuckers. I'll kill 'em. I'll—"

He stumbled, unbalancing one of the soldiers. The other attempted to right them, but in the confusion, Ogdell grabbed his weapon, broke from their hold and ran back toward the cottage. The soldiers lurched after him, but it was too late. Ogdell raised the gun and let a volley fly.

The weapon thundered. People screamed. Bullets pinged off vehicles and imbedded in windscreens. I watched, spellbound, as Blood, black in the artificial light, sprayed into the air. Terje, Evgeniya and two of their guards crumpled to the floor. The third haemophile dropped to his knees as the soldiers reached Ogdell, tackled him to the ground and forced the gun from his grip.

I ran toward them. Evgeniya, her face more petrifying than a living nightmare, was shrieking and straining against the tall haemophile's hold on her. Flesh hung from gouges in her arms and abdomen. Her face was spattered in red and black. She screamed and struggled, her eyes burning like furnaces, lips drawn back from her tooth-filled maw, the noise both deafening and terrifying.

The tall haemophile's eyes were hot and filled with darkness. His trousers were torn and his legs were injured and bleeding. His lips were drawn back from a set of teeth large and sharp as a lion's, but I could see in the deep, tight lines of his face that he was fighting — fighting to hold on to Evgeniya and himself.

I was suddenly back in that basement, staring at Terje's twisted face as the Blood took over. Brody screaming. Bones snapping. Blood pooling on the concrete.

The soldiers had fallen back, aiming guns and shouting useless orders. Evgeniya screamed and screamed, her feet digging gouges in the earth and snow as she fought.

"Hold her, Novák," someone shouted into the megaphone. "For God's sake, hold her."

The tall haemophile could only grunt in reply. The muscles in his huge arms bulged under his coat as he tried to overpower the flailing Magister. I scanned the scene desperately and finally spotted Terje sprawled on the floor at their feet. His face was turned away. The muddied snow around him was soaked black with Blood. I shouted his name and ran forward.

Evgeniya panted, weakening as I closed in. Novák finally overpowered her and forced her to the ground, pushing her face-first into the snow, muffling her screams and stilling her wild thrashing.

I dropped into the bloodstained snow at Terje's side. His arms were flung wide, his long fingers curled delicately against his palms. His eyes were half-open, gazing sightlessly into the middle-distance. His chest was a pulpy mess of ruined flesh and broken bone. I said his name over and over, pressed my hands uselessly against his arm, his face, loath to touch the Blood. The rich smell wafted in the cold air — autumn leaves, red wine, sun-warmed heather. But the acrid, fiery smell of discharged bullets and charred fabric swamped it.

I bent over his unmoving form, brushing my fingers over the cuts on his face. They'd stopped bleeding but weren't healing. "Terje?"

His eyes flickered. His mouth opened. I dragged him into my lap, ignoring the shouted warnings of the men closing in around us. His eyelids fluttered but his eyes didn't focus. Blood ran down from his mouth. Up close I could see just how vicious the bites in his neck and jaw were. I wanted to scream but I held my breath, held him close. "Terje?"

His eyes flickered again. For a second, they met mine. A breath rasped in his ruined chest. He lifted his hand and brushed his fingers over my chin.

"Alec," he murmured, so low I barely caught it.

"It's going to be okay," I managed. "They're going to get you fixed up."

His face changed, smile vanishing, and his eyes darkened. "Get away," he whispered. "Now…"

"Don't speak. Save your strength."

"I don't want to… I…" His face creased. His lips drew back from his teeth. Something flashed in his eyes and his whole body tensed. Everyone was screaming at me to get back but I couldn't move. They reached to pull me away, but then his eyes dulled, his hand dropped and his head slumped against my chest.

"Step away, son," a deep, accented voice murmured in my ear. A huge but gentle hand was on my shoulder while the other was trying to pull Terje from me.

"No," I choked. "Not yet. He's still alive."

"It's too dangerous," the voice said. "The Blood could still take over."

"Someone do something," I shouted. "Get the medic."

The large haemophile knelt so he was on eye level with me. Soldiers hovered nearby. The heat of Terje's Blood soaked through my clothes. I could taste it in the back of my throat. His body grew heavy in my arms. The tall haemophile's eyes were large, a shade of impossibly dark midnight-blue, filled with a very human-looking pain. There were bullet wounds in his powerful calves and sliced into one thigh. But he knelt next to me like he'd never even known the idea of discomfort.

"Let me take him," he said.

"Why aren't you getting the medic?"

"He's lost too much."

"It's not too late," I protested, pulling Terje out of his reach. "You don't die. I know you don't die, not like we do. He needs blood. That's all. Call the air ambulance and get him to a hospital."

"Novák, is it safe?"

The haemophile raised his head. An older woman in body armor, an officer by her epaulettes, stood just at the edge of the nervous ring of soldiers. Evgeniya was being loaded onto a stretcher behind her, weakly trying to push against the people pressing dressings against the wounds in her legs and abdomen. Her face was a tight, white mask but her limbs had lost their power. The manic fire in her eyes had been doused.

"This one's no threat," Novák said. "Too far gone."

I stared at Novák, his weird, wide, black-blue eyes holding mine, filled with unsettlingly deep sympathy. Slowly, carefully, he took Terje from me like he was no more weight than doll. I let him go, watched him being carried away, a stinging numbness that had nothing to do with cold settling into my guts.

"I'm sorry," the woman said gruffly, putting her hand on Novák's broad shoulder. "This wasn't supposed to happen."

"Blood begets blood," he said in a low, bitter voice, laying Terje on another stretcher. "All I can do is try to stem the tide."

"Did you know this one?"

Novák swept Terje's hair away from his face, then gently closed his sightless eyes. "No."

"Looks like he tried to stop her," she murmured, indicating his other wounds.

"Yes," Novák replied as they drew a blanket up and over his head. "That gives me hope."

"Wait," I cried. "Wait, please."

Novák's heavy gaze went right to the epicenter of my pain. The human officer watched me approach with a more wary expression. I hesitated then pulled back the blanket. If it weren't for the blood, he might just be sleeping. I placed a trembling hand on his cheek. It was cold. I took several deep breaths to steady my voice.

"Can't I help?"

"How?" Novák's face told me he knew exactly what I meant.

"He needs blood," I said. "Human blood. To fuel *his* Blood, which can still heal him. Right?"

"We'll get him to a hospital," Novák said. "We'll give him a transfusion. But he's already lost so much —"

"He can have mine," I said. "Give him my blood. Now. Give me a knife, and I'll do it myself."

"Don't be an idiot," the officer barked, but Novák raised his hand.

"A noble and selfless offer," he said slowly, "but highly inappropriate."

"Inappropriate?" I choked. "He's dying." I held out a shaking hand, my eyes fixed on the sheathed knife at the soldier's belt. "Please. Let me save him."

Novák held my desperate look for a long time before nodding to the men standing around the stretcher. They covered Terje up again and carried him off whilst I stood there, shaking, with my hand still held out for the knife they would never give me.

"It would take more than you have," Novák said.

"I don't care."

He sighed. "Another death will be another nail in the coffin of our future. Evgeniya has done almost as much harm as your friend and his Blood dealer."

"Jon Ogdell is no friend of mine," I ground out. "Drain him dry for all I care. It's less than he deserves."

Novák stood still and quiet until I met his eyes. "Jon Ogdell will answer for his crimes. You have my word on that. But remember… If your friend here fought his own Magister over this — over you — he wouldn't want any more being sacrificed for his sake — and certainly not your life."

I watched Terje being loaded into a truck alongside the now-incapacitated Evgeniya, feeling like my insides had been gouged out with a blunt knife. The rear doors slammed shut. The night was suddenly darker and colder than anything I had ever known.

"What's your name, son?"

"MacCarthy," I replied, voice dead and low. "Alec MacCarthy." I blinked a couple of times until the business card the haemophile was holding out came into focus.

"Ivor Novák. I'm sorry the circumstances of our meeting aren't more congenial." I stared at the card. "We need humans on our side, Mr. MacCarthy," Novák continued like he hadn't noticed my unraveling control. "I still believe we can exist together. But we need allies. Please. Take my number."

I took the card with numb fingers. "Will you tell me which hospital he goes to?"

He nodded gravely. "I will. Now you must excuse me. There's a lot to do here. You should let the medics treat you."

He paced away. The army officer hurried after him, talking animatedly. The last of the other soldiers were all climbing back into the trucks, which one-by-one rumbled away down the track. The headlights disappeared and someone shut the lights off in the cottage, allowing the night to crowd in.

The ambulance waited to one side, flooding yellow light into the snow with the woman in high-viz gesturing impatiently at me. I plodded over in a daze, my chest aching, head pounding, wound in my neck stinging. It was only when I drew close that I realized Ogdell was handcuffed to a seat in the back, a dressing pad taped on his forehead. His round face was puffy and bruised, his dull eyes red and watery. He slumped in the chair, pain etching lines around his mouth.

I remained silent and let the medic wrap me again in the foil blanket, put the oxygen mask on me and hurriedly clean and dress the cuts in my neck. She bundled me onto the ambulance gurney and told me to lie back and relax. She shut the doors, then the vehicle rumbled and started to move.

I scowled at Ogdell, contemplating hunting around for scalpels, scissors, anything to hurt him with. But instead, I just stared at his hunched, pathetic form until he finally lifted his head to glare at me.

"And you can stop with the filthy looks, arsehole."

"You killed him."

"Good."

"You opened fire in cold blood."

"Cold blood?" He laughed, a choking, bitter sound. "Good one."

"You really don't give a shit, do you?"

"And my sister? Matthew? Hans?" he ground out. "Where are they on your giving-a-shit scale?"

"Evgeniya needs to face the authorities, just like you do, to show the entire world that no one, human or haemo, gets away with shit like this."

"You sanctimonious prick. Entire governments get away with 'shit like this' every day." He shoved his swollen face into mine. "Real men take matters into their own hands. They know that the whole world revolves on who's on top. Who's getting fucked. Who's not. That's something I thought a fag would understand."

I hit him. It had no real power behind it. I was too exhausted. But there was a satisfying crunch as my knuckles smashed into his eye and his head snapped back. He howled in rage, clutched at the eye and made a swipe with the back of his free hand, but I shimmied up the gurney, out of reach. After he'd flailed enough to exhaust himself and sat panting in his chair, I continued.

"Your family tortured another living being for kicks. Don't sit there and pretend you're innocent victims in this."

"And what about you, huh?" he grated, glaring at me through his rapidly-swelling eye. "Fucking landed laird looking down at us all like pond scum —"

"It's you fucking people who think all that's so important," I growled. "I'm not like you."

"Very well, Lord Aviemore," he drawled. "Tell me. How was the Blood, huh?" I flushed hot then cold. A warm smell rose in my mind, a hot taste in my mouth and throat. My blood thrummed. "Yeah, that's it," Ogdell sneered. "You drank, all right. Can't forget it, can you? It's *in* you now." I wanted to hit him again but I couldn't move, his pin-prick stare holding me in place whilst the truck bounced and rattled over uneven ground. "You think you're so special," he went on. "Pro-haemo bleeding-heart lefty. Their defender, lover, whatever. But you're just another Blood junkie. The only difference between me and you is that I don't let them fuck me to get a fix."

"You know nothing about it."

"Tell yourself whatever you want, MacCarthy," he said, leaning back and closing his eyes. "In those long cold nights in prison, whilst the rest of us, the *real* men, are out hunting down every last one of the bloodsucking sons of bitches, you keep telling yourself that it really was deep and meaningful and not just your sad, desperate inability to connect with your own species. Did you catch any, by the way?" He cracked his good eye. "I know most of it went into the snow, but I bet there was enough to grab a couple of mouthfuls before it bled out, huh?"

A swell of anger like a bubble of hot lead rose up my throat and burst in my head. My cuts and bruises and frostbitten fingers pulsed. When I came back to myself, the medics were wrestling me off the screaming Ogdell. Someone pushed a needle into my neck and the world went dark.

* * * *

"Alec? Are you awake?"

I blinked my gummy eyes. My limbs ached. My bones throbbed. There were stinging scratches all over my skin, a pulsing pain in my neck and pounding in my head. My mouth tasted foul. Eventually a gray, tiled ceiling came into focus, the soulless mint-green of a hospital curtain at my side, the thin, bright light of strip lighting.

"Alec?"

Rolling my head on the stiff pillow caused the swirling to start anew and I had to wait a few painful moments for the fog to clear again.

"Meg?" My voice sounded rusty.

Her smile was warm with relief, her brown eyes sparkling, even whilst she forced her face into a mock-frown. "Jesus H. Christ, Alec MacCarthy. If you ever, *ever* frighten me like that again..."

"What's going on?" I mumbled stupidly. "Where am I?"

"Belford Hospital, Fort William," she said, dragging her chair closer to the bed and grabbing my hand. "You've got some cuts and scrapes, a minor concussion and some blood loss, but they say you're going to be fine."

"What about Terje?" I murmured, struggling to sit up.

Meg urged me back into the pillows with gentle hands. "Just rest for now."

"Meg, where's Terje?"

Her frowned deepened. "I don't know what Terje is."

I fought back impatience. "The haemophile. The one that was shot."

"Three were shot—" Meg started, face uncomfortable.

"You know the one I mean," I said, begging her with my eyes to understand. Her lips pressed together. Her eyes were pained. "Tell me, Meg. Please."

"He'd dead," a flat male voice said.

"David—" Meg scolded as David appeared at the bedside. His dark eyes were empty, but they had a sunken look and his jaw was tight.

"He's dead, Alec," he said again. There was no anger in his tone. No judgement. But there was no sympathy either.

"I don't believe you," I said. "Where are my clothes? Where's Ivor Novák's number? I need to speak to him."

"Novák was here," Meg said, face tight. "It… He…came to check on you."

"What did he say?"

David sat on my bed and pinched the bridge of his nose between his finger and his thumb. He appeared drawn, tired, older than he was, like he'd let go of something that had been holding him together.

"He said the blond one was dead on arrival, man. They tried a transfusion, though why you'd do that on a DOA I don't know." I flinched and David winced, flicking me a brief, apologetic glance and looking away again. "As I said, they tried. It didn't work." The room blurred. My head span. I jumped when David's hand rested on my leg. "I'm sorry, Alec. But maybe it's better this way."

Rage chased pain around my insides. I clenched my teeth together. I didn't raise my eyes from the stiff, white sheets.

"He's a hero," Meg said softly after a long moment. She tightened her grip on my hand and I wondered what she was trying to say to me that she didn't want to say in front of her brother. "He stopped the killer getting into Callum's apartment."

"Callum?"

"The actor from the Blood Party," she went on softly. "There's footage of the female trying to get into his place and the blond one trying to stop her. It's gone viral. It was…" She took a breath. "It was grim. He got hurt. But he did stop her. He couldn't keep her from going after Ogdell, though." I closed my eyes, trying to fight the information into some semblance of meaning. "Novák's going to use this whole thing as a publicity campaign," Meg went on. "He says it might repair some of the damage."

"How much damage is there?" I croaked.

"It's too early to say," David said gravely. "As soon as that dealer's body was discovered, it all kicked off.

Humans attacked vampires. Vampires fought back. Humans attacked other humans and…well…" He finally met my eyes. I had expected more anger, but he just looked weary. "It's not been good. Over a hundred dead, they're saying. And that's just here in the UK. But it's over now, more or less."

"But there's more, Alec," Meg said warily. David gave her a warning look but she ignored it. "You need to know… The police are waiting to speak to you."

"Ogdell," I ground out.

She nodded stiffly. "He's made accusations, but I've made my own too." She sat straight and tall in the chair. Her face had taken on a hard set. "I've been gathering evidence. Phone messages. CCTV from Lure. It's his word against ours, but the police believe me."

"You were supposed to leave Glasgow," I said.

"I know we were," said David, giving Meg a look.

"I wasn't going to run away," Meg said, "not when you were willing to face it." I squeezed her hand. "We'll have to submit to questioning at some point," she went on gently, "about the Blood Party and Brody Harris. But they've got forensics crawling all over Auchallater Keep. They'll find out what really happened and Ogdell will be the one to answer for it, not us."

"I'm glad," I managed to get out, though I couldn't make it sound warm. "Thank you, Meg." A pause. "Can I be alone now, please?"

Meg's face fell. David's hardened. There was a painful moment where their eyes met, like they'd expected this, then they rose. I sensed David fight himself and lose. He leaned forward and kissed me on the cheek. Dampness brushed against my temple. He held his face against mine a moment longer than was comfortable. I smelled his familiar smell of tobacco smoke and fresh, grassy aftershave and, for the briefest of moments, felt comforted and was grateful to him.

"I'm glad you're okay," he murmured in my ear.

"You too," I got out, emotion weighting the words. I grabbed his hand and squeezed it. He stared at our joined hands for a long moment then stepped back, swiped angrily at his face then strode off.

Meg called after him but he was gone. She chewed on her lip a moment before speaking again. "I'm sorry, Alec. About the haemo."

"Are you?" I hadn't meant for it to sound bitter, but holding it back was suddenly beyond me.

"Of course I am," she said with that infinite, unflappable patience that had allowed her to be my friend for so many years. I instantly regretted my anger and resentment, even though they continued to pulse inside me. I dropped my eyes so she couldn't see it, but she raised my face with a knuckle under my chin. Her rich, brown eyes were earnest. "You're hurt," she said softly. "I can see that. I can see whatever it was was…real. For you. I'm sorry I doubted that." She dropped her hand and turned to leave.

"Meg…" I took a breath as her eyes met mine. "I do love you, you know."

She pressed her lips together. Her eyes brightened with tears. "I know that, Alec."

"Not in the way you want" — I forced out, watching the pain mount in her eyes and hating myself for it — "but it's still there."

She brushed my hair back, bent and kissed my forehead, hesitated then pressed another, softer kiss to my lips. "I know," she murmured. "I love you too. Just not in the way you need."

"I don't know what I need," I whispered.

"Dear Alec," she murmured, a watery smile turning up her beautiful mouth. "Do you think anyone ever does?"

She left. My phone was charging next to the bed but I didn't pick it up. I didn't want to read the news or check the messages. I didn't even want to call Ivor Novák and confirm what I already knew in my heart…that I was alone, again.

Chapter Seven

I straightened my aching back after re-attaching the last tire of the Porsche 501. The chassis was gleaming, the new weld work smooth under its fresh coat of ice-white paint. Its interior was deep red leather, smelling warm and organic. The wheel arches curved like swan necks over jet black tires, their silver alloys gleaming, the raw power of the engine tucked away behind the elegant swoop of the bonnet.

It reminded me of Terje. It had done so for the whole six months I'd been working on it. Clem had accused me of drawing out the restoration. He warned me that the owner was getting impatient, but working on it had managed to restore the only thing close to peace I'd known in over a year.

The days were gradually lengthening. The ice and snow were loosening their stranglehold on the glen, even whilst the mountaintops were still capped in white. Meltwater swelled the gurgling burns. The workshop was fractionally above freezing for the first time in weeks. The storms of the previous winter hadn't returned with the same severity, but there had been moments in the long, dark nights when I had felt as trapped as when the snow had been ten feet deep the year before.

I knew I had no right to complain. Meg had been good as her word. She'd gotten our Obstruction of Justice charges dropped on the understanding that we both testified for the prosecution at Jon Ogdell's trial. Neither of us had had to think on it long, even though seeing that man across the court room, prison-chiseled lines in his sagging face and all, was something I had been unable to prepare myself for.

His black glare had never left me. When it was finally over, I'd thanked Meg, deeply and sincerely, and climbed into my car to drive straight back to Glenroe, politely refusing her offer to put me up for the night.

I had watched her shrink in the rearview mirror with hard hollowness in my bones. She might have saved us from criminal charges, but her law career was over. People didn't understand. Social media was rife with conspiracy theories. Activists on both sides were proclaiming their version of the truth and what they considered should be done about it. It would be a long time before any law firm wouldn't associate the name of Megan Carlisle with that infamous Scotland Blood Party that had sparked the terrible events of what was now being referred to as 'Blood Winter'.

I knew she needed someone who knew what had really happened to be close to her while she worked through it all. But I couldn't stay in the city and I couldn't think what to say to make it better.

At least David was back, staying with her while he looked for a local job. She needed him, and I was glad he was there for her, even more glad that'd he'd stayed clean despite everything, but things had been strained since that last kiss in the hospital. He knew I was hurting and couldn't understand why. I knew he secretly blamed me for my own unhappiness. I'd hardly known Terje, after all, and would possibly never have been able to understand much of made him what he was. To David, he'd been, at best, a toxic invader who'd messed up our entire lives in just a few short days. At worst, a predator who'd manipulated and abused me into a dangerous addiction that I couldn't even see for what it was.

He couldn't understand that Terje, in that tiny amount of time, had somehow become everything to me. He was the first being I'd ever encountered who didn't leave me feeling alienated and frustrated upon discovering I wasn't like everyone else. He had been deep enough and old enough to absorb every extreme and intense emotion that spilled out of me, responding only with patience and curiosity. He had been life and breath and heat, mystery, strength and beauty, even if — or because — he was something so far removed from what was considered human as to be classed as a different species.

He'd got me to admit things I'd never admitted to anyone. I'd felt unfettered and guiltless for the way my life had played out for the first time in my life.

I couldn't explain that to anyone and I couldn't let it go.

I suddenly understood how David must have felt when I'd ended it with him — and that stung.

I'd had to get a new phone line and mobile. Somehow, my numbers and email had been leaked and I was getting abuse and death threats on a daily basis.

It was an unfortunate for me but an acceptable — to him — by-product of Ivor Novák's media campaign. Terje and I had been made out to be the human-haemophile Capulet-Montague equivalent — star-crossed lovers, vengeful families. Our story had everything. Lashings of death and tragedy. And for what?

Necro-fag. Psycho. Corpse-fucker. Freak. Traitor.

Novák had at least managed to keep my real name and Glenroe out of everything, despite Ogdell's best efforts to smear me from prison. Not enough people had heard of the real me to believe his accusations, and the collapse of his business empire and his rapidly diminishing mental health were increasingly the focal point of most of the news stories he generated.

I'd spoken to Meg by text message only a couple of times since Ogdell had been sentenced, but she'd long since given up trying to maintain communication. She had started her own consultation business and, through it, had met someone. He was handsome, successful and by all appearances stable and secure both in his future and his outlook, and he trusted her version of the events of the previous winter rather than what he'd read on the Internet. I read her engagement notice online and was happy for her in a vague and distant way, but I also knew a certain degree of guilty relief.

I wasn't invited to the wedding.

The news sites, papers and radio continued to report on the pulsing waves of consequence from Blood Winter throughout the following year. Ivor Novák, along with a platoon of PR execs and government officials, had overall succeeded in pulling off the colossal juggling act of ensuring that blame did not land on either side and instead focused on the individuals. By the time the following summer had come to Glenroe, the hottest flames had been doused, though things were far from settled.

Freak. Faggot. Blood junkie. Child killer.

Evgeniya had been stripped of her Magister position and extradited to Russia to stand trial in one of the three specialist courts set up to try haemophile crime. I read, several weeks later, that she'd escaped custody, leaving several — haemo and human — dead in her wake. I was certain the world hadn't heard the last of her, but I couldn't bring myself to care.

"You should let it go, you know."

For a moment I hadn't recognized Clem's voice when he spoke to me one evening late that summer when, again, I'd not acknowledged his attempts to draw me into discussions about supply orders.

"Let what go?"

"Feeling something you can't understand…can't justify, even to yourself. It'll eat you alive if you let it."

I lifted my eyes, but he was packing tools away at the other end of the workbench, gaze intent on the tool rack. If I hadn't known better, I'd've sworn there was a flush rising above his beard. "I don't know what you're talking about."

One bushy eyebrow twitched. "I don't know the whole story of what happened — "

"Clem — "

"But I do know something's broken in you since," he went on like I hadn't spoken. Finally, his watery blue eyes met mine. "And you're too young for that, son. Too young to become your pa."

The anger was instant, even though I knew it was unjustifiable. "You don't know anything about it."

His face shifted, something like pity filling in his eyes. "I know his lordship wanted stuff he couldn't get his head around, too."

I put the filer down with a clunk. "Like what?"

His gaze went far away. "I really thought we could be happy, for a while. More fool me. Can't make someone happy if they can't handle wanting what they want."

A long pause whilst my mind somersaulted. "You...and Dad?"

"We were both young once too, you know."

"But...Dad? Dad wasn't gay."

His storm-cloud face twisted into a grimace. "I don't know if he was or he wasn't. There weren't labels for things like that back then. But we..." He definitely blushed this time. "We were close for a while, after your ma left." He picked at a loose splinter on the workbench. "I knew we could never tell anyone. But I thought..." I held my breath. I sensed that if I spoke, I'd break the spell. "He used to come to the cottage. In winter, mostly. I don't know if was because of the long nights or if he felt, I don't know, hidden by the snow. But winter was when I saw him most. It was the only time he was himself—the only time he knew the truth about himself."

"You can't be serious."

"Oh, I know what he was like," Clem continued, his familiar scowl returning. "A tough old sod. A right arsehole, even, sometimes. But that's what happens when a man fights himself for a lifetime." His gaze dropped to the oil-streaked floor. "It got so bad that in the end, the only thing he could care about was the damn house. It played its part, you see. Helped him look right. Protected his place in the real world." He snorted. "Your ma never understood what it was really all about. Of course, that was all before the drinking got too bad. After that, he couldn't even care about Glenroe, let alone anything...or anyone...else."

My knees had gone funny. I wanted to sit down but I didn't dare move.

"Your pa knew what he wanted," Clem continued after a moment, his voice even lower, "and hated that he wanted it. It destroyed him."

I gripped the workbench. "What if you can't have what you want?"

He methodically cleaned a spanner for a few moments. "You can still accept you want it," he said. "It's a good start."

He placed the spanner in the rack, folded the cleaning rag and put it in his pocket then raised his eyes to mine. For one surreal second, I thought he might put his hand on my shoulder, but he seemed to reconsider it, nodded briskly and left. I listened to his Land Rover drive away in dazed silence.

Long after everything had gone quiet, I still hadn't figured out whether the conversation had made everything better or much, much worse.

When he returned to work the next day, it was like nothing had happened. I caught myself looking at him out the corner of my eye, feeling at once uncomfortable, saddened and angry. He knew I was looking at him differently but he went about his work with only the occasional grumbled complaint offered as conversation, the same way he had my whole life.

It was like pieces of a puzzle I hadn't known I was trying to solve suddenly fit together. The picture they formed was sad, even if it completed something inside me that I'd never realized was missing. It didn't stop everything hurting, but at least I finally allowed myself to admit that it did hurt…and how much.

Late one night, when that summer had just started to sigh into autumn, Ivor Novák knocked at the Glenroe front door. Memory smote me as I pulled open the door, which hadn't been opened since Brody had knocked on it the year before. But the towering, broad-shouldered haemophile standing on the step in a long, ground-sweeping coat, impeccably tailored navy-blue suit and perfectly schooled expression couldn't have been more different from the sunny, slim Californian. His fine-cut appearance should have made me very aware of my oil-stained, unshaven state, but I'd already had half a bottle of wine and couldn't bring myself to care.

I heard myself trying to explain why I hadn't returned his calls or messages.

He raised a spade-sized hand. "It's okay, Lord Aviemore. You don't have to explain yourself to me."

"Why are you here?"

"To reassure you that you have not been forgotten," he said, his deep voice, faintly accented, rolling through me like a fine whisky. "And that your kindness toward Terje Kristiansen has not been overlooked."

The name renewed a pain behind my ribs that had, at that point, faded to a dull ache. "What kindness?"

"You attempted to bring him relief when he was suffering," Novák continued softly, "despite the danger to yourself. And you tried to save him during the confrontation with his Magister."

"How do you know that?"

He put his head to one side. There was something in his blue-black eyes that I couldn't identify. "Don't worry. No one is renewing the claims against you regarding Brody Harris. The boy was an unfortunate casualty, one that Terje would have answered for, had he been able to. But his death was not of your making."

My throat closed and my fingers ached where they clutched the wood of the door. I wished fervently that he'd leave.

"To answer your question," he went on smoothly, "the timeline of the true events of Blood Winter has now been fully established. I wanted you to know that your actions are appreciated by my people…and myself."

"Thank you?" I managed.

His gaze drifted over my shoulder to take in the hall, the staircase and once-grand windows over the gallery, now almost entirely blocked over with plywood. "Some people don't understand your attachment to this place," he went on quietly, "but I know what it's like, holding on to something that the world thinks is useless or antiquated." I struggled to untangle one question from the dozens that swirled in my head. "Glenroe is yours," he continued, holding out a thin manilla file, "for as long as you want to keep it. I have taken the liberty of funding a Blanket Prevention Order to last your lifetime, stopping anyone from approaching you about the sale of the property without facing legal action."

I took the file, feeling numb. "I don't understand. How do you know so much about me? Why — ?"

"Don't worry yourself, my lord," Novák said with a soft smile and a slight bow of the head. It was the first time anyone had used the title and made it sound real. "This is merely a small way for my kind to pay you back for the understanding you extended to one of our own in a time of need."

"I know you want me to do interviews," I said, voice flat and lifeless, "but I really just want to be left alone."

"I understand," he replied, though something in his eyes told me he wasn't dissuaded. "Please," he said, producing another business card from a pocket in his coat, "keep my number. Let me know if I can be of any more assistance. A new age is coming, Lord Aviemore. And this won't hurt forever."

He glided down the overgrown path, large feet barely making any noise on the weedy gravel. A car started on the road below, its headlights washing holes in the gathering night, then he was gone.

His words swirled in my head for days, but I hadn't been able to fathom what had lain behind them, if anything. I had my new lawyer look over the BPO and they found it to be airtight. Something loosened inside me as I filed the papers away in a kitchen drawer, like a knot that had been snagged in me for years had finally come undone, but it only eased a small part of the constant ache that still permeated to my bones.

* * * *

"Boss?"

I blinked, Clem's rough voice in my ear bringing me out of my reverie.

"What?" I asked, straightening from the Porsche. He was craning his neck, peering out through the window into the forecourt.

"I think someone's here."

I frowned, looking at the time. "It's very late. Didn't they ring the bell?"

Clem shook his hairy head. "Didn't even hear the car drive up."

I strode over to the window and peered out into the gathering dusk. A beautiful E-type Jaguar, gleaming British Racing Green, was parked in the forecourt. I went out to it but it was empty, though the keys were in the ignition. I took a moment to admire the walnut paneling on the dash, the creamy leather upholstery, then straightened to scan the forecourt and stretch of deserted road. There was still just enough daylight to see there was no living thing as far as the eye could see.

"What the 'ell?" Clem stood scratching his head in the doorway. "Is that a job?"

"Looks in perfect condition," I murmured.

"Well, it didn't drive here itself, did it?"

"I—" I froze. A figure had stepped from around a corner of the workshop and stood just out of Clem's eye-line. White-blond hair brushed the turned-up collar of a black wool coat. His skin was the color of fresh milk, marble smooth, the curving lips a fractionally darker shade, like sun-warmed fruit. A large pair of sunglasses hid the eyes from view but I could feel them on me, even at this distance.

"Clem," I called when he turned to look over his shoulder, "I think we'll call it a night."

"I got paperwork to finish up."

"I'll do it in the morning," I said, hurrying into the workshop and fetching his coat and keys. "I'll lock up. Have an early night."

"What about this?" he said, gesturing at the Jag.

"I'll take care of it. Goodnight."

He muttered to himself as I hustled him to his car. The Land Rover rumbled away and I rushed to the back of the workshop. Terje stood on a raised bit of land watching the retreating vehicle with a cool, blank expression. He appeared so unearthly in the rapidly diminishing light that I was utterly convinced he couldn't be real until he took off the glasses.

"It's good to see you, Alec."

It took me a long time to find my voice. "It can't be you."

He stepped off the rise and came within arm's reach. The early spring breeze shifted his hair. It was longer than I remembered. He was squinting slightly, shading his eyes with his hand so I couldn't see them clearly. He was thinner, his cheek bones sharper. But it was him.

"I'm sorry it's been so long."

"I don't understand."

"Can we go inside?" I couldn't move. Couldn't think. "Please, Alec," he pressed, softly. "It's still very bright."

I stared at him for another long moment, tentatively decided that, whatever I was seeing, it was real, then trudged up the path. His tread was so light that I had to check to be sure he was following. I drifted down the side of the house with my heart hammering and my brain blanked. I opened the newly repaired side door and let him precede me in, then followed him into the drawing room. He stood looking around at the sawn-up timber, dust sheets and buckets of plaster mix.

"You've started restoring it."

"I like this room." My voice sounded rusty, like I hadn't used it in years. "I wanted to make it livable."

"It'll be beautiful when you're done."

"You're dead. I watched you die."

His face went still. "I'm sorry you had to go through that."

"Through *what*?" A rage so intense that it frightened me bubbled from somewhere deep inside me. "What *happened*?"

His deep silver eyes had my senses flooding with memory. I could taste him, feel his fingers gripping strong enough to bruise. I remembered the sounds he made deep in his throat as he gradually lost control. Things I'd refused to let myself think about in months rushed through my head like a speeding train. I had to put my hand on the back of the couch to steady myself.

"I probably did die," he murmured, "in the way you mean the word."

"Novák said you were dead."

"As I said," he went on mildly, "in the way you think of it, I was. My heart stopped. My body shut down. I certainly remember nothing after Ogdell fired his gun." I shut my eyes, smelling the gunfire and spilled Blood all over again. "They put me in the morgue…" He blinked and in the unguarded moment, I detected discomfort on his face, but then it smoothed again. "I'm not sure how long I was there. But then I started to wake up."

"How?"

He shrugged. "Like I've said before. With us…things take time."

If I hadn't been so ragged with emotion, I'd have been warmed by the look in his eye. But my voice was no gentler as I said, "Surely Novák would have known. He could have told me there was a chance you weren't…?"

"There wasn't much of a chance," he said, voice level. "And, as far as the world is concerned, I am dead. It's better this way."

"Better?" I growled. "*Better*? Do you have any idea — ?"

"I'm sorry," he said it quietly, but it derailed my angry tirade.

"It's been over a year." My voice shook.

He stepped up to me, raised a hand and cupped my cheek. His skin was cool, despite the thick coat. I smelled fresh, light smells, like those carried on an autumn wind when winter is just starting to creep in. "I couldn't see you, Alec. I couldn't see anyone. I wasn't...myself. For a long time."

"You should have told me—"

"I couldn't," he insisted, gently, brushing my over-long hair out of my face. "You remember what it was like in the basement?" My mouth went dry. I nodded. "It was like that. For a long time. I had to hide somewhere where I couldn't hurt anyone."

"How did you...?" I heard myself asking without wanting to. "When did you...get better?"

He dropped his hand but took a tiny step closer. I could have gathered him into my arms, but I didn't move, wasn't sure if he'd let me or if I wanted to. In that moment I didn't know if I'd ever be sure of anything again.

"It took a long time," he said softly.

I swallowed. "Did you kill anyone?"

"No," he said, firmly, putting both hands on my face. "No. I swear I didn't hurt anyone. I...I fought the Blood." His voice was tight, like he was reliving something painful. "I managed to get myself somewhere where there were no people before it took over."

"If you didn't kill anyone, how did you get better?"

His brow creased slightly. He didn't drop his hands. "I...don't want you to know."

"I have to know," I gritted. "You owe me that much."

He slid his hands from my face onto my shoulders. I resisted the urge to put my own on his waist and pull him close. There was a wall of ice between us. When he spoke, his voice was low and slightly strained. "I fed on animals," he said, "to start with. Then, when I was more in control, Novák helped me."

I stiffened. "When did Novák know?"

"It doesn't matter —"

"*When*?" I insisted.

Finally he let his hands drop. "I'm not sure. Weeks…maybe months later. It was warmer."

"He came to see me," I said in a low voice, "last summer. He knew something. I knew he knew something. He almost told me, I'm sure…but I couldn't believe it."

He took my hand in both his own. He ran his long fingers over the marks and scars on the back of it like he was reading braille. My hand looked large, dirty and gnarled compared to his. "He brought me blood. Donated blood," he amended, pausing his fingers in their gentle exploration of my hand. I fought the flickering that was gathering strength below my gut in response to his touch and starting to work hot tendrils up my spine. "I grew stronger. I healed. I came back to myself…slowly."

"Why did no one tell me?" Pain tightened my throat so I barely got the question out.

"We couldn't tell you, Alec. There was still a chance…" He hesitated, then continued steadily. "The Blood brought my body back, but I might never have been myself again, not after having been gone for so long. It was better you didn't know."

I suppressed a shudder. "Did it hurt?" I asked, so quietly I barely heard myself.

He raised his eyes, a spark of that dark amusement deep in his eyes. "Dying?"

"This isn't funny."

His face smoothed over again. "No. Sorry." He took a breath in through his nose then breathed out slowly. The warm air brushed against my collar bone and ripples ran over my skin. "Yes. It hurt."

"Novák turned you into a martyr," I murmured, watching his face closely. "A tragic victim of human-haemo brutality."

His eyes flickered slightly, the long eyelashes fluttering in the dying light. "I'm doing more good that way."

"How can you say —?"

He gently pressed a hand to my lips to silence me. I smelled his skin and desire surged in me but couldn't burn through the cloying, damp fog of betrayal that still clogged my chest. "No one can know the truth," he whispered softly. "Evgeniya can't know I'm alive."

I stared at him. "She doesn't know?"

"No."

"You're not going back to the commune?"

His grip on me tightened. When he spoke, it sounded liked he was forcing his words out. "No."

"Would she hurt you?" My eyes flicked unconsciously to his jaw, his neck, where I remembered the ragged bite wounds she'd inflicted, but there was no trace.

"Yes. But that's not why I don't want to go back."

"Why, then?" I asked, trying not to sound too intense.

His mouth turned up in a soft smile. "I'm free," he breathed. "For the first time in my life, I'm free."

"She said your kind can't exist on their own. Can't exist outside a commune. It's not safe."

He leaned in. "I thought you could show me how it's done."

All my breath left me. "What are you saying?"

He closed the remaining space between us and kissed me. He put a hand on the back of my head, tilting it to deepen the kiss. I flicked my tongue over his sharp teeth, and my head filled with the taste of old wine and aged whisky. My body loosened, like I'd suddenly been freed from a cage of wire. I gathered him to me, wrapping my large shape around his now-slight one like I could absorb him into me. I backed him against the arm of the new sofa and leaned into him. He yielded to me as I attempted to possess him entirely—mouth, arms and body—losing any remaining shreds of control, letting myself believe he was alive, really alive, really here and, despite everything, somehow wanted me.

When we finally broke the kiss, his cheeks had warmed and his eyelids were heavy. I tightened my grip, not nearly done, but he pushed me back, gently but firmly. "You need to think about this, Alec," he murmured, his mouth looking so inviting that I could barely focus on what he was saying. "Everything I told you about relations between our kinds? It was all true. And I think you understand that more now."

"I'm not like the rest of my kind," I said. "And you're not like yours."

He bit his lip, such a stark display of vulnerability that it shocked me. The heat in me damped, allowed rational thought to sneak through, and I resisted recapturing his mouth and waited for him to go on.

"I don't age," he murmured. "Not like you will. I can't move around in the day. I don't feel things the way you do. I have to drink blood…"

"I knew all that before," I said. "It didn't stop me from wanting you." His forehead creased. I stepped back, letting him straighten up, but I kept my hands on his elbows. "I'm yours, Terje," I went on. "I'm yours in whatever way you need me. I think I've been yours ever since I realized how badly you needed someone."

His face tightened. "What made you think that?"

I took a moment to gather myself, sensing I was venturing into delicate territory. "In Ogdell's basement when you were tied to that bed… When you sat here in a blackout trying to explain yourself to me… When you put yourself between me and Evgeniya… Hell, when you called out in the snow after the Blood Party… It was like you were crying for someone to understand." He stared at me. A chill of doubt swept through my insides but I made myself continue. "You've been hurt—by humans and by your own kind. That time…" I had to stop to clear my throat. "That first time, here on the old couch…" I tightened my grip on his arms. He didn't move or take his eyes off my face. "It felt like you needed that as much as I did. You needed comfort, just like any human would. But instead, you chose to give it to me. But I could feel you holding back, feel that you needed more."

He examined me as though, for the first time, he was the one struggling to read me. "Do you love me?" he asked, so quietly that his lips barely moved.

My stomach flopped over. "I…don't know," I answered, truthfully. "I don't understand you. I don't know you, really. I don't know if I ever will. I'm not sure love can exist like that."

I didn't expect his eyes to lighten and his expression ease, but they did. "It's good that you see that."

I nodded. "I see it," I said, a little dourly.

He raised my chin with two gentle fingers. "It's a good thing," he breathed, leaning in close so he was talking against my lips. "It means this could work. For a while, at least."

"Just for a while?"

He brushed his lips along my jaw. His fingers threaded through my hair. He breathed in deeply and sighed the air back out against my ear. "If living this long has taught me anything, Alec, it's that you can never predict what the future might bring. Don't be afraid of that. We have now."

He kissed me again, slowly, languorously. He pulled me onto the sofa, never breaking the kiss or his fierce grip on my hair. I fumbled at unzipping my overalls without breaking contact. Somehow, he'd shed his coat and I was able to nuzzle the cool, smooth skin of his neck. He made a soft, low noise, almost like a purr, and it was as though my heart had started beating again for the first time in months. I worked at his shirt. He let out a soft laugh, then pushed me back and unbuttoned it, slowly, deliberately.

I hurried out of my clothing whilst he removed his with a spark in his eye. He was definitely thinner, his collarbone and hips more prominent, and I had a horrible moment imagining what he must have looked like when he first woke up in the morgue. The image of his ribcage shattered by gunfire rose and threatened to swamp the mood. But looking at him now, I could see no visible sign of what had happened. He was slimmer but still beautiful, all smooth muscles and fine, unblemished skin.

When he finally stepped out of his black jeans, I was pulsing with need. He took a gentle but firm hold of my arms and twisted me around to sit against the new cushions, then he straddled my hips. I gasped. He planted a series of slow, burning kisses down my neck and across my shoulder whilst he swept his long-fingered hands over my stomach and chest.

He lingered at the scarring on my neck where Evgeniya had bitten me. "I will never do this to you," he said softly, the words brushing against my mouth. I shifted, resisting the urge to push my hips up, so desperate was I for friction. I held his gaze to let him see that I understood. "If any of my kind ever asks this of you," he continued, "in any context, you must refuse. Understand?"

"I have no intention of letting any other haemophile this close to me." His mouth twitched, though I could see by his eyes that he was still deadly serious. "I promise," I went on.

He watched me for a moment longer. Then, apparently satisfied, he took my face in his hands and kissed me again. I whimpered, feeling as though I might burst. It had been so long. Too much had happened. But now he was here, more real than he ever had been, and he was bringing me too close too quickly.

He backed off, as if sensing it. His jaw tightened, like he was wrestling with something. He leaned back and I repressed a groan at the loss of contact, but then froze when he brought a finger to his mouth and pricked the pad with his canine. A spot of black-red Blood welled up.

"No," I managed, grabbing his wrist, though the smell was filling my senses, dizzying me, causing my own blood to pump into my head and my groin with the strength of distant thunder.

"This is different."

"How is this any different than me offering you mine?"

"It's completely different."

My hand on his wrist started to tremble. "How?"

"You can't hurt me by doing this," he said softly. "And you've not asked for it. I'm giving it to you because I want you to have it." His finger hovered a centimeter from my mouth. He locked eyes with me then gently smeared the drop of Blood over my lower lip. "I want you to understand."

The scent of it seeped through my head and filled my chest with light. I opened my mouth and could taste the smell against my tongue, my palate, in my throat. My heartbeat slowed but strengthened, thumping in my chest like a fist. Every inch of my flesh was hot, charged. I resisted a moment longer, simply to show myself that I could, then I licked my lip.

The world melted away, sloughing into nothingness. All that remained was the feel of the sofa fabric against the skin of my back and legs, the cool kiss of the air on my flesh and the suddenly warm, irresistible weight of Terje across my hips. My pulse throbbed, spreading a slow, steady burning through my entire frame that was hotter than any fire but felt like it could blaze forever. When Terje licked my lip, tasting himself in my mouth, he made a low noise in his chest and I swelled and brightened, like the very oxygen in my bloodstream had burst alight.

Everything surged and focused on the feel of him, the feel of me, his scent, the expert way he moved and touched me to awaken every layer of desire that could physically exist within me. Everything slowed. Even the sounds he made were deep, like he was finally able to speak to me in his own language. It was as though we were underwater, floating, free and warm and isolated from everything else.

When he drew me into him with a sound like someone letting go of something painful that they'd been holding on to for a lifetime, my eyes stung and my heart ached. Pleasure and heat rolled out from his tightness, pulsing around my painfully hard cock so strongly that I wondered if it would undo me. We started to move together like dancers in a routine so familiar that we could read each other's flesh. The world dissolved into the feeling of me being buried in him, of the smell of his skin surrounding me, the sound of his voice in my ears.

We came together in a way we never had before, even in my dreams. I don't know how long we made love or how long the tsunami of the final orgasm actually lasted, because time lost all meaning.

I got a glimpse of what it must be like to be him, to only feel things that were so deep and primal it was like being caught in a lava flow — to know things with such intensity that they would drive a normal human mad. It both awed and terrified me, and I had to cling to him tight enough to leave marks in order not to be swept away forever.

* * * *

When we were done and the effects of the Blood were fading like the sun setting on a hot summer night, hours had slipped by. He lay along my side, propped on his elbow, resting his head on his hand whilst he ran his other through the hair on my chest. I lay on my back, the cool air finally starting to prickle at my skin. My blood still sang, my skin still glowed and I could feel the hairline grazes his nails had left on my shoulders and back in minute detail, but I could no longer see clearly in the dark and my heart had slowed to a normal, human rhythm.

I raised my hand and brushed his cheek with the back of a finger in the darkness. "Thank you," I said, "for coming back."

"Thank you for being here when I did," he replied. He pressed his lips to my cheek in the darkness then eased himself away. I shivered and fumbled for the lamp on the new occasional table, marveling at his controlled movements as he dressed.

"Can I see the rest of it?"

"The rest of what?"

"The rest of the house."

I raised my eyebrows as I zipped up my overalls. "It's not exactly homey."

"It's rustic, with great potential. Not unlike its owner."

I frowned. "If I'm rustic, what does that make you?"

Another half-smile. "Timeless."

I smiled despite myself. "Does that mean...you want to stay here?"

Both his eyebrows raised this time. "Sorry, was that not clear?"

"You don't just want me for my nice, dark cellar, right?" I realized with a pang that I was only half-joking.

He stepped close. "There are many cellars in this world, Alec MacCarthy."

"Not many with access to a natural cave system."

His eyes flicked between mine. "I must admit that I didn't expect you to start getting cold feet this quickly."

"I'm not," I said hurriedly. "I just..." I sighed, rubbed my face. "I'm figuring this out as I go."

He took my hand. "That makes two of us."

I smiled too. Now that the heat of desire had ebbed, I was aware of a pang of uncertainty. Even the way he smiled was...different. My brain couldn't process it the way it would a human's. It took a second longer to decide what it was seeing. And in that second, doubt existed.

Everything we'd said was true. There was nothing certain between us, nothing that could be put into words. Love was a human word with human implications that somehow didn't fit what I felt. I couldn't even predict how he, or I, would feel in the morning. I realized with a jolt that I wouldn't even see him in the morning — or any morning.

But even though I was very aware of how little I really understood about what we were getting into, I wanted to learn. The thought filled me with an almost physical sense of anticipation. He gazed at me with something between curiosity and fascination in his eyes and I wondered if I offered the same challenge to him.

'I try to remember what it was like before,' he'd once told me.

"Would you change back?" I asked. "If you could."

He blinked. His smile disappeared. "Would you want me to?"

"This isn't about me," I insisted. "I just want to know."

He stared at the Jacob More over the mantlepiece. I'd scraped together enough money to have it cleaned. The frame gleamed in the lamplight. The moody, dark paints were bolder with all the dust cleaned away, revealing the twisted, storm-battered landscape in all its dangerous, raw glory. I wondered what my father would make of it being admired by Terje as he stood with his hand in mine. Clem's revelations had changed my memory of my father forever. But all that change had done had made me realize how little I'd really known him.

"This is who I am," Terje eventually said, his eyes still on the painting, "for better or worse. I couldn't change, even if I wanted to. That will have to be enough of an answer."

I hovered on the edge of a question that had lain, like a black stone, in my mind ever since the encounter with his Magister in the caves. With him here, alive and real in front of me and with my immediate need and elation drained away, I opened my mouth and it tumbled out. "Did you kill Shelly Morris?"

The silver of his eyes darkened to pewter. "No."

"You swear?"

"I swear. That boy…" He winced, though didn't look away. "Mr. Harris is the only human I've hurt in over fifty years. And that wasn't on purpose, you know that."

My voice, when I found it, was thin. "I heard what you told Evgeniya in the cave, but I want to hear it again. Who did kill her?"

"Alec, you knowing won't help—"

"I want the truth, Terje. All of it. Unless you think Evgeniya was right?"

His expression flattened and he looked away. "Okay, I'll tell you and in detail. I owe you that much." He took a breath. "I'd had a…disagreement with Evgeniya over a human I'd grown close to."

"How close?"

"That's not relevant."

"Terje—"

"Alec," he said, firmly. "I will give you the truth...but only the truth you are entitled to."

I chewed on that a moment, something spiky working its way around my stomach that I was half-afraid was jealousy, but then I nodded. He continued, his face schooled blank. "She didn't trust me to stay away. She was having me followed. This haemophile following me, they—" He broke off and took a breath. Something in his eyes reminded me of when he'd faced his Magister in the icy cave. Fear looked unearthly on him. I didn't like it. "They were what you might call 'private security'. They're registered, legal, but Magisters usually choose the strongest and...more conservative members of the commune for the role."

"And by conservative you mean—"

"Old-fashioned. Assertive. Unpredictable." He shook his head, a heavy frown darkening his expression. "And Olsen had never liked me. We were too different. Being told to keep an eye on me was apparently the last straw for him. When he saw the chance to implicate me in something he knew would shame and disgust me, he took it." Terje was still staring at the floor. "I didn't kill her—but I guess it was still my fault." He raised his eyes. I was shocked to see the brightness of tears gathering in their corners. "If I had just obeyed... If I'd just been like everyone else, the girl would still be alive."

I held his look. "If you were like the rest of them, Blood Winter would have been ten times worse."

"And that makes everything all right?"

"Not all right," I said, "but better than it could be. It's not your fault, Terje. Being different doesn't mean being wrong."

His gazed unblinking at me as the words he'd once said to me hung in the air between us. I felt like I was balancing on a cliff edge, my toes hanging out over nothing. I let myself smile and squeezed his hand. "What part of the house would you like to see first?"

His expression warmed slightly. "The master bedroom. There are pictures online. It's quite something."

"It doesn't look like that now."

"It could again."

I shook my head, fighting something unpleasant snaking around my belly. "That's Dad's room."

He leaned close and brushed his mouth over my ear. "Not anymore."

I shivered, tried for a smile and led him out into the dusty hall. The lights flickered and hummed when I switched them on, the wiring old and crackling.

"I don't go up here much," I said, picking my way up the creaking stairs.

"We'll soon change that," he said, gazing at the arched ceiling, the dust-caked chandelier, the plywood boards on the windows.

"What do you mean?"

"It's time you stopped living in someone else's idea of home," he said softly.

"It's not that simple."

"I understand that," he said, a hand on my arm. "But the answer is simpler than you think."

"And what's the answer?" I said, trying not to sound tetchy. His smile went a long way to remove the needled feeling, though it couldn't expunge it completely.

"We turn it into something that makes you proud, somewhere you can really live." He put his head on one side. "Or would you rather squat in the kitchen forever?"

I made an impatient noise. "Even if I wanted to, it would take millions…"

"I'll help," he said. "I have some means."

"You do?"

His eyes swept over the chandelier again. "I set up my own private means of income years ago. Evgeniya never knew. When I died, it went into trust with Ivor Novák." He met my eye, smiling slightly. "So I still have access to it without anyone else knowing."

"It must be one hell of an income," I remarked, trying not to sound incredulous.

"It's enough," he murmured. "Enough to make this place a home."

"The E-type Jag," I breathed. "That's yours?"

"Yours now."

"I can't accept it," I said, shaking my head, "any of it. It's too much."

"I *want* to give it to you," he went on. "I've no use for money. I set up the fund on the hundred-to-one shot that if a time ever came that I could start my own life — and now it has. I want to use it to make this place somewhere safe, for both of us."

"I never sold Glenroe because that's just what Dad expected me to do." My muscles stiffened and something hot surged up my back. "To abandon everything and run the moment I got a chance. The perpetual disappointment that I was, what else would I do?" I glared at the bannister without really seeing it.

"I don't think me being gay, in itself, bothered him," I murmured, Clem's words floating in my head, "but when I said that I'd never pretend, never marry, have children...that I wouldn't do what was expected..." Terje was watching me but didn't interrupt. "After Mum left, I was the only thing left of the life he wanted, and I was all wrong for that part. This house was all he had in the end...the only thing he felt he could rely on. It's too *him*. It can never be mine. But I can never let it go, either."

"Let it do for you what it could have done for your father," he said, drawing me close. "It's sheltered your family for generations, kept reality at bay and protected the part of the world you most care about." He brushed his lips over my brow and breathed in the smell of my hair. The cool touch of his skin was soothing. "It protected us," he went on, speaking softly in my ear, "when we needed it to, shielded us from the storm and from the Ogdells. I know what it's like to need a safe space. Don't deny yourself one any longer."

I buried my face in his hair. To my great dismay, my eyes prickled and my body shook. The Blood still thrummed deep in my flesh, but another feeling overwhelmed it now, one I couldn't entirely understand and which frightened me more. He held me until the shaking stopped then let me stand up and apart from him. I almost loved him then, for that effortless understanding of what I needed.

"The E-type is completely the wrong sort of car for these roads."

His mouth twitched. "It's for trips into town."

"There is no town."

"There are some very good architects and interior design firms in Edinburgh," he said mildly. "And I'd like to see the castle."

I raised my own eyebrows. "For someone who doesn't think about the future, you seem to have done a lot of planning."

"I'm an optimist by nature. And I believe in change. It's what put me so at odds with my commune."

"Novák knows you're alive, right?"

"He does," Terje replied carefully.

"Evgeniya could find out."

"She won't," he said. "It's in his best interest that no one ever finds out. Come on." He held out his hand. "I want to see that bedroom."

I paused before taking his hand. "But you won't be able to sleep up there."

He brought my hand to his mouth, gently brushing his lips over my knuckles. The Blood stirred in me again, making my heart thump heavily in my chest. "Not sleep, no," he murmured against my skin, "but there are plenty of other things to do at night besides sleep."

I swallowed. "What about your...other needs?"

He went still. He lowered my hand and took it in both his own. "Novák and I have made arrangements. You don't need to know the details."

"He knows you're here?"

"He does."

I studied the wall for a moment, the reality of the situation slowly taking form in my head.

"We'll have to make the cellar more comfortable," I said. "Get some heating down there."

His look softened. "I'd appreciate that. Alec..." His face was grave. "No one can know I'm here. No one."

"I know."

"I know you're a good person," he said, still serious, "and that you trust your friends. But—"

"I won't tell anyone," I said, fervently.

"I'm not trying to make it difficult," he said softly. "And it's not just Evgeniya. Us...being together, here. It would not be welcomed by many of your kind...or mine."

I tried to get my head around what I was teetering on the edge of committing to. I had visions of work starting on Glenroe whilst Terje kept from sight, of clients coming to the workshop whilst all the time a haemophile, a killer, whatever I thought of him, was just up the hill. Trying to act normal around Clem, day after day. A fridge filled with bottles of blood in the wine cellar. Terje drinking that blood, human blood, then joining me in the master bedroom.

Blood junkie. Freak. Traitor.

I blinked, fighting back the cold swell of uncertainty. His expression was guarded. I drank in the sight of him, the feel of his hand in mine, and fixed on the certainty that I wanted this, wanted him. "You're sure about this?"

"As sure as you are," he said.

Neither of us *knew* anything. We only...felt... something, something that didn't have a name. But it was real.

I kissed him again, letting everything fall away but the feel of having him close in a place that I, for the first time, felt I could own. No matter how uncertain it all was, it was mine—mine and Terje's.

I took his hand and led him upstairs.

Want to see more from this author?
Here's a taster for you to enjoy!

My Bloody Valentine:
Blood Red Roses
S. J. Coles

Excerpt

Rick slid his key into the lock. It caught, again. The thing had needed replacing for months. But, for the first time in years, the thought of another financial outlay barely registered. He wrestled the door open and hurried inside. Ella rose from her seat at the kitchen table, a half-drunk cup of coffee forgotten amidst a drift of bills and credit card statements on the kitchen table.

"Well?"

Rick was quiet just long enough for her face to tighten then he smiled. "I got it."

The worn lines of care at the corners of her eyes smoothed away. She laughed and flung her arms around him. He laughed too, squeezing her tight.

"I *knew* you had this, bruv. I told ya, right? Didn't I say?"

"This is it, El. We're sorted…finally sorted."

Ella wiped at the wetness in her eyes but her smile never wavered. "This calls for a celebration, right?" She went to the fridge and produced a bottle of cava.

"When did you get that?"

"Lidl had them on offer. Come on. A toast." She poured the sparkling wine into two mismatched beakers and held one out. Rick took it, and Ella raised her own but then lowered it, her face growing serious.

"What is it?"

She huffed out a breath. "Before we drink... *Fuck*." Her expression darkened. "Sorry... It's just I'd kick myself if I didn't ask this..."

"El—"

"Just let me, please?"

Rick sighed and gestured for her to continue.

"Are you sure this is what you want?"

"El—" he said again, but she cut him off.

"I'm serious, bruv. I know this feels like the answer. And I know Dad..." She took a breath then smiled a wan smile. "Dad would have been so chuffed. Beyond chuffed. But is this really, *really* what you want?"

"A job with Swanson and Gerrard is above and beyond 'want', sis."

"But your music."

Rick glanced at the rack in the corner where his battered Martin acoustic, Fender Strat and Gibson Les Paul sat gathering dust. "Music was Mum's dream," he said softly, feeling a familiar clench in his chest. "But Dad was right. It was just a dream."

"Money's not everything," his sister replied. Rick glanced at the bills littering the table. She followed his gaze and grimaced. "We could manage," she went on. "We've managed this far."

"This isn't managing."

"We could find another home for Mum—a cheaper one, outside London. We could move back up north, even—"

"It's not just the money," he said. "This job means I've made it...finally made it."

"But—"

"Leaving now would be going backwards. I can't go backwards."

"Now you sound like Dad."

"The bloke did talk sense occasionally."

She sighed. "All right, Ricky. So long as you're sure. Cheers." She clinked her glass with his. "In which case, enjoy your moment. Christ knows you deserve it."

"We both do." He drank. Ella drained her glass and poured another. "Don't you have a shift tonight?" he asked.

"Not until six," she said, topping him up. "And it's not every day your little brother lands a job as a junior analyst with one of the biggest finance firms in the country, is it?"

"No, it bloody isn't," Rick said, a little grimly, and drank deep from his own glass, enjoying the light taste and the fizz. "My first payday I'll get us some of the real stuff," he added with a grin.

Ella's eyes were bright again. "Last time I had real fizz was at my wedding."

"That was Italian. Real fizz is French."

"Well, get you. Got a taste for it all now, huh?"

"Champagne and caviar from now on, sis." Rick winked at her, loosened his tie and sat, grateful to take his weight off his feet. He emptied his glass and reached for the bottle.

Ella sat next to him, pressing her lips together as he poured the last of the wine into her glass.

"What now?"

"So they really didn't twig?"

"Would they have given me the job if they had?"

"I dunno," Ella said, shrugging. "I don't have the first clue about how these big places work. But you'd think they'd be the sort to know if you lied on your CV."

"I didn't lie on my CV," Rick said carefully. "I just was…you know…selective with the details."

"That's lying, Rick."

"Swanson and Gerrard would never look at the likes of me without something to make it worth them looking."

"But you could dance circles round anyone else," Ella went on. "Dad always said you had an insane talent for this stuff. That's all that should matter—not where you grew up or the fact that your first job was at Maccie Dee's."

"It shouldn't matter," he agreed, "but it does. But it's fine. I got the job and I'll do it well. They'll have no reason to dig any deeper."

"But—"

"This merger they've got in the pipeline is worth several billion. They hired me because I know everything there is to know about Egerton, Baines and Russel. And that's not a lie."

"Who?"

"EBR…another finance firm. I studied them at uni for my dissertation. I can help Swanson and Gerrard make this the deal of the decade. *Then* I'm in for good. Five-figure salary from day one, plus bonuses. An advance bonus mid-January. Job security for life." He pulled his chair closer to hers, and she raised her slightly worried eyes to meet his. "Believe me, El. I can do this. I owned that interview. Cecily Swanson even invited me to their New Year's booze-up at The Savoy on Saturday."

"*The* Savoy?"

"Uh-huh."

"Fancy." She examined his face. "You didn't tell her, did you?"

"Tell her what?" Rick asked, searching the half-empty fridge for his last cans of Stella.

"You know what."

Rick passed Ella a can and cracked open his own without meeting her look. "It's not like that."

"I saw the way she looked at you," she said, the mischief she'd never completely lost dancing in her eyes. "Like a cat what's got the cream."

"Yeah, right."

"We don't get the likes of her in the cafe, Rick. I mean, *ever*."

"She must've heard about your coconut cake."

Ella gave him a sardonic look. "Or she followed you in."

"You're dreaming."

"Rick, I *watched* her do it. You came out of that bank with a face like a back of a bus—"

"I'd just flunked another interview—"

"And she watched you come down them steps, cross the road and followed you like a posh cat after a mouse."

"Nah," he said, shaking his head.

"I'm *telling* you. She saw something she liked. You think these West End types buy sympathy coffee for just anyone?"

Rick swallowed more beer, hoping it would drown the nervous tingling in his belly. "Even if you're right, she's engaged."

Ella snorted. "You clearly don't read Twitter."

"Not these days. Why?"

"Everyone knows that engagement's bollocks," she went on, pouring her lager into the empty cava glass.

"Harry Whateverhisnameis is the nephew of one of your new firm's partners and cousin of some other."

"Harry Gerrard-Hanson. Yeah, he's related to one of the senior partners in EBR and to a former partner of S&G. These sorts of companies are always inbreeding. The marriage is why the deal's on the table at all. So?"

"So," Ella went on, flicking through something on her phone. "The wedding hype? The cover stories in *People* and *Hello!*? The huge ceremony at some stately pile on Valentine's Day? It's all a sham. The likes of Cecily Swanson ain't gonna be sticking to no vows for this fat bugger's sake." She showed Rick a picture of Harry Gerrard-Hanson on some gossip site. His eyes were watery and dull, his hairline receding, his face and neck those of a man that ate too much and moved too little.

"There is nothing between me and Cecily Swanson."

"I know *you* know that. I'm just not sure *she* knows it."

"I can't tell them I'm gay, El," he said. "This shit matters in places like this, especially for someone like me. They're…old school."

"Bigoted, you mean."

"Okay, maybe. But if they can make our lives better, then screw what they think. We deserve this, right? You said it yourself."

"So what happens when she finds out?"

"She won't."

"She might notice when you don't fall into bed with her at this fancy-arse drinks party."

"You're worrying too much. So maybe she likes what she sees. She's only human, right?" He smirked but at the look on Ella's face sighed. "But whatever. You don't give JA jobs to eye candy. She knows I can help land them this deal. That's what's most important to her."

Doubt warred with the hope in Ella's deep-brown eyes for a long moment. The hope won. "If you say so, bruv," she said, brushing his lapels, "but maybe playing on it a little can't hurt. So we need to take you shopping."

Rick winced. "I don't get my bonus until after New Year. And the last lot of care home fees maxed the Visa."

"So I'll pick up a couple of extra shifts. Oh, and I found a shop that'll buy my rings for a decent price — "

"No," Rick cut in. "No, El, I can't let you — "

"Rick, I'm doing this," she insisted. "We're in this together, remember? And besides…I'm ready to let them go."

He took in his sister's earnest expression. For a moment she looked so much like their mother his heart broke all over again. "Ella…"

"You know what I think about this walk-the-walk bullshit," she cut him off, "but if you say you gotta play the game then I'll help you play it…at least for now. And a big bit of playing a part is *looking* the part."

Rick glanced down at his winter-sale Matalan suit and his father's last decent tie and sighed. "Fine."

"Atta boy." She raised her glass. "To new beginnings."

"To a new life," he said, lifting his own, "and to dreams coming true."

PUBLISHING

Sign up for our newsletter and find out about all our romance book releases, eBook sales and promotions, sneak peeks and FREE romance books!

About the Author

S. J. Coles is a Romance writer originally from Shropshire, UK. She has been writing stories for as long as she has been able to read them. Her biggest passion is exploring narratives through character relationships.

She finds writing LGBT/paranormal romance provides many unique and fulfilling opportunities to explore many (often neglected or under-represented) aspects of human experience, expectation, emotion and sexuality.

Among her biggest influences are LGBT Romance authors K J Charles and Josh Lanyon and Vampire Chronicles author Anne Rice.

S. J. loves to hear from readers. You can find her contact information, website details and author profile page at https://www.pride-publishing.com